The Summer Job

Michelle Meenan

Susi,

I hope you enjoy it!

Michelle

x

Dedication

I dedicate this book to my husband for always
encouraging me to get it done!

Acknowledgements

This book is only possible thanks to JimBob,
Spanner, Dave and Liz for providing such
amazing inspiration and friendship.

1

One

"Why do short people always get the extra legroom seats on aeroplanes?" I muttered crossly as I wedged myself into the row behind the coveted exit seats. I cursed under my breath as I rested my chin on my knees and peered between the seat backs at the short legs of the people in front.

"Are you going to Portugal on your own love?"
The middle-aged woman next to me had been eyeing me ever since I put my bag in the overhead locker. She leaned towards me slightly as I fiddled with the arctic air conditioning above my seat. Her peach velour leisure suit matched the lipstick on her tiny, pursed mouth exactly. She was fanning her face with an in-flight sick bag; her dark hair had pure white roots, an inch long, and it was sticking to her forehead in thin strands. Her Thames Estuary accent was right out of a 'Carry On' movie.

"Yes," I forced a nervous smile, "I'm starting a new job. Why don't these things ever work?" I exclaimed as a freezing blast of air blew down onto my head.

"I'm glad of it to be honest," she puffed pulling at the front of her velour top.

"What work will you be doing?" she asked, running a paper tissue across her forehead. Small, damp balls of tissue settled into the perspiration slicked tracks of her skin.

"I'm going to be a rep for a small holiday company," I answered excitedly as I gave up trying to turn the arctic blast off and directed it at my companion instead.

3

"Oh, that's lovely," she gushed leaning back and putting her face under the cold stream of air. "Which company is it?"
I watched as the balls of paper tissue dried and blew away.

"It's a small company; you might not have heard of them. Complete Holidays?"
Even as I said the name, the butterflies in my stomach started to flutter again.

"No, I haven't heard of them," she said becoming animated, "'Ere, are you sure it's all boney fido? If I was your mum, I'd be dead worried. They'll have you working all hours you know. Have you got a proper contract? They'll have you selling cheap shots to teenagers on bar crawls! Oooh no, I'd watch yourself, my love."

"Right, thanks," I sighed as the plane surged forward, picked up speed and lifted seamlessly into the sky.

"Oh, I do hate flying," my neighbour said as she clutched my forearm, eyes clenched shut, "especially this take off bit. Are you a good traveller? Well, I suppose you'd have to be in your line of work, I say. I couldn't be doing with it myself. All that heat and airports," she chuckled.

"I'm Judy by the way and this is Pete," she touched the arm of the man sitting next to her, "I don't know why I bother going abroad, I really don't. I don't do well in the heat at my time of life!"
I smiled kindly, "I'm Jo," I said and nodded at Pete, a balding, red-faced man with a beer belly who hadn't uttered a word so far. He was probably well used to his wife speaking for him. Again, I smiled and nodded at Judy even though I was no longer really listening to her.

As the plane levelled out, the seatbelt signs were switched off and the cabin crew began their slow trip down the plane with the drinks trolley. My neighbour began foraging in her bag for her purse.

"Do you suppose I can pay in sterling?" she asked. "I haven't had time to get any escudos yet..."

The cabin crew dragged the trolley past me, banging my knee and rolling the wheel over my foot. I turned into a pretzel to fit my legs behind the seat back in front, as my neighbour ordered her drinks, talking to me all the while. As she droned on and on, my mind drifted off and I turned to stare out the opposite window at the whipped, white clouds beneath us.

My stomach was churning with nerves. I was travelling to a new job and life in a country I'd never been to. I was a late twenties singleton with a string of dull, unfulfilling jobs behind me. When I was a young girl thinking of how my life would be; I imagined a fabulous career, perhaps a husband, maybe some children, and definitely a beautiful home. I did not imagine a dead end job working as a PA to an egotistical bully of a finance director, a failing relationship and a poky, damp flat in Kilburn.

My relationship with Andrew quickly began to fall flat. As his career took off and mine stalled, we grew apart. He mixed with trendy, aloof media types who rendered me mute in their presence leaving me dull and flat next to their glossy sheen. I became invisible, like a spectre, looking in at the ruins of my life. Constantly dreaming of a different, exciting life away from the grey skies of London kept me going. I drifted through each day, gazing constantly at the palm tree fringed beaches in the photographs I stuck to my computer, dreaming of escape, excitement, a chance to reinvent myself and start again.

Just when I began to believe nothing would ever change; one of my incessant job browsing sessions turned up an advert for Complete Holidays, who were looking for Representatives for resorts in Europe. My stomach gave an excited little flip for the first time in months and I applied without a second thought! I didn't give myself the option of overthinking it and backing out, like I always did. The crippling anxiety which held me back from achieving so many things wasn't going to win this time. Besides, I'd been here before; applying for an amazing job, only to receive the inevitable rejection. I'm not sure what was different that day; maybe I had reached the end of the proverbial tether, I don't know. If I did know, I would have bottled it, manufactured it and opened my own shop to sell it. I was not going to let this opportunity bypass me this time.

I can't begin to explain the excitement, then sheer terror, when I was invited to an interview. After fretting and overthinking in the days previous, I found a friendly, welcoming company excited to meet me. When I left the building that day, I wanted the job with every ounce of my being and silently prayed to the universe the whole way home.

After four, never ending days, I got a call offering me a job in the Algarve programme in Portugal. Oh, my word, I don't know how I managed to speak. I felt every emotion - excitement, shock, disbelief and, my old friend, fear. However, this time the fear was not winning.

I had two weeks before my flight to resign from my job, give notice on the poky flat and dump

Andrew. It speaks volumes about the esteem I was held in, to say there was no resistance to my plans. My friends just couldn't understand why I'd want to do such a job or even why I'd want to leave London.

I busied myself with admin and shopping as I got used to the wriggly, nervous feeling in my stomach, which was becoming ever present. The job offer made me feel confident and capable... until now, on this plane. What *was* I doing?

The flight was soon descending towards Faro. The land still looked very green and fertile, but it was still April and the programme manager, Gaby, told me it might still be very wet at this time of year. The plane bounced a little on the tarmac and then touched down, the engines roared as the brakes applied, pinning us all back in our seats until the speed slowed and we began taxiing to our docking space. I unfolded my legs into the aisle and stood, rubbing my lower back. The nerves started to wriggle and squirm in my stomach again as I would soon be meeting my new boss.

"Oh, good luck dear and I hope it's not too awful!" Judy smiled, patting me on the arm, still fanning herself with the sick bag.

"Err... thanks, have a nice holiday," I replied smiling through the haze of nausea I was now feeling.

The line of people down the middle of the plane began to move and I started forward eager to get through baggage reclaim. As I stepped through the door onto the top of the plane steps, gorgeous warmth hit me. This was going to be a little different to the dreary, grey, rainy London I'd left behind.

Two

I'd been told to look out for Eleanor Barton, the area manager for the team; she was meeting the flight and then, hopefully, taking me for a drink. I suddenly felt tired and overwhelmed. I made my way through passport control, without incident, and through the security doors into the arrival hall. I spotted a red, Complete Holidays, sign and made my way towards it. The woman standing next to the sign was chatting into a mobile phone. She seemed to be a similar age to me and was tall with a slim figure. She was wearing a simple black shirtdress and had a pair of sunglasses pushed back on her head into her shoulder length brown hair, which was streaked with expensive looking lowlights in caramel and honey.

She looked up and smiled as I tried to steer the trolley in the right direction. She pressed a button on her phone and smiled, holding her hand out to me,

"Hi, you must be Joanne, I'm Ellie."

"Oh, please call me Jo," I said smiling broadly as I returned her firm handshake. Her voice was deep, husky and haughty. She was attractive but had a rather large, hooked nose which, as I soon came to learn, had already earned her the secret nickname of Beaky. She chatted away easily as she guided me towards the exit leading to the car parks. The warm air was again a shock after the air-conditioned airport but also a welcome change after being so frozen on the flight.

"I'm sorry I haven't managed to sign up your apartment yet," Ellie apologised as she pulled one of my cases across the road, "the owner's been away on business. You'll stay with me tonight and you might have to share with one of the others for a few days until we get you moved in."

"Oh, ok, sounds fine to me," I said struggling with my suitcase wheels and a high kerb, "right now, I could do with a very large drink!"

"I think you'll fit in fine," she laughed clicking open the small car, "we can be in my local in forty minutes!"

As Ellie switched on her car ignition, I opened the passenger window to let in the sweet evening air. The radio started and played the dance tune, 'If everybody looked the same.' There was a scent of jasmine wafting in the atmosphere and the sun had begun to set behind the green and blue mottled mountains, which I could see in the distance. My initial overwhelm was calming down and Ellie chatted away asking about England, the weather and current affairs.

"You've been lucky arriving today," smiled Ellie pushing her shades up her nose, "it's been raining for a week. This is the first gorgeous day we've had in ages."
I smiled turning my face towards the sea as we left the airport and followed the coastline towards Ellie's flat in Quarteira. Spring was in evidence now with fresh blooms everywhere and the unmistakeable blazing pink of bougainvillea trailing from balconies and terraces. We passed small roadside villages, large supermarkets, and giant, colourful billboards screamed Portuguese advertising that I didn't understand. In the distance, the setting sun was painting streaks of lilac and orange across the sky as it sunk deeper into the horizon.

"It's so different from what I expected," I said, "I thought it would be dry and brown everywhere.

"It will be! Give it time for the summer to really start but then, there are always green woods and flowers here. See those hills over there?" Ellie nodded into the distance, "That's where you'll be living."

"You know I don't speak any Portuguese, don't you? Will I be ok up there?" I asked, suddenly terribly worried, "will anyone understand me?"

"Don't worry," said Ellie seriously, her voice deepening, "many people speak some English and if you have any serious problems, I can help you and Tom speaks Portuguese too. He'll help you loads anyway."

"Tom?" I asked.

"Another of the reps," Ellie smiled, "I'll fill you in on the rest of the team over a drink, ok?"

I smiled in reply and wondered if there would be any decent male talent in the team, though that was the last thing I should be thinking of after my recent relationship demise.

We were soon settled into a comfortable sofa in the corner of Ellie's local bar which overlooked a golden beach and a gently, lapping sea. Thrusting a gin and slimline into my hand, Ellie gave me the rundown on the rest of the team.

"Ok, first there's Daniel. He's been in the Algarve for a while so knows his way around if you get stuck. He's handsome and knows it; prefers men, sadly, and can mood swing with the best of us. Don't take it personally, you'll get used to it. I've been working with him for a while now. If he likes you, he'll be the fiercest friend ever.

Next up is Tom. He's from Cornwall but has been living over here a while, much like Dan. He's great and will help you loads, especially if you have any issues with the language. In fact, both Dan and Tom have been covering your area, so they'll bring you up to date on everything. Then there's Emma who is covering the west coast and Monchique. She's from Somerset so another one from the west country! So many yokels!"

She threw her head back and laughed a deep, throaty laugh as she picked up her sunglasses from the table and pushed them back into her wavy hair to keep it from falling in her face. I looked across the table at her, pursed my lips and asked,

"What's Emma like?"

"Well, she's small and blonde and, I suppose some people would say she's pretty. She's been travelling abroad for a few years and this is her first real job in quite a while. She doesn't seem to like rules, so we'll see how she gets on," she sneered.

I wondered what Emma had done to make Ellie dislike her so early on in the season and decided I liked her already.

"And finally," she sighed, "there's Beth, our admin. She's a bit older than the rest of you, and I hope, more sensible. She'll go through all the paperwork with you on Friday and keep you in check about it.

You'll get to meet them all in the next few days and can make your own mind up. We do get together quite a bit and try to have some fun. The company pays for us to have a monthly night out for morale building," she said drawing speech marks in the air.

11

"Another drink?" she asked, waving at the barman.

I'd nodded an enthusiastic yes before I excused myself to the ladies loo.

This was going to be an interesting season I thought. I couldn't wait to meet my fellow reps. I was excited and nervous in equal measure, but I'd taken the biggest, scariest step just to get here and I couldn't wait to see what the season had in store.

Three

I awoke late the next morning with a headache and couldn't think where I was for a moment. There was a bright light coming through my eyelids and it was warm, really warm. I opened my eyes and the first thing I focussed on was a cup with steam billowing from the top.

"Don't expect this treatment all the time!" I heard Ellie's throaty voice from the doorway. "I'm making breakfast if you want any?"
Ellie had bought a considerable amount of alcohol last night, none of which seemed to affect her in the slightest. I rubbed my eyes as I stumbled to the kitchen in search of more coffee to be met by Ellie, showered, dressed and loud.

"Good sleep? Don't get used to lie ins like that. Come on, look sharp, we've got things to do."

She'd left a little tower of toast alongside butter and a variety of other toppings like jam and marmalade. Ellie tottered off on her shiny heels onto her balcony, which was hidden behind white, voile curtains, billowing in the breeze, and began chatting in Portuguese on her phone, which seemed to be permanently attached to her ear.

After a morning filled with inductions, forms and company policy, we were on our way to Tom's place on the eastern side of the Algarve. For the next few days, until my apartment was ready, I was going to be sharing with Tom in his apartment in Tavira on the eastern side of the

Algarve. Ellie mentioned the company provided dinner each month for the team and tonight was the second outing. Great timing always was my strong point and it meant that I got to meet the rest of the team all at once. I'd be lying if I said I wasn't a little worried about meeting them all. The team had been together for a month already and what if they'd bonded as a team without me? As it turned out, I worried over nothing. What a wonderful bunch of people I was about to meet.

As we pulled up outside Toms apartment block, Ellie blew the car horn. I looked up the building, squinting against the sun to see a dark outline give us a cheery wave. We parked under the shady, bamboo awning provided for vehicles and climbed out of the car. It was a pretty ugly building with long rusty watermarks running down the render underneath each balcony. The balconies themselves were ugly square breezeblock constructions, most of which had clothes airers or washing lines strung across them.

"Hello," I shouted.

"Hi!" he bellowed back.

"You'll be fine," said Ellie, sensing my nerves and giving me a reassuring pat on the arm, "I'll see you both later on," she shouted up at Tom. "You know where we're meeting, don't you?"

"No problem Boss," he shouted in reply with a thumbs up, "wait there, Jo, I'll come down and help you with those bags."

Ellie stayed long enough to make the introductions, as Tom emerged from the front door of the block, and then sat back in the car, mumbling something about phone calls to make. I hauled my huge suitcase out of her boot, muttering to myself about the lack of help she'd offered. Tom was there in a flash to help me pull the last of the bags out.

"Thank you!" I said flushing a little. Ellie reversed the car out of the space and drove off without another word. I smiled at Tom who watched Ellie drive away and then announced,

"Time for a drink then!"

He picked up my suitcase easily and threw it over his shoulder and set off into the building and up the stairs. I followed him with my other smaller bags hooked over my arms. Looking up at this strange man running upstairs in front of me, I could tell he was well over six foot, with broad, tanned shoulders. He was wearing navy board shorts and grey flip-flops that slapped his feet with each step.

"I'm doing a few drinks and some nibbles for everyone tonight before we go out," he said as he opened his nondescript, brown front door and showed me through into the narrow hallway of his apartment. The long, narrow kitchen was immediately to the left and the countertop was full of bottles and party food. I threw my bags down onto the floor and had my first proper look at Tom, my new flatmate, as he popped the tops of two bottles of beer and handed me one, clinked his bottle to mine and led me out onto the balcony where I'd first seen him. He was tall with dark, dark short hair that was messy on top. He already had an enviable tan, which certainly helped emphasise his toned torso and made his broad shoulders even more appealing. His eyes were light, but I couldn't tell if they were blue or green.

"What music is that?" I asked referring to the cool tunes playing from somewhere in the flat.

"That? Oh, that's the Buena Vista Social Club. You like it?"

"Very much," I smiled.

"I'll do you a copy if you like?"

"Sure! Thank you!"

"No problem! How have you been finding everything?" asked Tom in his broad Cornish accent.

"I'm a little overwhelmed so far actually; there's so much to take in!" I replied a little shyly, safely gazing at him from behind my sunglasses.

"Ellie been scaring you, has she? Don't worry about her, she'll let you get on with things and it's really not that bad. I'll help show you around. You'll be fine – trust me. You'll get on really well with the rest of the team, I'm sure. We're going to have such a great time this Summer!"

He flashed me a broad smile as he raised his eyebrows. I grinned at him as my stomach did a little happy flip.

"I think we're going to get on great Tom!"

"Yeah, me too," he smiled as he clinked his bottle against mine, "Cheers me dears!"

We spent a happy hour swapping background stories of where we were from, what we'd done before, how we'd ended up here. I liked him more and more as he shared some of his story with me; he was so open and honest; and I felt more relaxed and ready to meet the rest of the team.

I finished my beer and jumped in the shower to get ready for the night ahead. The beer had relaxed me somewhat and I was more excited than nervous. I looked at myself in the bathroom mirror, my dark blonde hair dripping down my shoulders. I looked tired but my blue eyes were sparkling more than I'd seen them do in years. In this light, they were my favourite cornflower blue. I wrapped a towel around my head and began to apply some light makeup, before drying my hair and slipping into a simple white t-shirt with wide-legged cotton trousers. Once ready, I parked myself next to the drinks table. If all words failed me and I got tongue tied around so many new people, at least I could pour them a drink as they arrived.

"Wow," said Tom, smiling at me approvingly, "you look gorgeous!"
I blushed and smiled back at him.

"Thank you!" I said as the doorbell rang. Tom had changed into denim board shorts and a simple white t-shirt and looked delicious. As he opened the door, a champagne cork flew into the room.

"Where is she?" a high-pitched Somerset voice shouted, "My fellow female! Where are you?"

From Ellies description, I guessed this must be Emma. She was a real beauty with blonde hair, but unlike my own, hers was sun-bleached, almost platinum and her petite but curvy figure was clad in figure hugging white vest and cerise pink shorts.

"Hello lovie," she smiled as she came forward to kiss my cheek and handed me the bottle of champagne. "I'm so glad you've arrived, trying to put up with these two blokes on my own has been a nightmare!"
The top of her upturned nose wrinkled slightly when she smiled. I found it hard not to look at her; she was so pretty!

"Oi!" protested Tom but he was laughing with her.

"Piss off Tom," she laughed in return.

17

"Where are Beth and Dan?" she asked me.

"I'm not sure, they must be running late. I've not met either of them yet," I said.

"Oh, you'll love them!" reassured Emma giving me a big beaming smile. "I'm so glad you're here and can't wait to have you on the team and work with you."

What a welcome! I could feel my muscles beginning to relax and I briefly wondered why I'd been so nervous and worried as the old admin job and poky flat got even farther away in my mind. This bright, sunny place had already lifted my spirits more than I ever thought possible.

"Beth is probably in the Alentejo by now," laughed Tom. "She's only been to my place once before and she has the worst sense of direction I've ever known! She'll be late, trust me!"

"Anyway Emma, why did you bring champers when you know I've got loads?" said Tom.

"Ha ha," she laughed, flicked her long hair away from her face and turned to me, "That's Toms cheap Lidl special – champagne for a quid. He buys crates of the stuff for the clients and then we drink it all when we run out of the good stuff! Don't drink it unless you've already had a few," she winked at me conspiratorially.

Emma poured me a glass of the good champagne and as we clinked our glasses the doorbell rang again.

"Let me in you Cornish Pixie; I'm too hot and I need a bloody drink!" came the excited voice through the intercom.

"That'll be Daniel then," said Emma rolling her eyes but smiling at the same time.

A few moments later, a very large duvet appeared in the doorway and all that could be seen of the person under it was a pair of hairy calves.

"Get me a drink; I've had a terrible day," said the duvet before it dropped to the floor revealing what must be Dan.

"Hiya! You're here! You must be Jo. Thank God for you! Welcome!"
This tall, tanned, toned and incredibly groomed blonde flew over to where I was sitting and planted a kiss on my cheek.

"Pleased to meet you," I smiled completely amused by this whirlwind that had entered the room. He ran his hands over his short hair and shouted,

"Tom, a drink for your guests please! Don't make me ask again."

"Do you want some of this?" Tom waved the Lidl special in Dan's direction.

"Is that that Lidl crap? No, I don't, give me something that doesn't taste like piss."
Emma came to the rescue and gave him a glass of her "welcome" champagne.

"Mmm lovely," said Dan as he sipped his drink and slipped into the chair next to me.

"So," he said cocking his head on one side, "tell me everything! I didn't think we were going to have such an elegant lady joining us!"
I smiled and looked across at Tom who was grinning at me.

"Watch him," he said, "he may be gay, but he has a fetish for women and their boobies!"

"Tom!" shouted Dan, "I do not! Don't tell such porkies!"

"She is a lady," said Tom winking at me, "It's good to have someone who is elegant on the team! Makes a change!"

"Rude!" shouted Emma and Dan in unison. Dan then turned to face me, "I think you'll find we're a very cultured bunch here!" Emma and Tom both raised their eyebrows and laughed as the doorbell rang a third time.

"Hello!" said Tom into the intercom.

"Hello Tom, it's me Beth."

A few seconds later, a very attractive brunette appeared at the door. She was clutching her car keys so tightly that they were leaving indentations in her hand. She was chewing the thumbnail on her other hand and her eyebrows were pulled together giving her a worried, tired look.

"Hi Jo, how are you? Really nice to meet you!" she said as she dropped her thumb away from her teeth and approached me planting a kiss on my cheek. She had rather plummy tones to her voice but didn't seem to be a plummy sort of person at all. I liked her immediately.

"I don't know how I found you, I really don't," she said waving away Tom and his Lidl champagne. "Could I have some water please?" she asked, "I've only been here once before, and you know what my sense of direction is like!" she said tucking her dark hair behind one ear. Emma laughed, "Only you can get so lost Beth!"

"I knew I'd got it wrong when I got to Cabanas and there was a sign for Spain," Beth wailed.

"Seriously?" said Dan, "we need to get you a sat nav. You shouldn't be allowed out by yourself without one!"

"I know," laughed Beth, "I'm an absolute liability. Good job I'm based in the office else I'd be stuck up a mountain somewhere; I'd never find any of the villas."

The room was full of chatter and laughter. Some low music was playing somewhere but I couldn't make out what it was. I'd never met such a friendly group of people before and they were all gorgeous! It was like walking into a teenage soap opera of sorts.

"Guys! Best drink up soon. We have to leave or Ellie will be sat waiting like a lemon on her own!" said Tom.

"Oh, let her wait! Won't do her any harm to be kept waiting for a few minutes!" said Emma with a wicked glint in her eye.

"Oooh Em, you are evil. Come on best go, we don't want her giving up, going home and not paying for our night out!" said Dan.

"Always so caring Dan," laughed Emma ruffling his hair as she passed him.

We set off to meet Ellie in a restaurant on the other side of the river about a fifteen minute walk away.

Tavira is a beautiful old town, full of narrow, cobbled streets that retain the heat of the sun throughout the night. The whitewashed buildings tumble down a slight hill towards the river and the beautiful Ponte Romana de Tavira (Roman Bridge to you and me). Large squares on the banks of the river were filled with tables and chairs. Candles and lamps shone through the darkness creating a wonderful glow. Whole families were enjoying the spring evening with children playing in the bandstand that stood right on the riverside. Lights were strung on wires along the river and hung on ornate lampposts that continued over the bridge as we crossed. It looked like a beautiful, fairy-tale town. A few metres after the end of the bridge, we turned down what seemed to be an alleyway but there, down on the left was the restaurant façade. This

21

was the "Aquasol," an Italian eatery run by a Portuguese family.

Ellie was sat at a large table eating olives and had already drunk the best part of a bottle of wine.

"Where have you been?" she said hissing at us, "I've been here for ages! They were about to boot me onto a table for one!"

"Sorry boss," said Dan, shrugging his shoulders, "we're here now. Are you ok now honey?"

"It's ok; you can climb out of my arse now!" said Ellie rather loudly.

Dan didn't respond to the comment and placed himself at my right side. There was silence as we studied the menu.

Emma had told me, on the walk down, that Dan and Ellie had been reps together the previous year and had been really close friends. Ellie's promotion and the shift in power had totally changed the dynamics of their friendship and now Dan didn't know how to behave around her at all. Even here the office politics dripped into people's lives.

As a group, we all decided to have pasta. Most restaurants also provided bread, olives and sardine pate for nibbles before your meal came out.

"It's all beige," said Dan, "carbohydrate filled beige food. It's what we live on!"

I studied the menu intensely, trying to translate the unfamiliar words. Tom came to my rescue and read the options to me.

"Thanks Tom," I said, "I think I'll need you to just follow me about translating everything!"

"You'll get used to it and will start to pick up words here and there," he said kindly. Dan was most attentive and gentlemanly, always filling my glass when it was empty.

He asked me question after question, "Where did I come from? What did I do before? Was I attached to anyone, you know, romantically? Did I like dancing? And on and on.

"Dan you know there is such a thing as a conversation where you get to know someone," said Tom, "you don't need to bombard poor Jo like the Spanish inquisition!"

I laughed, "it's really ok. No one has shown this much interest in me in a long time."

"Has life been like that?" asked Tom sadly.

I blushed, nodded and tried to join another conversation before he asked me more. It was far too early to get deep into my emotional past. The meal, when it finally came, was delicious and everybody was having a great time. I didn't get a chance to speak to Beth and Emma much as they were on the other side of the large table in the noisy restaurant.

Emma shouted across at me, "we need to arrange a girl's meet up to have a proper chat, yes?"

"Yes," I shouted back, "That would be amazing!"

She gave me a thumbs up and did the international "I'll call you" sign.

As we left the restaurant, Tom and Dan linked arms with me and confirmed themselves as my new best friends. I feared they were both rather drunk as they tried steering me in different directions. We still decided to go for another drink. The next day was a fairly easy one for all of us except Beth who had to be in the office at 8.30am. She decided she'd had enough.

"Beth, don't leave us!" Tom slurred as he flung his arms around her neck.

"I'm going," she said firmly, "I've been drinking water all night, unlike you! I'm driving home. Anyone need a lift?"

"I'll come with you if you don't mind, I'm really tired," said Emma yawning.

"S'not like you to miss a party," said Dan surprised.

"Yeah, well I've got health and safety checks to do first thing," she said dully, "and I've got to sort out my cots and highchairs."

"Fine, leave us to our debauchery," shouted Dan theatrically.

"Very sensible, for once," said Ellie, "I'd like that full list of baby equipment by tomorrow please. We need to know what we have out there."

Emma sighed, "yeah, yeah, whatever! Right guys, speak soon and lovely to meet you Jo." They both gave me a quick hug before they walked away towards the bridge.

Four of us remained as we entered a salubrious looking establishment that had no name, just a door in a wall with a beaded curtain across. The place was empty with just two guys at a pool table.

"Mmm, it's kicking in here!" I said sarcastically.

"Oh, come on, who cares? Let's have a drink," shouted Dan.

The bar seemed to be some kind of a motorbike/cowboy/farm theme bar. The bar stools were, in fact, old saddles for drinkers to straddle. There were old petrol pumps turned into cigarette machines and an enclosure full of straw with hay bales around the outside. The best bit, by a long shot, was the DJ stand. In front of where the DJ stood were motorbike handlebars. These bars had headlamps attached to them that flashed along in time with the beat of the euro pop he was currently assaulting our ears with. No one was dancing but the DJ, who was waving his arms above his head and sporadically shouted something indiscernible into the microphone. Neither the glass polishing barman nor the two, pool-playing guys seemed very interested. We ordered some vodka and sat at a beer barrel table. Tom began to copy the DJs moves, which only heightened his excitement.

"Oh my God," groaned Ellie, "we can pretend we don't know him if that helps!"

I was amazed by her capacity to hold her drink. She had drunk far more than the rest of us, never mind what she'd had before we arrived but appeared to be completely sober unlike Tom, who was drunk.

"Come on," said Ellie after we'd drunk our vodka, "let's try somewhere else. This is not where I want to be."
As she stood, her right leg gave way, and it was thanks to Dan who caught her by the elbow that she didn't fall flat on her backside. It was a chink in her armour – a small one – but a chink, nonetheless.

We all weaved our way into the next bar where a dark skinned man of about forty was sitting. HIs face was strong and characterful with a long chin, startling, crinkled green eyes and a large roman nose. His cigarette hung from the corner of his mouth as he cracked pistachio nuts on the bar. He wouldn't have looked out of place in an old black and white French film. His eyes drifted over all of us and settled on Ellie. He watched her as we walked towards the bar and looked admiringly up and down her body.

"I think you have a fan," I whispered to her nodding in the man's direction. As she turned to look at him, he spoke.

"Good evening, may I join you for a drink?" His voice was deep and smoky with a French accent.

"Sure," said Ellie, "why not?"

He ordered Bacardi with a twist of lemon, smiled at Ellie and as he lifted the glass to his lips smiled, "Good Health!"

"Cheers!" we all said.

Ellie leaned over and hissed in my ear, "May I join you for a drink actually means will you buy *me* a drink? Cheeky git!"

Tom was already making friends with the stranger and had established that his name was Bernard pronounced in the French way – *Bernarr*. Ellie and Tom were the only Portuguese speakers in the team – a fact that was not lost on Bernard. Whatever he was saying to Ellie was making her blush, but I couldn't tell if she was flattered or not. As Tom embarked on a long drawn out joke, I asked her what he had been saying to her.

"He keeps telling me I'm beautiful. He wants me to go to his house in the hills. I think it's probably time to go home."

I nudged Dan who was snoozing on my shoulder and helped him to his feet. My shoulder felt slightly damp. Tom had already stumbled outside.

"Oh my God, how embarrassing," cried Ellie covering her face "This is how not to behave Jo! What must you think of us all?"

"Ellie, you shurrup," slurred Dan, "go on and snog your mate or summink."

"Don't worry, I will. You are all disgustingly drunk!" she shouted as she ran to catch up with Bernard who was a little way up the street sitting on a doorstep adjusting the laces on his roller skates. Funny, I hadn't noticed him wearing them in the bar. Everything was getting way too surreal tonight.

The sun was beginning to rise, and it cast a pale blue light across the town that was getting warmer every minute. I found Tom sitting on the kerb not far from Bernard and helped him to his feet as Dan caught up and the three of us followed Bernard and Ellie home. They were silhouetted against the rising sun as they led the way. Bernard, on his skates and not skating very well, was holding Ellies hand.

"Bless them, it's like a Mills and Boon! This has been, without doubt, the weirdest night I've ever had." I laughed.

As we kept giggling and shouting, Ellie kept yelling back at us to be quiet. As we neared Tom's apartment, we stayed a discreet distance behind as Bernard gently kissed Ellie, his hands in her hair. They spoke for a brief moment and then Bernard was off, zooming past us on his skates.

"Bon soir!" he shouted and was gone. We walked to the door of the building where Ellie was waiting. We tried really hard not to laugh, but one look at each other and we all sniggered and giggled.

"Not a word, any of you. Not one word."

Four

Someone had obviously glued my eyes together. The same person must have removed my tongue, replaced it with a swollen sponge covered in sandpaper and then savagely beaten me around the head which throbbed and pounded. I managed to stand and eased my way down the hallway into the kitchen and downed a pint of water whilst trying to decide if I felt hungry or sick. I decided on hungry and opened a cupboard door to explore the food options. The smell of Bombay mix hit me hard, so I decided nope, I felt sick, and closed the door breathing hard.

Peering at my watch, I could just make out it was 10.30am. We didn't go to sleep until sunrise, which meant we'd had about four hours sleep. Last night had been the most fun, wonderful, funny, surreal night out of my life! I wondered if it would set a precedent for the rest of the season. A grunt behind me announced the arrival of Dan.

"Water! Give me water!"

"Shh," I said handing him a glass. After he had drunk it, he looked at me and gasped,

"Jo, you look really, really awful! Do I look as bad as you?"

"Thanks, and if I look as bad as I feel, then yes, you look as bad as me."

"Huh?"

"Jo! Dan! Help me!"

It was Ellie screeching. She was pounding Tom around the head with a pillow screaming at him to get off her. Tom's flat had three bedrooms; I'd had one, Dan must have had the second so, for some reason, Ellie had ended up sharing

28

Tom's bed. Sharing a bed with a dead drunk
Tom was not fun as Ellie was now protesting.
He was wrapped around her, gripping her tightly,
still fast asleep and snoring gently. I couldn't
help but feel slightly envious as I patted Dan on
the shoulder, "Help the nice lady. I'm hitting the
shower!"

Showered and dressed and several cups of coffee
later, I was on my way to Faro airport with Ellie,
who had finally escaped poor Tom's clutches,
for more training and airport induction. We had
left Dan making enough toast to feed the whole
apartment block, if required. Tom had made it as
far as the bathroom and hadn't reappeared before
we had to leave.
Ellie chatted on about clients, health checks,
keys, expectations and duty cover and I tried to
nod in all the right places. Was this woman
immune to hangovers? For the second time in a
few days, I'd seen her seemingly immune to the
effects of alcohol. I wondered if she had duped
us all last night by drinking tonic water but her
red-rimmed eyes told me otherwise. She was
putting on a front. She was the boss. She was in
control at all times.
She had managed to secure my new apartment,
in the tiny town of Sao Bras in the hills about
twenty miles inland. I was excited and nervous
about moving there, not speaking the language
and not being as close to the rest of the team.
        "You'll be fine," assured Ellie, "I'm
sure neither of the boys will be too far away
from you at any point. You've certainly made an
impression on them both."
        "I have?" I asked surprised to hear this.
I didn't remember making much of an
impression on anyone and I thought of how
bored and uninterested Andrew had seemed

29

when I told him I was leaving him for a job abroad.

"Honestly, Jo," said Ellie with exasperation in her voice, "drop this shyness! Is it an act? It doesn't suit you and will annoy your clients."
I really didn't know what to make of that or really understand what she meant. I was just being me.

"Uh, what?" I replied feeling hurt.
"This is all new to me and I'm finding my feet."

"Well, find them faster. Your first lot of clients will be here soon and you can't be shy in this job."
I felt my heart sinking to the depths of my stomach. I knew my lack of self confidence would begin to show in the end.

We sat on the roof terrace of the airport, "it's lovely up here," promised Ellie, as she grilled me about health and safety. Planes roared across the sky ready to land every few minutes as I cowered under the twirling sun umbrella in the middle of our table trying to get some shelter from the hot sun. I was trying not to think about what she'd said to me earlier and concentrate on the training. I knew Ellie was aware my eyes were shutting behind my sunglasses at times. I was so tired after such limited, alcohol induced sleep.

It was late afternoon before I picked up my new car, a sparkly, new, silver Corsa, with some trepidation, as I'd never driven abroad before. Ellie sat in the car with me and took me on a few laps of the airport roads until I was confident enough to drop her off and bid farewell and make my way back to Tom's apartment. As I put the key in the door, I was sure I could hear singing. I went through the kitchen and out on to the back balcony, which looked onto the inner courtyard of the building, and there was Tom, up to his elbows in soapsuds scrubbing clothes on an old washboard. The boys didn't have washing machines in their apartments and the laundrette was too expensive.

"Hi," I said.
He jumped a foot in the air. "Don't DO that!" he shouted as he turned to greet me, but his mouth fell open before he grinned, his green eyes (I noticed) twinkled.

"What have you done to yourself?" he began to laugh as he led me back into the apartment and placed me in front of the bathroom mirror.

I gasped at the sight. I obviously hadn't done a very good job of sheltering under that umbrella. On my chest was a bright red, sunburned V, the same shape as my top and my hands were the same crimson shade. I looked like I was wearing a pair of pink Marigold gloves.

"OH NO! Look at me! I look ridiculous!" I cried only to be met by much snorting and laughing from Tom. I stuck out my bottom lip and then laughed along with him until my stomach hurt.

Five

Later that evening, Tom announced his dinner plans.

"Seeing as it's our last night as flat mates, I thought I'd cook my speciality – pasta á la Tom!"

"Great," I smiled taking the beer that he was thrusting at me, "Are you still ok to help me move tomorrow? I don't really know where I'm going!"

"Of course," he smiled as he turned the radio on. Britney Spear's Baby One More Time filled the room.

"Don't worry, I can show you where some of your villas are along the way. Now go and sit down because you're not allowed to see how this dish is done. It's my secret!"
I didn't argue. As I sat with my feet up enjoying my beer, Tom slaved away in the kitchen and told me about his day photographing boilers, testing gas bottles and checking sun loungers. I smiled to myself as I thought how easy living with him had been and how relaxed things were between us.

"Right," he yelled, "it's ready."
He entered the living room brandishing two huge plates of food.

"Wow, it smells amazing," I said.

"I hope you like cheese because there's a lot of it in this dish."

"I love cheese!" I replied enthusiastically.
He had cooked a four cheese pasta with fresh salmon. It was delicious and accompanied by a lovely, white wine, which he announced had

come, of course, from Lidl. I laughed remembering Emma's review of Tom's taste in wine.

"Do not even think about the calories in this," he said as we tucked in.

"I wasn't going to," I mumbled, my mouth full.

"My girlfriend always moans about the fat content, every time I make this, she moans!"

"Your girlfriend?" I asked almost choking.

"Yes, Tammy. She's back home studying for an MA in Business Admin. We met at the college when I had nearly finished my MA. It's been, let's see ooh.. must be a year and a half now we've been together"

A little pang of disappointment ran right through me and I felt annoyed with myself for feeling it. Why wouldn't he have a girlfriend? What was I expecting? The happiness I'd just felt a moment ago seemed to dissipate. I gave myself a mental talking to. This one tiny thing, which was hardly surprising, was not going to ruin this experience. "Pull yourself together," I said to myself as I smiled through the disappointment that had taken up residence in my gut.

"More wine? How about a game of backgammon after dinner?" he asked blissfully unaware of my inner turmoil and emotion. Tom had been trying to teach me the game all week and I had a sneaky suspicion that he was making up rules to allow himself to win.

"Ok you're on, but no cheating this time." I replied forcing a laugh.

"As if I cheat," he laughed, clearing the plates into a pile and taking them out to the kitchen.

The girlfriend revelation had hit me harder than I'd expected, and it surprised me. I tried to push it to the back of my mind as I set up the board game. The most gorgeous bloke I had met in ages was taken and I don't know why I was surprised. That's the way it always seems to work out, doesn't it?

Six

I was up bright and early finishing off my
packing when Tom appeared sleepy eyed and
yawning but ready to hit the road and show me
the way to my new home.

"Right then," he said, "let's get this
stuff into your car and get you moved shall we!"

The road north wound upwards through forests
and tiny villages and down long, dusty stretches
of road. I followed Tom's blue car at a short
distance so the dust didn't blind me. At certain
points along the way, he'd thrown his arm out of
the window and pointed down narrow tracks. I
guessed these were where some of my villas
were to be found.

We were soon at the sign for my new hometown,
Sao Bras, as our surroundings turned from
country to town. We passed small restaurants
and shops before arriving at a huge square. The
traffic was very busy and there didn't seem to be
any rhyme or reason to the traffic flow. Cafes
with pavement seating and pretty, yellow
parasols to protect the customers from the sun,
greengrocers, estate agents, a small cinema and a
newsagent lined the square. Two wide main
roads seemed to run off the square leading north.
Tom was indicating right to turn into the first
one, so I followed him into a wide, tree-lined
Avenida. There were plenty more little
restaurants and cafes on this road which led
north out of town to more mountains. We turned
left before the town limits and pulled up outside
a whitewashed apartment block. I stopped the
car and got out, taking in my surroundings.
There were three different blocks that all looked

the same, all four storeys with balconies jutting out at each level.

"Welcome home!" said Tom as he jumped out of his car, "I believe you are on the second floor. Let's get you up there, shall we?"

The sound of clanging metal came from somewhere nearby and Tom told me the sign above the door at the bottom of my block indicated there was a gym inside. That would be the sound of weights been lifted and replaced.

"Lucky you!" said Tom.
I laughed, "The last time I was in a gym was when I was in school!"

"Well, now you have an opportunity! It couldn't get much closer!"

"I think getting my stuff up all these stairs will be exercise enough for now," I said opening my car boot.

Several trips later, I flopped into the nearest chair breathing heavily. Four flights of stairs with two suitcases and various bags had nearly killed Tom and me.

"That," I said out loud, "is the last time I'm moving those bloody suitcases until November. Thanks for everything this week, Tom," I said, "You've been a star!"

"Not at all my love. The pleasure has been all mine!" he smiled as he gave me a huge hug.

"Here," he said handing me a bag, "I got you a moving in present."

"Tom, you didn't have to do that. Thank you."
I unwrapped the gift to find a very fine bottle of port. I was so touched by the kind gesture that I

felt myself blush and tears pricked the back of my eyeballs.

"Just make sure you keep some for when I come to dinner."

"I will. Thanks Tom." I gave him a kiss on the cheek swallowing back the tears as he turned, walked through the door and left me alone in my new, very empty apartment.

I sat down in the extremely large, very empty living room, staring into space, not knowing what to do first. The thought of unpacking was not a motivating one. I don't know how long I sat there before I glanced at my watch and groaned. I was due in Quarteira to go through the paperwork with Beth. With all the might I had, I hauled myself out of the chair and back down to the car.

Seven

The traffic through the market town of Loulé was unbelievable. People seemed to have no spatial awareness and the car behind tapped my bumper several times while braking in the queue. Cars came out of side roads and then stopped abruptly to offload passengers who then decided to have a further chat with the driver. I beeped my horn angrily.

"Come on, come on," I shouted. The lack of order was really stressful; I could feel my blood pounding through my veins.

Moving down a narrow street with walls on either side, there was a lorry unloading some goods, leaving only one lane open. The traffic was squeezing through. As I approached, the car coming the other way flashed its lights at me and I pulled out to pass the lorry. It was then I realised the other car was coming straight at me. I had nowhere to go and instinctively, I pulled the steering wheel to the right and winced as I hit my wing mirror hard against the side of the lorry. I got past and put my foot down. I looked at the space where my wing mirror used to be.

"Oh shit shit SHIT! I'm SO dead!"

This must be a record for the shortest car hire time before an accident. EVER!

I would have to pay for the mirror to be replaced myself. I thought of the £150 excess on the insurance and tried not to think how much worse it could have been.

What was that crazy driver doing driving straight at me? Maybe flashing lights meant something different in Portuguese? I'd only had my car a few days. Ellie was going to kill me!

My head was racing with so many thoughts and worries. The snakes had awoken in my stomach and sweat was beading on my top lip and soaking through my t shirt.

By the time I pulled up outside Beth's apartment, I was shaking. I kept telling myself it could have been worse. I got out of the car and rushed round to the passenger side where I let out a huge gasp.

"OH MY GOD!" I brought my hand to my mouth. I hadn't just knocked my wing mirror off. From the front of the car to the back window was a deep gouge that marked a tramline on the glass and had ripped the metal on the doorpost. The back quarter light window was shattered and the bottom of the doors were deeply scratched. It was bad, really bad.

I ran across to the office apartment, pressing on the Complete Holidays bell. Beth buzzed me in and by the time I arrived at her front door on the first floor, I was shaking violently.

"Jo, what's the matter? You look terrible!" she said taking my hand and guiding me into the flat.

"Oh Beth, I've broken the car. Ellie will kill me!"

"What do you mean Jo? Honestly, I'm sure it's not that bad," she said calmly, "Come in! You're shaking Jo, what's happened? Come and sit down."

She gently led me to a bright orange sofa and sat me down, putting a blanket round my shoulders. Shakily, I told her what happened as she made me a cup of tea with lots of sugar.

"I'm sure it's not that bad Jo. And even if it is, it can be sorted. It's just a car. It can be replaced. You can't. Now, take this and sip it slowly and I'll go and have a look."

39

She handed me the tea, slipped her pedicured feet into pink flip-flops and disappeared out the door. A few minutes later she came back, her face a little paler.

"Oh Jo, you were so lucky! If that had been on your side… Anyway, that doesn't matter. Are you sure you're ok? Can I get you anything else? Have you stopped shaking yet?"

"Yes, thank you Beth. I don't know what I would have done. I'm feeling much better now but I need to speak to Ellie, don't I?"

"Oh, don't let her scare you! She's all bluster and not much else. She has a go at me all the time. You kind of get used to it and ignore it after a while."

"Really?" I asked unsure, "because she's said some pretty mean things to me."

"That's her own insecurity Jo. Don't let her knock your confidence."

She dialled Ellie's number and handed me the phone.
In a wavering voice, I explained what had happened as she silently listened. I must have caught her in a good mood as she was surprisingly sympathetic and understanding, knowing I'd never driven abroad before. She even blamed herself for not driving with me longer as I got used to the left hand drive. She assured me she would sort everything out and I wouldn't have to pay the insurance excess if she could manage it. I put the phone down with a sigh of relief.

"Beth, she was ok. She's just been really nice to me. I was expecting a right dressing down. Maybe she's ok after all."

"Mmm," said Beth doubtfully, handing me another cup of tea, "you might have caught her on a good day, in a good mood. Now, honey, if you're sure you're ok and feeling better, let's make a start and get the paperwork out of the way. I need to explain it all before airport day so you'll be ready. I'll help you tape the broken window on the car so you can drive until you get it swapped out. And then, we'll have a proper chat. Sound ok?"

I nodded, thanking Beth again. She had been so calm and caring, looking after me and helping me sort it all out. She really was so very kind.

Eight

My alarm screeched at 7am on the morning of
my first airport day, a few days later. I prised
my eyelids open and made my way to the
shower. What was this day going to bring? My
stomach was already a mass of nervous knots
and churned with nerves. Today would be my
first day in uniform in front of clients. I was
supposed to know my area inside out and had
spent the last few days driving around looking at
restaurants, discovering quiet beaches, visiting
the tourist office, gathering leaflets of local
attractions, making welcome books for each
villa, and generally settling into the area, all
while getting very lost and hot.

Sao Bras had almost everything a villa
holidaymaker would need with plenty of
wonderful, inexpensive restaurants, cafes,
bodegas and a stationery shop owned by possibly
the most miserable man I have ever met.
I needed to buy some envelopes and pens to
write my "Welcome notes" for the airport and
decided to use the local shops rather than the
hypermarket in Loulé, which, as I'd already
discovered, was busy, chaotic and choked with
traffic.

I entered the small, dark shop to be greeted by
the sight of an older man, slouched over the
counter reading a newspaper. His yellow t shirt
strained against his ample gut as he scratched his
sparsely haired pate. There was an
overwhelming smell of very ripe body odour
emanating from him, causing me to mouth

breathe. He didn't even look up as I entered so I looked around the small room for what I wanted. The room was messy with cardboard boxes scattered around the perimeter. There were no shelves for me to browse and I wondered if I had the right place. The man looked up briefly, rubbed a grubby hand across his stubbled chin, and returned to his paper.

"Okayyy," I thought, "this will take some negation skills. You can do this Jo." I took a breath and said, "Qual o seu nome?" I hoped to build rapport by finding out his name. He slowly lifted his eyes to meet mine. They were actually very kind eyes, appraising me and there was a glint of mischief there.

"O que voce quer?" he asked gruffly. I had no idea what he had just asked me but guessed he didn't want to tell me his name. I continued speaking in English, flapping my hands as if that would help me be understood, feeling a total hot mess.

After half an hour, lots of sketches of envelopes and references to my phrase book and waving of hands, I had what I needed. I felt a little stupid and embarrassed. The smelly man took my cash and pushed my goods across the counter with no enthusiasm or grace. I did detect a hint of a smile as I bade him "Good Day." Or at least, I think that's what I said!

As the shop door closed behind me, it's little bell ringing happily, I breathed a huge sigh of relief. That was not an easy transaction and I vowed to learn some of the language so I could communicate and I wondered if Tom could give me some lessons. It wouldn't be *so* terrible to spend some extra time with him.

Even though I'd been busy the last few days, it was always lonely coming home to a large, empty flat. It seemed a little cavernous with two large bedrooms, a huge bathroom, living room and a wide hallway. The living room itself was large enough to house another family and I felt lost and alone in there, even with its cheery rainbow coloured sofa and chairs. I chose to spend most of my time in the clean, white tiled kitchen which was just big enough to fit a small table and chairs. This was where I completed all my paperwork and where I listened to Portuguese radio stations. The big selling point of this room, however, was the patio doors which led onto a balcony which stretched the length of the apartment. The views from here reached cross the northern part of the town across fields and trees to the hill beyond where the Sao Bras Pousada nestled. I could just see the red tiled roof peeking through the greenery. I would enjoy a cold Gin and tonic on this balcony over many nights in this apartment. After a few days of solitude and local fact finding, I was looking forward to seeing the rest of the team.

I double checked my paperwork several times and pulled on my red uniform dress, which was a very flattering cut and suited me well against my dark blonde hair. I pinned my name badge on, loaded my rep bag with welcome notes, clipboard and snacks and set off down the stairs to the car. Beth had helped me temporarily fix the car. Masking tape and cardboard was holding my back window together and I prayed it would hold a little bit longer until I got to the airport car park.

The morning was promising another beautiful day with clear, blue skies as far as I could see.

The sun was already warm even at 7.30am. It was easy to be up at this time on a Sunday morning like this. Who would want to waste this day? At least the incoming clients would be happy with the weather. I had only one family arriving this week and was glad I could ease in gradually before all twelve of my villas were full. One of our many jobs was to buy welcome hampers for each client. We had a weekly budget to buy basic provisions for people arriving at their villas including tea, bread, and milk – that kind of thing. It was an easy task to perform when you only had one family to buy for. I wondered how I would cope when I was buying twelve of everything.

I parked safely at the airport with the back window still in place and made my way to the car hire desk where I found Tom checking the car hire list.

"Morning," he chirped, "what's all this about you having an argument with a lorry? Are you ok?"

"Yes, I'm fine! I see good news travels fast. It wasn't my fault you know!"

"I only heard about it this morning! Otherwise, I would have called and made sure you were ok. This is Carlos. He'll sort out your car for you."

He indicated the man in the kiosk who was grinning at me, his white teeth flashing. Carlos was not the manager of the car hire desk but seemed to be in the hierarchy, taking his role very seriously. He was also a total flirt, older and maybe in his mid thirties, and charmed every holidaymaker, male or female.

"How long you been here Jo? A week? It's a record! No one wreck a car in less than a month before," he laughed batting his dark lashes at me.

"Right, I'm a record breaker," I said sarcastically. "Can I have a new car please?"

"Certainly, madam," said Carlos rubbing his hand over his perfectly clipped black, goatee beard, "and may I say what a pleasure it is to be working with such a beautiful woman. I'm bored of looking at these boys!" He waved his hand dismissively at Tom as he handed me the keys to a new car, catching hold of my hand as he did so and winking.

"Carlos! Really?" said Tom, "is there any woman you won't try it on with?" I'd come across men like Carlos before. He may have been handsome and charming but he was also oily and lecherous.

"I think I can take care of myself Tom," I said laughing.

"We'll see how you feel in a few weeks," said Carlos winking. I rolled my eyes and pulled my hand away from his clutch.

"Sorry," he said, "I was just messing," he said looking a bit put out.

"Save the charm for the clients, Carlos," I said smiling, "and thank you for the new car!"

With all the paperwork complete and a huge weight lifted from my mind, Tom guided me to the company stand in the arrival's hall.

"Where are the other two?" I asked, looking around at all the other rep's milling around waiting for the next flight.

"Emma's in the car park looking after car returns and departures and Dan's probably up there." He nodded up towards the small café on the first floor. It was the place where all reps could be

46

found drinking coffee whilst waiting for flights to arrive.

"He's most likely up there doing his welcome notes. I think he was out last night."

"On a school night?" I exclaimed in mock astonishment laughing.

"I know. He's a rebel," he smiled, "right then, this lot should be through in a minute. There's not many today and only one family on this flight. You'll be able to spot them a mile off in a few weeks."

The security door opened and holidaymakers began to pour through, pulling suitcases and trying to hold on to small children. Most of them headed towards the reps from the bigger holiday companies. We lifted our clipboards high displaying the company logo, scanning the crowd for our family.

"Bingo!" shouted Tom, indicating a family of six who had burst through the doors. Tom stepped forward. The parents looked tired and I tried to keep their four children together while Tom ran through the car hire procedure. I helped them with the paperwork and successfully kept all the children together out into the car park before handing them over to Emma.

"Hey," she said quietly, "let me get rid of this lot and I'll see you guys for a coffee ok!"

"Great," I answered smiling and headed back into the airport. I'd welcomed my first Complete family and it had gone swimmingly. With a huge sense of relief, I headed up the escalator to the café where Tom and Dan were already tucking into huge doorsteps of hot toast.

"We would have saved you some, but we didn't," said Dan wiping melted butter off his chin.

"You're all heart Dan Davies," I laughed and went to buy a coffee.

"I feel rough," said Dan as I arrived back at the table, "I went to the Klan Bar for a drink last night and somehow ended up dancing in some club with random people and I think I was a bit drunk! It was so quiet though. This place is like a ghost town at this time of year."

"The Al-Grave!" laughed Tom.

"Exactly," moaned Dan, "we really need to have some fun and soon. It's been all boilers and gas fittings so far – not very glam is it? Are there ANY gay men in this country?"

"Isn't there a gay bar in Vilamoura?" I asked, "I'm sure I've seen some flyers for it."

"Really?" said Dan, his eyes bulging, "Right, we'll be going there to have a look then!"

"That big club near Albufeira is opening in a few weeks too!" said Tom.

"That's a definite on the calendar if we can sneak it under Beaky's radar," said Dan whispering.

Our social planning was interrupted by the arrival of Emma who was accompanied by Beaky herself, who had a face like thunder and spent no time getting down to business.

"I've had the questionnaires from Easter back," she said, "and they're not good." She threw copies across the table at Tom, Emma and Dan who read them looking gloomy. Each client received a questionnaire on their arrival back home asking their views about all aspects of their holiday, including their rep's performance.

"I can't believe I got 'poor' on some of these! I ran around like an idiot at Easter. Bloody hell!" moaned Emma.

"You obviously didn't run around enough!" said Ellie sternly, "and how many times do I have to tell you to take that jewellery off?"

"What's wrong with it?" asked Emma shrugging her shoulders nonchalantly.

"What's right with it? That stud in your ear looks like a bullet. The dangly earrings have to go. Take the necklace and the toe rings off and, for god's sake, tie your hair up. It looks a mess! You look a mess."

"Thanks a bunch! I'll ask you the next time I want fashion advice," mumbled Emma removing the offending items and plaiting her long, platinum hair.

Ellie glared at her before turning to the boys.

"It's just not good enough. What more do I have to do? We're almost bottom in the performance tables. I want to see dramatic improvement in these scores, or you'll all be back in training. Now let's sort out the budgets for next week and I'll leave you to get on with it."

Her words had left us all feeling deflated and demoralised. No wonder we needed a monthly morale boosting meal. We'd need one every week at this rate. Ellie was not winning over any new friends with this management style.

"Maybe she's getting it in the neck too," said Tom later once Ellie had dished out the budget and left the airport. "She's got a lot to prove this year - going from rep to manager – if she wants to keep the job."

"Oh, don't even try and defend her," said Emma replacing all her jewellery and removing her hair ties, "she was a total cow to me. There's just no need."

"I'd like to know who stole the Ellie I knew last year! We used to have a laugh. She was my mate!" wailed Dan who was poring over his questionnaires again with a hand in his hair.

"I very much doubt that," said Emma rolling her pretty eyes, "she's power crazy!"

"Honestly," said Dan sadly, "there's actually a lovely girl under all that front."

"Must be buried deep," mumbled Emma.

The mood had definitely changed since the morning and we still had several flights to greet. Luckily, they all arrived on time and the clients were fairly happy apart from my one, and only, family who were led by the most stressed man I had ever met. He had shouted at me, then Dan, then Carlos. I was glad that I had put lemons in their hamper – he was going to need a lot of gin and tonic to relax out of that mood! I wondered why people paid so much money for a holiday and then spent the whole time doing nothing but complaining and moaning.

Dan agreed to accompany me on my first visit to the family and I was eternally grateful. A bit of hand holding would not go amiss as I really didn't know anything much about Portugal and Dan knew loads. Well, he was a better blagger than me anyway!

"We'll make a star rep out of you yet," Dan announced putting his arm around my shoulders, "we'll show Beaky that we can be the best team in Europe. Wait and see!"

Nine

The next day I met Dan in the lane leading to my
villa, Casa do Campo, where my first family had
arrived yesterday. It was another bright day but
with a slight chill in the early morning air.

The villa was one of my favourites being in an
elevated position providing views all the way
across the Algarve to the sea, which twinkled in
the far distance. It was a beautiful, airy house
with large, bright rooms and huge windows to
take advantage of the view. The patio led to a
gorgeous, turquoise blue pool, which had heating
available for the cooler months. Pink
bougainvillea trailed from a pergola that shaded
the chiminea and barbecue area. It was simply
stunning.

"Morning darling!" chirped Dan, air
kissing my cheeks.

"Hi," I replied, "hope this guy has
calmed down since yesterday!"

"Don't worry," he said waving his hand
dismissively, "you'll be fine. He'll be fine.
How could you not be in a place like this?"
The client, Mr Robins, greeted us as we walked
up the driveway.

"Good morning," he bellowed, "just
admiring the gardens here."

"Morning!" I replied, "Is everything ok
for you?"

"Oh, it's wonderful, simply wonderful!
Please come in."

As we entered the hallway, Mr Robins shouted, "Put the kettle on Margaret! Make yourself useful!"

A small, birdlike woman who I hadn't even noticed at the airport came scurrying out of the kitchen, nodded and scurried off again.

Mr Robins led us into the vaulted living room and lowered his ample frame into a large easy chair. He folded his arms across his middle and looked us both up and down. The atmosphere was thick. Margaret appeared with a tray of coffee and distributed the cups around the room.

"No biscuits?" asked Mr Robins, "I guess Jo didn't put any in the hamper."

"Well actually Mr Robins..." I began, feeling irritated but Dan interrupted me,

"So, what can we tell you about the area? Is there anything in particular you're interested in?"

Margaret had settled herself on the edge of a wooden chair and lit a cigarette with shaky hands. She glanced nervously towards her husband and then disappeared back towards the kitchen.

"Would you excuse me for just a minute?" I asked as I left, looking for the tiny woman.

Margaret was leaning over the kitchen sink flicking cigarette ash on to the draining board. The sun was streaming in through the window, spotlighting the tiny woman. Her arms were thin and bony, the skin so transparent I could see her veins shining through. I coughed to announce my presence and asked,

"Is there anything I can do for you Mrs Robins?"

She sighed deeply, and turned to face me, crossing her arms.

"No love, everything's fine. I'm sorry about my husband – he can be so rude. Don't take any notice; it's not personal to you at all."

"It's ok, it's not your fault," I said kindly, smiling at her.

"It's not ok though, is it?" she sighed, "I don't know how I'm going to cope with two full weeks of him, twenty four hours a day, barking out orders like I'm a member of staff. He's so rude to everyone like he's so bloody important! I'm sorry; you don't need to hear this and I shouldn't be saying this to you."

"Really, it's ok," I said feeling desperately sorry for this frail woman. "Maybe there is something I can do to help you. How can I help make this a holiday for you too?"

"I don't know, my dear, he'll be organising me into trips and golfing days and all sorts of stuff I hate. I'd just like the chance to swim in that beautiful pool in peace."

"Golf? Your husband plays golf?" I asked as I'd picked up on one of the things we could arrange and book for clients.

"God yes, all the time. I really don't mind being a golf widow though!"

"Well, we have a few contacts in the golf clubs here. Maybe I could book him a few games on the championship courses while he's here? That would you give you some time to yourself to get in that pool. All the courses are a good forty minute drive from here plus a few hours on the course, then there's the 19th hole, of course!"

Margaret's shoulders seemed to relax down immediately.

"Really? Do you really think you could do that? He would love it; I would love it. He won't even be bothered about what I'm doing. It would be great!"

"Let's go and place the idea in his mind then, shall we?" I smiled and led her back towards the living area.

Mr Robins and Dan were busy discussing Portuguese wine and local vineyards.

"Wondered where you'd got to," said Mr Robins, "Margaret hasn't been boring you too much I hope."

"Not at all," I smiled as Margaret placed herself next to her husband, "In fact she's been telling me all about you and how great you are at playing golf. She's asked me to book some rounds for you this holiday, if you'd like that? If you tell me when you would like to play, I'll sort that out for you."

"Well Jo," blustered Mr Robins, "that would be absolutely marvellous! I say, yes indeed. You don't mind do you Margaret? You can do some shopping or something or whatever it is you ladies get up to. Thank you."

His red face brightened considerably as a huge grin spread across it. Margaret mouthed a thank you at me from beside her husband.
Dan's mouth fell open and then formed into a smile as he winked at me.

Later, over lunch, Dan asked me, "What happened back there? What did Margaret say to you in the kitchen?"
I explained briefly as Dan shook his head.

"Well," he said, "if poor Marge has got anything to do with the questionnaire, I would say you've just earned your first 'excellent.'"

Ten

Later that afternoon, I was due to meet Tom in
Santa Caterina da Fonte do Bispo. This small,
typical village was halfway between our
apartments and was also the location for a
fabulous café 'Rosarhinas.' Most of the tables
were outside taking advantage of the wonderful
view across the valley, which led to the sea. The
air was hazy and shimmered in the afternoon
warmth. Each table had a large umbrella to
protect the customers sitting underneath and,
what made it so pretty was, each umbrella was a
different colour creating a gorgeous rainbow
across the otherwise uninteresting gravelled
ground.

Tom was already seated at an outdoors table,
surrounded by several piles of paperwork
weighed down with various stones and pebbles.
        "Hi Tom!" I greeted him
enthusiastically, "Another bica?" Tom adored
the coffee, much like an espresso, and drank far
too many.
        "Oh hi!" he replied, smiling as he
removed his sunglasses. "Yes please, can you see
my pen anywhere?" He continued lifting stones
and bits of paper as he looked in vain.
        "It's behind your ear," I laughed as I
walked to the café kiosk to order.
When I arrived back at the table, Tom was half
standing, swearing under his breath, his hands
clasped in his hair making it even messier than
normal.

"What's wrong Tom? Something tells me you're a little stressed."

"Oh, it's these safety checks! They drive me insane. You'd think I'd be organised with it now, doing them every month but I can't remember where I've been, what I've checked, what I haven't...."

"Maybe I should have got you a camomile tea instead of coffee!" I said soothingly as I pressed his shoulder to get him to sit down in his chair.

"Why don't I help you with some of this this afternoon? It might take the pressure off you a bit?"

"Oh Jo, that would be just great! But...hang on a minute! What's in it for you?" he asked suspiciously, his eyes narrowing.

"Tom, I'm helping you out of the kindness of my heart, of course." I said in mock horror, my hand clasped to my chest, "and, well, I could also do with going back over it myself to be honest. Ellie went through everything so quickly. I'm not really sure what I should be doing when!"

"And..." he said quizzically.

"Ok," I said, in answer to his raised eyebrows, "I thought, maybe, you could show me The Waterfall. I think I'm going to need something up my sleeve to win clients over this season. I told him about the clients at Caso de Campo. If they're all like that, I'm going to need some help! Please!" I begged, my eyebrows raised in question.

"Shhh...you know that place is my secret weapon," he whispered conspiratorially looking around for eavesdroppers.

"It can be *our* little secret weapon, can't it?" I whispered back lowering my head and looking up at him from underneath my eyelashes.

His face broke into a huge grin, crinkling the skin around his green eyes.

"How can I resist you?" he replied and my heart skipped a beat. "If you help me sort out all this," he indicated all the paperwork, "then you're on. I'll show you the waterfall."

The next couple of hours were swallowed with visiting villas, checking emissions from gas boilers, the safety of balcony railings and chlorine levels in swimming pools; and most importantly, completing all the paperwork. Tom kept his half of the bargain though, being more than grateful for my admin skills. We drove back into the hills on the main road from Tavira to Sao Bras, on our way to find The Waterfall.

"I'm really excited to see this place," I said.

"How do you even know about it?" he asked, "I thought it was a big secret."

"Not that big," I laughed, "both Emma and Dan have told me about it but had no idea where it is or how to get there, just that it's off this main road."

"Oh yes," he said, "I brought them here when we first arrived. We had a couple of hot days and Ellie let us have some time off from the training."

"How do you know about the waterfall?" I asked.

"Last year, I made lots of friends with the locals and the villa owners. A couple of them told me about it and one day, one of the managers drew me a map and I explored. You'd never find it without a map! It's very hidden away, as you'll see."

Tom indicated and turned the car right down a very narrow track that was marked off the main road by a tiny wooden arrow. If you didn't know it was there, you'd miss it. The dusty, rough track led to a dry riverbed, full of large stone boulders, where we parked on the riverbank.

"In winter, this is a fast running river," said Tom, "you can only get to the waterfall in the summer months. Even when we came here in April, we had to wade across the river."

The sun had begun to set but the heat hadn't abated at all. Tom scrambled down the dry riverbank and held out his hand to help me down. We picked our way across the boulders and sand and climbed up the opposite bank. This side of the river was packed with dense bamboo plants that were dry and brittle, dusty and full of flies. The dust invaded my nose, making me sneeze, and stuck to my skin. However, we made our way through easily as others had already blazoned a trail, pushing the plants aside to create a very rough path.

"I hope there's a Michelin map available for this place," I joked, "How did anybody ever find it?"

"I do have a map, like I said, but I only give it to people I really like. Most clients will never know this place exists. All the locals know about this place and sometimes, you get here and it's packed with people!"

After a few minutes of walking through the brown, brittle plants, Tom parted the last few and I got my first glimpse of 'The Waterfall.'

Below me was, what I could only describe as, a lagoon of beautiful, clear, azure blue water surrounded by rocky outcrops that provided shady seating. Trees surrounded the waterhole, providing some dappled shade and, at one end, water was cascading down black rocks, which were slick and glistening with blue-green algae. The noise of the falling water was all I could hear as it fell into the lagoon below. The setting sun was bouncing off the water making it sparkle and shimmer and as the sun shone through the water, little rainbows appeared. It was a magical spot and we were the only people there to appreciate it.

"At this time of year, there's a lot of water flowing down. Give it a week or two and it will be more of a trickle."

"Wow, Tom it's beautiful!" I gasped, "I didn't think it would be anything like this!"

He'd been watching my face closely and he grinned broadly as he saw my reaction.

"Come on," he yelled, "last one in buys dinner!"

He'd already kicked his trousers off as he pulled his t-shirt over his head and jumped the five feet down into the water. I laughed as I pulled on my dress zip before stopping, crippled by embarrassment.

Tom had already surfaced, breaking through the water, wiping water from his eyes. With beads of water on his bronzed torso, I couldn't help but stare, my mouth hanging slightly open.

"Come on," he yelled, "what are you doing? It's gorgeous in here!"

"It certainly is," I thought as I wriggled out of my dress and stood feeling self-conscious in my underwear. I scrambled very awkwardly down a rocky outcrop and jumped into the surprisingly cool water. It felt amazing on my skin after such a hot working day and the dusty walk through the bamboo.

"Dinner's on you then slow coach,"
Tom yelled splashing water at me as I surfaced.
I splashed him back as the cool water ran down
my head taking my makeup with it, but I didn't
care. How right I was to send that job
application; I wouldn't have missed any of this
for the world.

Eleven

After an hour of blissful swimming, we were
headed back to Rosarinhos, where I'd left my
car. The daytime café had now been transformed
into a candlelit restaurant. The large parasols
had been removed and strings of white light
bulbs lit the perimeter.   "Tom, it looks so
pretty! Can't we just eat here? It is halfway
between our places and, well, it's just easy!"
He smiled at me and nodded, "Sure, great idea,
Jo," he said as he guided me to an empty table,
complete with lit candle. The fact it was such a
romantic setting was not lost on me. I'd managed
to at least brush my wet hair, which was still
damp and dripping, leaving dark patches on my
dress.
We settled ourselves into our chairs on opposite
sides of the table and began to peruse the menu.
It was typical of the area with seafood, meats and
salads. We ordered prawns, piri piri chicken,
rice, vegetables and salad. While we waited, the
waiter brought the usual beige accompaniments
of bread, olives, sardine pate and oil. I have to
say, sometimes this was the best part of the meal
and I'd cultivated quite a taste for it. Being
careful not to have too much to spoil the main
event, I took some bread and pate and nibbled on
an olive.

   "Now you've settled in, what do you
think of it all?" asked Tom. His hair, too, was
still damp and glistened in the low light.

   "It's been such hard work these last few
weeks," I replied, "so many clients just like to
moan about nothing. If I were lucky enough to

61

be on holiday in any of these villas, I wouldn't even bother my rep. Why would you need to?"

"Well, that's why they love Complete," he laughed, "I swear some of them just like to make us rush around after them. It's like a sport to them."

"You're not wrong there," I replied sighing and rolling my eyes.

"I'm worried about Villa Das Avores, it's so dark and dated and I'm just waiting for someone to start really kicking off. The outside is ok but go inside and it's like a cave. Though last week's family moaned about the leaves in the pool. They actually asked me if I could visit each morning to scoop them out!"
Tom was laughing at me now. "Oh Jo, you do make me laugh. What did you say to them?"

"I told them there was a long pole with a net attached and that's what they needed to use to scoop the leaves themselves. I also, very politely, pointed out that Villa Das Avores actually means Villa amongst the trees; trees have leaves, duh!"

"I bet that went down well," said Tom, sipping his drink and peering at me over the rim.

"Oh, I know, I shouldn't have been so sarky but, honestly! Maybe I'll make all of you look really good this month when the questionnaires come through because I'll be getting all the 'poor' marks."
Tom sniggered, nearly spitting cola over me, "I wouldn't be so sure! Don't forget I had a warring couple for over a month, living amongst my clients! They were arguing all the time. Hardly the calm, restful atmosphere people were expecting on their holiday."
Tom had a block of luxury apartments, managed by a married couple, who were now separated

after a month of loud, emotional arguments
which included china and plant throwing!
We laughed together, "Oh, we work hard!" I
said, "we can't make other people be perfect any
more than we can be perfect, can we?"

"Amen to that," sighed Tom.

The waiter had brought us prawns cooked in
garlic butter and we mopped up the juices with
the bread we still had as we tucked in, hungry
from our swimming. The prawns were large and
succulent with flecks of chilli which caught my
tongue.

"Oh my, these are delicious!" I
mumbled as I caught a dribble of butter about to
run down my chin. Tom was mopping up his
butter with his bread.

"Not exactly figure friendly, all this
beige, is it?" I laughed.

"Like you need to worry about your
figure!" he replied rolling his eyes.

"How do..?" I trailed off, "I thought you
didn't look when I got into the lagoon!?" I
replied placing my hands on my hips and
pouting.

"I didn't, but might have accidently
seen you climbing out," he said laughing.
I was glad the light was so dim as my face felt
was on fire with embarrassment. I hid my face
in my hands and groaned.

"You know what, Jo? You need to get
some confidence. You are a beautiful girl! You
have so many qualities and skills and you've
already helped me loads when you didn't have
to. Be proud of who you are!"

Tears prickled the backs of my eyes and I
rammed my fists into my eye sockets before
blowing my nose on my napkin. Tom smiled

sympathetically and reached across the table for my hand taking it in his.

"Has life been so hard Jo?"

Holding back the tears and swallowing the hard lump of emotion in my throat, I nodded.

"When I graduated, I thought life would be amazing. That's what they told us at uni. 'The world is your oyster.' In the year after leaving, I sent over 300 job applications and didn't get a single interview. I rang people, hand delivered CV's, temped to get more experience but nothing made any difference. I watched my friends get the second or third job they applied for and I was left behind, still living at home. I could never figure out what I was doing wrong so I figured it must be something wrong with me! I guess that thinking has just stuck."

"Oh Jo, I'm sorry." Tom squeezed my hand and listened intently.

"It was only when I met Andrew that I was able to move out of home and into a flat with him in London. I still couldn't get a job I was interested in and ended up working as a PA. I hate office work! But then I saw the ad for this job and, well, here I am."

I took a really, deep breath and let the emotion out with a shaky sigh. I hadn't spoken like this to anyone before.

"And here you are! I'm really glad you saw that advert Jo," he smiled encouragingly. My heart missed a beat as I smiled back at him.

"Me too," I replied.

Twelve

The days passed quickly and the season was in full swing. The temperature had really climbed and was hitting the mid to high thirties most days. Most of our properties were full every week and the majority of clients were happy and enjoying their holiday. However, there were still the few who liked to moan; "I can't put loo roll down the toilet", "the water pressure isn't high enough", "the maid doesn't speak English", "the local restaurants only serve Portuguese food", "there's leaves in the pool" or even, and my personal favourite, "the sun is too hot". These were among the most common complaints and things I could do absolutely nothing about.

The job was busy and I lost count of the hours I spent drawing locations of restaurants on maps, ferrying highchairs and cots back and forth across the Algarve to my colleagues and smiling. I had to smile a lot, even when I was cursing in my head.
Dan had been dining in with his clients, hoping for a top class job offer for the end of the season. Emma had been so caught up with work, I hadn't seen her for a few weeks outside of welcoming the new arrivals. I would sometimes see Tom tearing along the main road, on route to one of his properties, and give him a wave. The relaxed dinners in the week were consigned to the past for now.

Airport day was becoming part of the routine and we worked as a well oiled team should. We covered for each other when necessary, fitted baby seats into cars, drank more coffee than was good for us and kept the clients moving through the airport and on the way to their luxury holiday.

After a particularly long, trying airport day, we drove our cars in convoy to Quarteira for a well deserved drink at the Klan Bar. This bar was a step away from Dan's apartment and meant he always relaxed much more than the rest of us. After ordering a round of drinks for us all, he closed the parasol so we could enjoy the sun setting into the sea in front of us. Dan was so lucky living right on this beautiful, golden beach, which was wide and expansive. The tide was in and the sea lapped gently in a rhythmical, calming wave. The sun was turning the sand a deep orange and the shadows were lengthening as the restaurateurs along the front were readying their tables for the evening diners to come. Streaks of pink, lilac and orange painted across the sky, reflecting on our upturned faces.

"I don't know about anyone else," moaned Emma, breaking the moment of peace, "but I'm SO bored! We never have any fun. It's been weeks since we've all been out. All I ever do is sit on my balcony drinking wine by myself, listening to the radio, and wishing I lived closer to you lot."

"Don't worry Em," I said, "that's all I ever do too."

The others nodded their agreement sadly.

"We're in danger of becoming professional at our jobs," moaned Dan, "and you know what that means?"

"We're BORING!" wailed Emma and Tom in unison, then laughed at each other.

"I haven't been out of that office in weeks," moaned Beth who had joined us.

66

"Ellie is doing my head in! She comes in every morning at 8.30am on the dot and if I'm not there, ready to work or already working, she starts cracking the whip at me! She doesn't even knock before she comes in. It's so rude. It is still my apartment as well as the office!"

"Oh, that is rude," I said, "she rang me last night to tell me my last questionnaires weren't that great. I needed to know that on a Saturday night. She couldn't wait until today to make me feel rubbish."

"Yes well, I know why she's especially uptight at the moment," said Beth.
Beth was a great source of information about the workings and gossip of the London office. She had absolutely no qualms in telling us any information she knew.

"There's an educational coming out next week!" she said, "Gabriela is coming too for one of her jollies badly disguised as a contracting visit!"

An educational was sent out to various programmes several times a year. London sales staff came to view the properties and areas so they could better advise people wishing to book a holiday with Complete, having actually been there. Occasionally, the contacts team came out to visit potential properties for the programme and, if suitable, sign them up. Gabriela Becker was the Contracts Manager and had interviewed me and, although I got on with her very well in interview, I felt nervous at the thought of her coming here.

"How do Gaby and Ellie get on then? I take it they don't hit it off?" I asked Tom. He sucked the air through his teeth and took a gulp of beer,

"They get on fine. Most of the time. I like Gaby! She's a good laugh!" he said rather unconvincingly.

"Excellent," smiled Emma, becoming more animated, "There's nothing like a good bitch fight! I can't wait for this!"

Emma went to the bar to order more drinks and appeared to be deep in conversation with a handsome looking Portuguese guy.

"Who's Emma talking to?" asked Dan craning his neck to get a better view, "He's well fit!"

"And not gay," added Tom.

"Of course he's gay," scoffed Dan waving his hand dismissively at Tom. "He keeps looking at me! I bet he's asking her about me!" He began to smooth his hands through his hair, preening himself ready.

"He's probably wondering who the perv is in the corner who's staring at HIM!" I said laughing.

Emma was making her way back across the bar, pulling down the hem of her blue sequinned dress while teetering on her platform heels and flicking her blonde hair away from her face. She was looking very pleased with herself and blushing slightly.

"Well?" we chorused in anticipation. Dan was waiting, poised like a meercat, ready to make his move.

Emma looked at him with pity, sighed slightly and smiling broadly, babbled,

"His name is Rogerio. He's 22 and works for a car hire company. We're going for a drink tomorrow night," she squealed waving the

piece of paper he'd given her with his name and
number on.

"I hope you appreciate your good
fortune," said Dan huffily, sitting down heavily
and folding his arms, "because you're going to
be really upset when he tells you he's gay!"

Emma had just taken a swig from her glass as
she laughed blowing beer out of her nose.

In typical fashion, after a hard airport day, we all
drank a bit too much. Beth weaved her way
home with Tom as escort. By the time he
returned Dan had downed a couple more drinks
and was totally drunk.

"I wanna dance," he slurred, "dance
with me Jo."

He pulled my arms trying to make me stand to
dance but I kept shaking him off. Other drinkers
were watching him in amusement as he threw his
body into weird shapes. The bar was not very big
for Dan to wave his arms and legs about, so he
had moved onto the pavement next to our table.
When Dan drank a lot, he became very
suggestible and easily led; a fact we took
advantage of at every opportunity.

"Dan!" shouted Tom laughing, "Do the
twist! Chubby Checker!"
Obediently, Dan began to twist down to the
ground, a serious expression etched on his face.
This was Dad dancing at its finest.
I laughed so much I thought I might pee my
pants.

"Smile Dan, smile!" said Emma.
Dan smiled as he tried to twist back up again but
his legs would not lift him and he stayed
crouched down on the floor, still trying to twist.

"Help me Jo! Help Danny!" he pleaded with me but I was feeling a bit cruel and just giggled at his plight, tears rolling down my face.

"Right sailor boy, I think it's time we got you home, don't you?" Tom laughed, shaking his head and standing, readying himself for the task ahead.

"No! I wanna dance more," he wailed grabbing onto the back of a metal chair and gyrating.

"Come on Dan," said Tom gently but firmly, feeling a hundred eyes upon us, "we've all got to face client visits in the morning."

Dan's reply surprised us all, "You're all boring! This is boring! I'm bored. I'm going home." Dan heaved himself up from the floor, stood for a second and took a few zigzag steps across the floor. He did not look stable or safe.

"We best go with him before he locks us out and we have nowhere to stay tonight," I said to Tom, as I stood keeping an eye on the weaving Dan, "Emma, are you staying over too?"

"I might just stay here a bit longer," she smiled looking over at Rogerio who was now alone and smiling her way, his white teeth flashing.

"Emma, be careful, yeah?!" said Tom giving her a hug, "come up soon."

"Ok, ok, go before that drunk locks you out!"

We left the bar and ran around the corner to see Dan swearing at the front door to his apartment building "Torre Azul." The name makes it sound rather beautiful but that couldn't be further from the truth. It was an ugly, concrete block plonked on the edge of the beach. Cars were parked everywhere around its base and litter blew around the door. Awkward balconies stuck out at different places at each floor height.

"Someone's broken my key, it won't work!" he wailed.

"God Dan, you really are pathetic when you've been drinking," I shook my head as I took the keys from him and used the right key to open the door. With me on one side of the swaying Dan and Tom on the other, we got him safely into the lift and up to the tenth floor, apartment D.

"Look, D for Dan! They must have known I was going to live here. D for Dan! D for Dan!"

He was being so loud, we kept shushing him as we navigated him to the front door and unlocked his apartment. Stumbling through the small entrance, I pushed Dan through to the living room where he veered to the left, headed straight for his bedroom and fell face down, diagonally across the bed and began to snore loudly. I looked across at Tom with a raised eyebrow and we both laughed.

"Look, you make tea and I'll cover him up and make him move over to one side," I said panting slightly with the exertion of getting him this far.

I pulled off Dan's shoes and he snorted loudly. I tried to make him move and he just kicked out at me over and over. He really was like a petulant toddler when he'd been drinking. I grabbed a blanket, threw it over him and left the room.

"I'm sorry Tom," I said taking the cup of tea he offered me, "It looks like you and me are going to have to share the sofa bed. I can't move Dan, he's a ton weight and...."

71

"Hey, I don't mind if you don't," he shrugged nonplussed.

"Right then, ok," I said trying not to look embarrassed or awkward.

I went to use the bathroom and to change and when I got back, Tom had pulled the sofa bed out and found some blankets.

"I've made a little nest for us," he said indicating the bed, I don't think I've done too bad."

I laughed, a little too loud and uncontrollably, climbed under the blankets and turned onto my side facing the wall. I felt anything but relaxed as Tom got in behind me and snuggled down.

"I hope Emma will be alright. She won't do anything silly will she?" asked Tom.

"She's a big girl, she'll be ok," I replied sleepily, "Stop worrying about us all you Mother Hen."

There was a silence and then I felt an arm slipping round my waist. Tom pulled me towards him, and I could feel his warm breath on my neck. I smiled in the darkness, slipped my hand into his and fell asleep.

Thirteen

A phone was ringing somewhere in the distance, and for a moment, I had no idea where I was. I prised my eyes open to see rays of light coming through blinds and I remembered this was Dan's apartment. The ringing continued and I groaned as I tried to get up to answer it. Tom's arm was still wrapped around my waist, pinning me to him and I couldn't move. I gave up with a sigh and relaxed back down into my pillow. The ringing stopped for a few minutes and then started again. Something must be wrong. I would have to answer it.

Just as I was trying to wriggle free from Tom's arm, Dan flew into the room. His hair was standing straight up on one side and he had crease marks from his sheets down his cheeks. He picked up the phone,

"Hello?" He rubbed his eyes and yawned as he listened.

"What? Where? Really? No, I can't," he replied curtly to the caller, "I can barely see, never mind drive!"

After another pause, he bellowed down the line,

"Well, that's not my problem! Call Car Hire or something. What do you want me to do? Yes, they are but they're still asleep…ooh… right next to each other. Look, I don't know. Look it up where? You look it up! I'm going back to sleep. Bye!"

He replaced the handset and, groaning and scratching, shuffled back to his room.

"Dan," I yelled, "who was that? Is everything ok?"

"Yeah," he mumbled, "It was Emma."

"Dan? Dan! Where is she? Did you ask? Is she ok?" I threw Tom's arm off me and swung my legs over the side of the sofa. Standing up, I felt a little dizzy and grabbed the back of the nearest chair to steady myself.

"Dan?" I shouted in frustration. There was no response as I went into his room and poked him. "Dan, is Em ok?"

He squirmed at my poking, "Ow! Stop that! She's broken down somewhere and asked to be rescued. I don't know the phone number of the car hire desk, do you?"

"Well, yes actually. I've got it on me all the time in case any clients break down, as should you! Did she say where she was?"

"No, she did not," he said huffily pulling a pillow over his head.

"How can you be so selfish? She could be anywhere. She's on her own, Dan!"

I was so cross with Dan but also with myself. I should have made her come back with us last night. What was she doing driving after last night? Maybe she'd gone home with Rogerio. I was worried now and tried to dial the last number received. No number had registered; she must have called from a pay phone.

A sleepy Tom was yawning and stretching asking me what was happening.

"Maybe she'll call back in a minute," he suggested, his brow furrowing, "what is wrong with Dan?"

"I don't know but he's bang out of order; she could be in real trouble" I said fuming with anger.

"God, it's time we were on the road soon. I've got fifteen sets of people to see today!" moaned Tom, "What can we do about Emma?"

"You've got time for a cup of tea and no one will want to see you at eight in the morning, eh? We don't know where she is, thanks to Dan, so there's not much we can do unless she calls back. I'll be worried all day!"

I rang Emma's home number and left a bit of a frantic message asking her to call as soon as she got home. Tom did the same, concern etched on his face, and accepted the cup of tea I handed him.

"Listen," he said looking at the floor and colouring a little, "I'm sorry about last night...you know...hugging you..."

"Oh no," I said my face flushing, "it's fine. We'd been drinking...it's a small bed and it was cold and stuff..."

I tailed off not knowing what else to say and avoided meeting his eyes. I didn't want him to see what was growing within me. The silence hung in the air for a second.

"Look, maybe you could come over for dinner later in the week or something?" he smiled, eyebrows raised in question.

"I'd like that, thank you," I smiled, breathing out heavily, relieved that the awkward moment had passed.

There was no waking Dan, so we left him still snoring gently under his blanket as we dressed, drank more tea and readied ourselves to drive back east to see our happy clients in their villas.

Later that day, I still hadn't heard from Emma and was getting very worried. I'd checked my messages many times and, for once, was not relieved to find there were none. I left even more messages for her and continued with my paperwork slowly, imagining all kinds of scenarios. Finally, the phone rang as I was in the middle of my accounts.

"Jo, it's Dan!" he barked down the phone at me, "Why didn't you wake me up this morning?"

"Hi Dan, I'm fine thank you. You looked so peaceful; it seemed a shame to disturb you."

"I missed all my morning clients! I had so many messages on my phone. I didn't wake up until 11.30am. I had to make up an emergency!"

"Dan! It's not my problem you didn't set your alarm. Have you heard anything from Emma?"

"No, why should I?"

"You don't remember her phoning this morning?"

"Stop pissing about Jo! What phone call?"

"Emma is the emergency," I said then explained what had happened that morning,

"Well, I don't remember talking to her and even if I did, it's not my problem that she broke down!"

"Right, don't worry about it Dan…It's just no one has heard anything from her since." I sighed.

"Oh. I'm sure you'll find her underneath that handsome local!"

"Dan! This is worrying! What if she's not ok?"

"I'll bet my salary she's fine. Anyway, what was going on between you and Tom this morning? You looked very cosy wrapped up in your little sofa bed!"

"Nothing, just sleeping, that's all! Like we had to because you were star-fished on your bed, leaving no room for anyone else."

"Yeah, right. I'll be keeping a watch on you two. Does the lovely Tammy know about you?"

"Grow up Dan," I said moodily as I hung up the phone.

Immediately, I felt bad and decided to call him back. Maybe my behaviour was proving his theory correct. I shouldn't be so reactive and defensive. Before I could pick up the phone to call him back, the phone rang again. It was Emma.

"EMMA! I've been so worried about you. I tried to call you back this morning..."

"Hey, don't worry," she said calming me down, "I'm ok, honestly, and I know what Dan's like when he's been drinking. I was just ringing really hoping that you or Tom would answer."

"Believe me, it wasn't for the lack of trying. What happened to you last night?"

"Well, I stayed in the bar with Rogerio, had a few more waters...oh Jo...he's so fit! We got on so well and I stayed so long that I didn't want to come and wake you guys up to let me in, so decided to drive home. I was halfway home on the N125, when I felt really tired, so I pulled off into a quiet area and fell asleep. I woke up sprawled across the front seat and my car wouldn't start because I'd stupidly left the headlights on. I got out and walked for ages until I found a pay phone and that's when I spoke to Dan."

"Oh Em, then what happened?" I asked.

"I found the Car Hire number in my diary and then had to wait for the people to come rescue me. Oh Jo, it was so embarrassing. If it wasn't bad enough walking along the N125, at 8 in the morning, in a sparkly dress and platform shoes with cars beeping at me; I was expecting one of the guys to come rescue me, but this van turns up with the WHOLE team in the back, including all the really cute driver boys, and insisted that I go with them for lunch! Jo, my hair was fluffy and knotted and I had mascara running down my face – I could have died right there on the spot. They were all laughing at me especially when I used their mobile to call clients to apologise for my no show! God, if Ellie hears about this, I'm so sacked!"

"I'm just glad you're ok, Em. I've been so worried. I wouldn't worry about Ellie – if she knew even half of what goes on, we'd all be sacked."

"Yeah, well she rang me today and I know I could hear tennis balls being hit in the background. I asked if she was at the tennis club and she denied it. All she does is play tennis and lie on the beach. Who's got the best tan out of all of us?"

"Yeah, you're right. She'll have to make a bit more of a show when Gaby arrives. I can't wait to see some fur fly. Anyway, what you doing tomorrow? It's my day off and I fancy exploring the fine shopping in Faro. We could have lunch and spoil ourselves?"

"Sounds good to me. I'll see you tomorrow."

Fourteen

Emma arrived at my apartment at 11am with a baby bath under her arm.

"I forgot to mention this last night. The family that moved to Moinho do Monte from The Roundhouse made me buy this for their child. I'm guessing they'll want it this week too. We could drop it off on the way and win some brownie points!"

"Good thinking! Hopefully, I'll be able to slip in quietly, leave it and sneak away before anyone notices I'm there. You know what they're like on your day off!"

"Don't I just!" Emma rolled her eyes. "We'll sneak in and they'll never know we've even been."

It was a beautiful day and heat haze was already visible on the tarmac. I took extra care putting on the seatbelt as I'd burned my thigh more than once on the metal buckle. We wound the windows down and blasted Moloko's "Bring it Back," on the short drive to Moinho do Monte. I hung my arm out of the window to feel the cool air, just like the locals did. The air flow moved my hand gently and dried my palm.
Turning the music down as we approached the gateway to the property, I coasted my car into the car park as quietly as I could. I wrote a short note to leave with the baby bath and made my way up the driveway to the apartment door of the Bowden family.

This property was set high on a hill and had panoramic views across the rolling hills to the north and down to the sea in the south. It was made up of six apartments all with private terraces and built in the round so no one was overlooked. Every apartment was separated by well placed rosebushes and hedging kept the individual lawned areas separate. All the clients had access to a large, well kept swimming pool and barbecue area edged with trimmed lawn and shrubs. Large palm trees, which shushed gently in the breeze, provided some shade for the bright blue sun loungers. The whole building was covered in bright pink bougainvillea that fluttered gently around in the constant breeze, which came up from the sea, creating a gorgeous, scented confetti.

The French owners, Philippe and Sandrine, had created the perfect hideaway and worked hard to maintain the landscaped gardens and peaceful atmosphere. Their dog, a black Labrador named Pepe, struggled to his feet to greet me with a wag of his tail.

I whispered a hello to him and knelt to give him some love and tummy rubs. He was such a silly, docile old dog. Standing up was obviously far too much effort in the searing heat, however, and he waddled off and collapsed under the shade of a nearby carob tree and fell asleep.

The calm and peaceful idyll was shattered, as I neared the Bowden's apartment door, by the sound of raised voices.

"Oh lord," I thought, "I hope I'm not about to walk into the middle of a domestic."

As I got closer, it became apparent that it was two women who were arguing. There was no way I was going to be sneaking in and sneaking out again. I carefully rounded the edge of the pathway, hoping I could just leave the bath on the patio, and was shocked to discover the source of the voices were Mrs Bowden and Sandrine, who were stood just inside the open doorway.

"Ah non, it is not the behaviour of civilised people!" tutted Sandrine.

"They're just children, for goodness sake. You have cleaners don't you?" Mrs Bowden remonstrated with her.

"Excuse me!" I said but they neither saw nor heard me.

"No other children behave like this!" said Sandrine tossing her blonde fringe to one side, her voice raising. Her eyes were flashing like I'd never seen before. She was normally the epitome of calm, teaching her guests how to paint in watercolour.

"They're only babies!" replied Mrs Bowden waving her hands around her head in frustration and pushing frizzy brown hair back off her hot, red face.

"EXCUSE ME!" I shouted.
They both stopped abruptly, mouths open, and turned to look at me.

"Thank you," I said, "does someone want to tell me what is going on here?"

They began shouting accusations at each other. Mrs Bowden was swiping her hands around almost hitting the smaller Sandrine. I couldn't decipher anything with them both shouting. Holding both arms up to calm them both I said, "Mrs Bowden, if you would please tell me what's going on here please?"

"My children are only tiny. They don't have, what you would call, table manners yet and yes, they do make some mess. We're on holiday and don't want to be cleaning up every five minutes. That's what cleaners are for! Madame Bovere came to bring us the walking maps of the area I had asked for and just started yelling at

81

me. This is not what I expected from Complete Holidays and I will be writing a strongly worded letter of complaint about the attitude of your staff!" she sneered at me.

Sandrine had folded her arms in front of her chest and, tapping her foot, gasped and tutted disbelievingly at every word Mrs Bowden had said.

"Mrs Bowden," I said calmly, "I'm sure this is all a misunderstanding and if we all keep calm, we will be able to sort this out. Now, Sandrine, you tell me, what happened here?"

"One of my cleaners, Fernanda came to me a little while ago to say that this apartment was," she sniffed holding her small nose in the air, "in a disgusting state. She refused to clean this kitchen and I came to look for myself. When I saw the dirt, all over the walls and, mon Dieu, the ceiling, I had to say something to the family and Mrs Bowden began attacking me. That's where you came in."

They both started arguing with each other again, not listening and talking over one another.

"Will you please be quiet!" I said, my voice raised more than I ever have before, "Mrs Bowden, will you please go to the pool area. I will speak with Sandrine and come and find you when we have decided on a solution."

"Ok, but I'm not staying here if it's not cleaned," she said and flounced out of the apartment in the direction of the pool and the rest of her family.

Emma, bored of waiting in the car so long, had come to investigate. She appeared at the doorway of the apartment, pulling her long hair into a low bun, she asked me,

"Jo, is everything ok? Is there anything I can do?"

"Ah, the solution!" said Sandrine, "If she wants this place cleaned then I suggest you do it! Otherwise, find her somewhere else to stay!"

She marched out of the door, without another word or looking back, and turned away to her private quarters.

"Oh God, sorry Jo! What on earth is going on?" asked Emma, looking dismayed.

I explained what had happened as I looked at the damage in the kitchen.

"How could a small child possibly have got spaghetti up there?" I asked pointing to the ceiling where several strands of the pasta were being held in place by dried tomato sauce.

"I'm afraid if we're going to have any sort of day off, I'm going to have to clean this myself and deal with the fall out later!"

"No way!" said Emma, "That's not fair! Just because she can't control her children and Sandrine can't control her cleaners shouldn't mean you end up cleaning up after them all. I didn't have this issue with them at The Roundhouse."

"I know but I don't think there's any other option if I want to get out of here today!"

"Right then," said Emma, "I'm going to help you. We will have that lunch, or maybe dinner, if it kills us," she said looking at her watch. "Come on, quicker we start and all that!"

"Emma, you are a star and I owe you a very big one!"

"Yes, you do and don't think I'll let you forget it," she smiled throwing me a pair of rubber gloves she had found under the sink.

83

It took us several hours to rid the apartment of sticky, tomato sauce, which had found its way into every nook and cranny of the kitchen. We could not work out how a nine month old baby and a three year old could create so much mess while eating. I had to spend nearly an hour with Mrs Bowden to calm her down and persuade her to stay in the property. I think it was only due to our cleaning efforts that she agreed. She admitted to being slightly embarrassed by the whole affair and agreed to apologise to Sandrine. Equally, I had to spend time with Sandrine, who was so upset she was angrily throwing paint at a canvas when I found her. An accomplished artist, she was creating something quite similar to the sauce patterns we had just removed from the ceiling of the apartment kitchen! She accepted Mrs Bowden's apology with grace and said she was sorry for the things she had said about the children.

I couldn't be sure how sincere she was but, for the sake of her business, she backed down.

By the time we left the property, we were tired, dirty and hungry. We drove back to my apartment feeling deflated, dirty and tired. Some day off!

I checked my messages and groaned as I listened to the clipped tones of Ellies voice summoning us to a meal with the rest of the team and Gabriela, who had arrived that morning. It promised to be an interesting evening!

Fifteen

Later that evening, I drove Emma to the Klan bar where we were meeting the rest of the team before the meal. Tom and Beth were already in place, drinking red wine.

"Hi guys!" said Emma.

"Hi!" said Tom flashing me a smile, "How was the shopping trip?"

"Urgh! Don't even go there. We're cursed when it comes to the day out we've planned for weeks!"

Tom and Beth were both looking questioningly at us both so Emma continued, "We didn't get to go because we spent the afternoon scraping pasta off a ceiling!" said Emma in frustration.

"Don't even ask!" I said in response to Tom and Beth's amazed expressions.

Tom went to the bar as Beth gave us the gossip from the day so far.

"Well," she said looking around the bar before leaning into the table and talking in hushed tones, "Gaby arrived this morning and turned up at the office. Ellie wasn't there to meet her and Gaby was not impressed. She rang her on her mobile and told her to get to the office pronto. Well, I'm sure you can imagine how Ellie took that! She turned up an hour later and by that time Gaby was fuming. It's all a power struggle, you know. The educational is arriving in a few days and Gaby wants to make sure we have everything in place. Ellie doesn't like it because it's not part of Gaby's job. She's just here on one of her jollies. Her philosophy is 'Let's drink loads, eat loads and put it on the company credit card.'"

"Good philosophy!" said Emma rubbing her hands together, "I can't wait for tonight. Once there's some alcohol flowing...ooh I could just go a good bitch fight."

"Where are we eating tonight anyway?" I asked Beth, ignoring Emma's bloodthirst, "I'm starving; we didn't get to have lunch."

"Well, I'm not sure where it is but we are going to a Fado restaurant. Ellie thinks it's time you were all cultured."

"Oh my god!" said Emma, "I can handle the fur flying but listening to Fado? I don't know if I can handle that."

Fado is a music genre and part of traditional Portuguese culture, which originates in Lisbon. It's song usually with a melancholy theme, accompanied by a guitar. Most of the time it's improvised and, history buffs, it was once banned on the grounds that it was deemed harmful to social progress. The best Fado is still to be heard in Lisbon but some tourist restaurants in the Algarve offer the art to their customers as an added extra.

Just as we were all pondering the thought of a Fado based evening, Dan arrived resplendent in a pink shirt and tight, dark blue jeans.

"Are you sure it was a wise idea to wear jeans that tight when you're going to be eating?" laughed Emma naughtily.

Dan was not known for his restraint when it came to food.

"Ahem, I see you made it back from the N125 then," he said sniffily, ignoring her comment.

"No thanks to you," she smiled in a fake nice voice.

There was a prolonged silence as Emma and Dan stared at each other, almost daring each other to start the argument.

"Ahem, come on, let's go or else we'll be late," said Tom trying to diffuse the situation as tactfully as he could, standing and herding us towards the door.

The restaurant was situated on a corner and had black canopies above the windows. There were some bistro tables outside underneath these canopies where some smokers were seated with after dinner coffee. I followed the team through the front door, blinking as my eyes adjusted to the dim lighting. The room was also very smoky and very hot. We were led through to a large circular table where Ellie and Gaby were already seated arguing over the wine list. Everything about this restaurant was dark including the black tablecloths, dark drapes at the windows and the only lighting was occasional wall lamps and the kind of table candles where the new candle was just pushed into the remains of the old over and over again causing a big mountain of melted wax which had set in weird shapes and had completely hidden any candle holder from view.

We settled ourselves at the table. I sat as far away from Gaby and Ellie as was humanly possible; Tom sat on my right and Emma beat Dan to sit on my left. He settled himself next to Gaby and immediately embarked on full on suck up mode. Ellie took the opportunity to order the wine she wanted.

"Now, listen you lot. I've ordered cheap stuff that you can throw down your neck. But I've also ordered some really expensive wine that I'd really like you to drink slowly and try to appreciate! That includes you Emma!"

Ellie had ensnared Emma in a death stare, her eyes narrowing.

"Wow," Emma whispered at me, "I didn't realise we were getting wine tasting lessons as well! What have I done to upset her?"

"You're too pretty, that's all," I whispered back.

She didn't have an opportunity to reply and I smiled as the waiter brought and poured the cheap wine. I took a large gulp exclaiming that it actually wasn't bad at all. The Fado singer was introduced. He seemed a pleasant enough chap of average height with a well built middle and a moustache that any Portuguese man would be proud of – dark, thick and bristly. As he launched into his first song, Emma gripped my left forearm and bit down on her glass to stop herself from laughing. I exchanged looks with Tom who also seemed to have an unbearable urge to laugh as he covered his mouth and did a fake cough behind his hand. None of us could look at each other as we knew it would just cause more giggling.

The singing really was very bad. I hadn't heard any Fado before but this was not good. He was out of tune and, according to Tom, some of his lyrics were questionable. I looked across at Beth, who was sandwiched between Ellie and Gaby. She had a pained expression on her face and downed a good half of her glass of her wine. I mouthed, "are you ok?" at her and she gave a wan smile in return, rolling her eyes with a barely discernible shake of her head. Dan was leaning into Gaby and whispering into her ear. Gaby was responding by flicking her long, dark

fringe out of her face, tucking it behind her ear
and laughing lamely at his witticisms. He lit a
cigarette, held it up in the air between his fingers,
stuck his chin in the air and pursed his lips. This
was Dan's flirting pose, which he used on men
and women alike. Ellie was watching the two of
them, her mouth pursed, looking annoyed and
tetchy. She was tapping one fingernail on the
table. I sighed. It was going to be a long night.
By the time we had finished our meals, we were
all a little weary of the restaurant and its
oppressive darkness.

"I tell you what," said Emma, draining
the last dregs of her glass, "they ought to employ
that guy every night. He's so bad that it almost
forces you to drink loads to tolerate it. They
must have made a fortune at the bar tonight!"

"He wasn't that bad," said Tom trying
to be more positive, "it makes a difference when
you understand what he's singing about."

"You don't have to speak Portuguese to
know it was about something bloody depressing.
You, my darling, are too bloody nice. You know
that? Jo knows that, doncha Jo?"

Emma elbowed me as she said this before
tipping her glass back to drain the last dregs.
I ignored her insinuations but felt myself
blushing in spite of myself. Did everybody
know how I felt about him? Was it that obvious?
I thought I'd done a great job of being the good
friend.

"Don't think we haven't noticed how
much time you're spending together," she said
looking at us both, "you even look cute
together."

I felt like I'd taken a punch to the gut and the
embarrassment crept up my body, lifting my hair

89

away from my head in a prickling, hot sensation. I wanted the floor to open up and swallow me right there. I sneaked a look at Tom and he smiled broadly.

"Emma," he said, "you are drunk! Yes, we've spent time together because Jo is great company and we live really close to each other."

I raised my eyebrows in surprise at the complement. He looked to me now, "well you are! Don't look so surprised. You're great value; funny, intelligent, who wouldn't want to be around you?"

He smiled and those amazing green eyes crinkled in the corners of his tanned face.
I blushed to the roots of my hair again and couldn't find any words, so I kept quiet and just smiled back.

Our attention was diverted to Gaby and Ellie who were arguing over whose credit card was paying the bill.

"This looks like it's heating up quite nicely," Tom said with a wicked glint in his eye, "there'll be an argument before the night is through. Mark my words."

"I'm banking on it," said Emma, as she refilled her glass, "otherwise this is going to be such a boring night. All they've been doing is trying to outdo each other with wine and hair flicking. I, personally, need to drink a lot more wine to get through the rest of this evening."

Gaby was making a big show of refusing Ellie's card as the bill came and waved her credit card around before sending it away with the waiter.

"Thanks Gaby, you're a darling," said Dan wrapping his arm around her neck.

"Could he get any further up her arse?" whispered Emma downing another glass of wine.

We left the restaurant and headed back to the Klan bar. Ellie grabbed me on the way and pulled me back to create some distance from the rest of the group.

"Jo, she's doing my head in! How am I standing up to her? I don't look like an idiot, do I?"

"N..No Els, course not. She's a very strong personality that's all. I'm sure it's nothing personal," I replied not sure of what to say.

"Just back me up if I need you to, ok? She's really pushing all my buttons and I need my team to rally round. Pass the word on to the others. I think I've lost Dan though. If anyone can help him in his career, he's right up their arse." She laughed her throaty, hoarse laugh.

"Right, Ellie, I just want to have a good time tonight. Don't take it all so seriously, yeah? You'll just end up in a fight," I said trying and failing to calm her down.

"Ok, seeing as I paid for the meal, Ellie can buy the first round!" announced Gaby as we entered the bar.

I could see Ellie fume as she got her purse out and ordered the drinks for everyone.

"Listen guys," said Beth, "I'm going to call it a night."

"Nooo!!" we all chorused.

"No really, I'm expecting a phone call and I'm going to be caught in the middle of all this enough without witnessing it all tonight!" she whispered to us, "have fun. Fill me in tomorrow."

91

Beth disappeared off home leaving the four of us watching Ellie and Gaby who were deep in animated discussion at the bar.

"This is so boring!" said Dan, "There must be another bar in Quarteira! We always come here. Come on, we're going to another bar!"

He hurried us to drink up and follow him back out into the street.

We finished our drinks and were out the door before anyone could stop us. Emma had linked arms with me and we sang as we followed Dans pink shirt up the hill.

"Do you believe in life after lurve..?" we sang.

"Darlings, anything but Cher please!" said Dan.

"You're gay, you're supposed to like Cher," said Tom joking.

"Mmm and I also love Judy Garland, Barbara Streisand and Liza Minnelli!" said Dan sarcastically.

"Really?" asked Tom innocently.

"Hey, didn't I see a Wham CD in your flat?" laughed Emma.

"What is this? Let's all have a go at Dan night? Well, we're going to a gay bar now so it might open your eyes a bit."

"What..?" said Tom.

We went through a door that was draped with a heavy red curtain that shielded the room beyond from prying eyes. It was a lovely bar filled with large, overstuffed sofas and chairs. There were large, fluffy white rugs scattered about on the floor and dimmed lighting added to the cosy effect. There was only one problem – it was empty.

"Seriously!" moaned Dan, "Why have gay bars if there are no gay people? Where is everyone?"

Tom headed straight for the fruit machine while the rest of us hit the bar downing several shots. Ellie and Gaby had trailed behind us and we awaited their arrival eagerly. Maybe they would like each other more after a few more drinks.

"Where are they?" said Emma, "If they're going to have a bitch fight, they could at least do it in front of us!"

About half an hour later, Ellie appeared alone. She was in floods of tears and inconsolable. Tom came over trying to find out what was wrong. She buried her head in his shoulder and then seemed to think better of it as she dried her eyes.

"I've just drunk too much," she said, "I'll be fine. I just need to wash my face." She disappeared off to the toilets leaving us all bewildered.

"What do you think that's all about then?" asked Tom, "she's really upset about something but won't, or can't, talk to us. I think it's sad."

"You're right," I said smiling at him, "I'll go see if she's ok."

I walked past the bar where Dan was still downing shots of vodka, trying in vain to chat up a very bored bartender. As I entered the toilets, I spotted Ellie's feet sticking out from underneath the cubicle door.

"Ellie, are you ok?"

"Yes ..... sniff...fine...go away!" she
sobbed back at me.

I started to leave but stopped and turned back,
"Ellie..." but I was drowned out by the
unmistakeable sounds of sickness. I decided to
leave discreetly. She'd hate it if she thought I'd
heard or knew she was being ill.
    "How's Ellie?" asked Tom as I
reappeared in the bar.
    "She's talking on the big, white
telephone," I said.
    "Huh?" said Tom confused.
    "She's having a technicolour yawn,"
giggled Emma.
    "Having a chat with Shanks Armitage,"
I added.
    "She's puking, Tom!!" screamed Emma
laughing and throwing her head back in glee.
    "Well, why didn't you just say so?"
sang Tom as Emma rolled her eyes.

Just as we went to order more drinks, Gaby burst
into the bar looking furious.
    "Why did you all run away and leave
me? I've been in every bar between here and the
Klan bar looking for you lot!"
    "And had a drink in every one by the
state of her," whispered Emma.
    "You were with Ellie when we left the
Klan," I said, "you were right behind us!"
    "Where is she? She will be lucky to
keep her job after what she's done to me
tonight!" bellowed Gaby.
    "Oh my God," said Emma, "this is it;
bitch fight central is about to start!"

Gaby disappeared in the direction of the toilets,
reappearing a few minutes later with Ellie who

was looking dreadful with a puffy, white face and watery, red eyes.

"How dare you make me look stupid in front of the team," said Gaby as she pushed Ellie against the bar.

"I thought you were doing a pretty good job of that yourself!" replied Ellie wiping her face on the back of her hand.

"Who do you think you are? What you said to me earlier was unforgivable!" screamed Gaby. "I am Country Manager for the Portugal and Madeira programme and you would do well to remember that!"

"Oh please," replied Ellie slurring a little, "don't think you can come out here on one of your jollies thinking you own the bloody company!"

Gaby's mouth was open in a shocked O, "We'll talk about this tomorrow when you're sober but you would do well to remember if your results don't improve, it's your job on the line," she said threateningly before grabbing Ellie's arm and hooking hers through it like they were best friends.

The two of them snaked across the room as they left the bar without a word to any of us.

"Oh to be a fly on the wall of Ellie's apartment," I said, "I bet there's one thick atmosphere."

"Doubt it," said Tom shrugging, "I think Ellie will be unconscious the minute she sits down!"

"I'm really disappointed they didn't have a proper full on fight," wailed Emma, "We've been robbed! I'll call Beth tomorrow and find out what Ellie said. She'll know everything."

"I think it's time to go home," I said looking affectionately at Dan who had passed out on his stool at the bar. His face was resting in a little pool of beer and he had unidentifiable stains all over his pink shirt. The four of us must have looked a sorry sight as we dragged Dan home again, his arms resting on our shoulders and drool spilling from the corner of his mouth.

Sixteen

I didn't have time to hang around the next morning to find out what happened between Ellie and Gaby. I was due to have lunch with the owners of Casa Verde to discuss the various ins and outs of the letting of the property for four months of the season. Ellie was also meeting me at the property to do a spot of PR with the couple, so maybe I could find out exactly what happened straight from the horse's mouth.

Gerry and Caroline Bertram were ex pats extraordinaire. Both in their sixties, they had left England's green and pleasant land fifteen years previously to live life at a calmer pace and enjoy the year round Portuguese sunshine. Caroline suffered with arthritis, which eased incredibly with the temperate climate. Gerry had suffered a heart attack in England, due partly to his hectic lifestyle as a top TV producer. A somewhat eccentric couple, they were well known locally even though the local Portuguese people found it sometimes difficult to understand their rather posh home counties accents.

I dashed into São Bràs to my local florists, who had tied me a beautiful bouquet for Caroline. I say dashed – it took some time and some drawings and pointing at various blooms to buy the bouquet. But it was beautiful and colourful, and I hoped she'd like it. Paulo, my local wine merchant, advised on a good bottle of red for Gerry. I liked Paulo; his English was wonderful and he hadn't sold me a bad bottle of wine yet.

Casa Verde was five miles from the edge of my market town, located in a small hamlet with only five other properties. The villa was painted in red and cream and was built on a fairly steep slope surrounded by carob trees, which provided lovely shady areas around the terrace. A pool area overlooked the road, and I could partly see a wall painted with a mural.

Ellie's car was already parked outside. I took a deep breath and headed to the front door and knocked. I'm sure we've all met those people who love the sound of their own voices. I know I have, and I was about to meet yet another. Caroline Bertram!
The door of the villa was flung open and a large woman with white hair barked, "Yes?" she said, looking me up and down.

"Mrs Bertram? I'm Jo, your rep, I'm meeting Ellie here?" I felt very self conscious under her gaze as I was inspected. I thrust the flowers and wine towards her, not knowing what else to do.

"Well, come in, come in, don't stand there with your mouth open dear."

She stood to one side to allow me in and I squeezed past her into the hallway.
This was a beautiful villa and rather than the open plan style that most new properties were, this still had designated living areas. I noted the BAFTA award in the hallway which had its own plinth and pride of place. It was also secured to the plinth with screws, to prevent theft I guessed. To the left was a living room with large red sofa's and walls lined with books. Fluffy rugs lined the floors giving a cosy feel to the area. Straight ahead of us was the kitchen, which is where Caroline was indicating I should go to. I

obeyed and went through still clutching the flowers and wine, which I put down on the first surface I came to.

Ellie was sitting here in the kitchen, holding a glass with some kind of clear drink inside. She still looked rather puffy from last night. I wondered how her head was feeling. Her face brightened considerably as she saw me but I think that was more from relief I'd shown up than pleasure at seeing me.

"Ah Jo, Caroline was just telling me about the problems we've had in the past," she said, "You know, with clients and stuff."

"Yes," boomed Caroline, as she fussed about the kitchen in her voluminous white dress, "you simply must make the clients aware of the need for decent behaviour in this house. This is our home after all, and it is full of personal possessions."

Caroline had difficulty moving at any speed, due in part to her arthritis but not helped by her considerable size.

"Yes," I replied, "I realise that and I believe that's what attracts people to this villa in the first place!"

"What do you mean?" she asked me glaring at me again with beady eyes that seemed to bore straight through me.

"Well, I think people like to come to somewhere that's a home from home, some villas are bought with the sole aim to let and lack the personal touch. People coming to your beautiful home would be delighted to see all the books and the cushions and lamps; you know the little touches that make it feel like a home."

Caroline continued to stare at me; did this woman even blink? After what felt like an eternity, she blurted, "Well, try telling that to the family who broke my Magimix last year!"

"Accidents do happen, Caroline, and I'm sure it wasn't deliberate. You know we take a deposit to ensure any breakages are covered and that will be held by Jo until the final inspection of the villa," said Ellie with an audible sigh.

"Ahem Jo, while you're here, I'd like to show you how the cisterna works," said a thin, wiry man from the side door. I assumed this must be Gerry who had slipped in quietly. As much as Caroline was loud and brash, Gerry was the very opposite. Here was a quiet, softly spoken man, his face lined with the years that had passed but it was a gentle face, a nice face. He was wearing bright red trousers and a grey shirt with the sleeves rolled up to the elbows.

"Of course, please excuse me," I said to Caroline and Ellie.

"Don't let him waffle," shouted Caroline after me, "he's being playing with that thing all morning!"

I followed Gerry out on to the front terrace where he opened a door into, what I assumed must be the pump room. It was a small and dark with a low ceiling and was full of pipes and gurgling boilers. Gerry flicked a switch and the space was illuminated. He pulled a pair of half moon glasses from his breast pocket and placed them on the end of his nose; his head lifted back to allow him to see through them as he launched into a very longwinded explanation of how to turn on the emergency supply of water. I could feel my eyes glazing over as he stuttered his way through the process.

"Now, you must make sure that this lever is perpendicular to this pipe here. Oh, maybe you don't know what that means, mmm, I mean… vertical to…. Yes, that's it. You must make sure that this lever is in a vertical position…"

He droned on and on and I almost wished I were back in the kitchen listening to Caroline's booming voice. This couple had been together for forty years; I wondered how that had worked so well. They were like chalk and cheese and I couldn't actually see how the marriage had been successful.

"I've taken the liberty of drawing the system here for you," he said handing me a piece of paper with a complicated drawing on it, "it will help in case you forget the process, yes that's right."

"Do you mind if I have a look at the pool while I'm out here?"

"Be my guest," he smiled.

I climbed a flight of stairs to the terrace and gasped. This was the money maker for the villa. The pool was a large square patch of turquoise blue with a mermaid depicted in tiles at the bottom. The red tiles around the edge were hot and the heat was searing through the bottom of my sandals. A painted wall mural had only been hinted at from the car port and now, here it was in all its glory. It mirrored the mermaid at the bottom of the pool but here many different colours of paint had been used to create a gorgeous picture. I looked closely at the bottom of the wall and it was actually signed by Gerry Bertram. He was obviously a very talented guy! On the other side of the pool area, another set of steps led down to an outside patio area, which

101

was more shaded and several fat cats were sleeping here.

I walked back down towards the pump house.

"What a wonderful mural Gerry," I said, "am I right you painted it?"

"Oh that? Yes, yes I did that a few years ago. Will probably need a touch up of colour after this summer. The sun does bleach the colours, you know…"

"Well, she's very beautiful," I smiled meaning every word.

He smiled in thanks as I said, "Thank you Gerry," I said, "if that's everything, I really must get back to Ellie and Caroline to discuss the villa rentals this summer."

"Of course, of course my dear," he said distractedly, running his hand through his thinning hair, as he set about a nut and bolt with a large spanner.

Ellie had set the table ready for the lunch when I returned to the kitchen. Leading from the kitchen, the dining room was long and narrow with the most gorgeous heavy wooden table running its full length. There were twelve chairs around the table, plenty for the guests who would be staying.

Caroline was still in full flow about clients as she bustled around the well equipped kitchen. Ellie looked tired as she rubbed her temples with her eyes closed. I excused myself to have a further look around the villa that would be opening to clients the following week.

The house itself was beautifully decorated and felt light, airy but cosy and comfortable at the same time. The living room had floor to ceiling bookshelves and were crammed with all types of books from Wilbur Smith to Jackie Collins to Thomas Hardy. The bedrooms were fairly small but well furnished and the bathrooms were meticulously clean. It really was a beautiful house.

Lunch was finally announced, and I went through to the dining room and took my place at the table opposite Ellie.
Caroline had cooked a mushroom sauce with tagliatelle and the table was heaped with differing types of fresh local bread.

"What university did you go to Joanne?" asked Caroline as she ladled the pasta onto plates.

"Exeter," I replied, "I studied English."

"Our daughter read English and she's working in IT now. Sometimes I wonder why on earth she bothered! A friend of hers was reading Arabic! I mean, what on earth was she going to do with that?" she said, her face flushed from the heat of the kitchen.

"Well, these days, it's not so much what you study but the fact that you have a degree at all. It does still make a difference," said Ellie.

"Not for long though. I hear they let anybody in these days," said Gerry who had appeared from the cisterna rubbing his oily hands on a rag, "you can study knitting now for goodness sake! What in heaven's name is that going to help you with?"

"Gerry, wash your hands for heaven's sake!" pleaded Caroline.
I glanced at Ellie across the table. She rolled her tired, red eyes and smiled back at me. For the first time I felt a connection with her and gave a small smile in return.

"Well Caroline," said Ellie as we finished our pasta, "that was delightful. If you'll let us wash up, we really must be getting on."

"I won't hear of such a thing and there's still dessert to come. You young people are always rushing about!"

She collected the plates and shuffled to the kitchen returning with a large dish of strawberries and a jug of cream.

"Now these are just ripe for eating and won't last another day so you must finish them all," said Caroline piling up our dishes with the lush red fruits.

"None for me, dear," said Gerry, "the seeds get stuck in my dentures. Don't get old," he said to me patting me on the arm. I smiled back weakly, suddenly feeling faintly nauseous.

Ellie was also looking slightly green as she dug into the dessert. I put this down to her hangover, but I could see she wasn't really eating, and the strawberries were being pushed around the bowl more than being eaten. Caroline attempted several times to replenish my plate but I resisted all attempts. There's only so many strawberries you can eat when they're covered in thick, heavy cream. Another helping would also equal another half hour of discussion on the knives that the clients could and couldn't use. We insisted on sending back the remaining strawberries to the kitchen with the jug of cream and eventually Caroline relented and allowed us to finish and make ready to leave.

We finally made our escape. Our lunch had lasted for over three hours and I still had afternoon visits to make. Ellie was still looking slightly green.

"Are you ok?" I asked her tentatively, noticing how she was drinking a lot of water.

"Not really," she said, "I'm allergic to th-awberries! Look!"

I began to laugh as Ellie protested sticking her red, swollen tongue out, "It'th not funny! I need an anti-hith-amine tablet."

She looked angry but then started laughing too. It was a bit of a relief, to be honest, and good to see her humour emerge. She was much more attractive when she smiled. After much rummaging in her bag, she pulled out a pack of antihistamine tablets, pushed one out of its blister packaging and threw it into her mouth. I thought I'd take advantage of the humour and asked her about Gaby.

"What happened last night Ellie? With Gaby? You were so upset. It was awful to see you like that."

"Look Jo, me and Gaby have never got on that well. T-he thinks all I do i-th lie in the th-un with my feet up and go out raving every night. T-he doe-thn't under-thand how much I do! Just look after the educa-thonal, th-mile and nod in all the right placeth and th-he'll be gone in a few day-th. That-th all you need to know."

Although hard to understand with her swollen tongue, I got the gist.

"Right," I replied lowering my gaze and realising I wasn't going to get anywhere with her. She wasn't going to confide in me; why should she? Her lips were starting to swell also as she jumped in her car and sped off down the lane towards the main road.

105

Seventeen

The four-strong educational team arrived from London a week later. They had a successful day's viewing with Tom the previous day and were going to view my properties today. It was really quite bad timing for me as I had managed to clear two days this week and had planned on spending both of them on the beach. I must have been the palest person living in the Algarve. My stash of beach reads would have to wait, however. I would be spending the whole day escorting two members of the sales staff on their villa viewings.

I met them outside Casa do Campo and waited for them on the terrace as they looked round. Thankfully, the family staying there had gone out for the day, so we didn't have to creep about. I was so grateful as it would be quite embarrassing to be showing people round a property with clients in attendance. The educational team had split into two and the two I had seemed nice enough girls. Sarah was a pale, freckled tall redhead who looked up at me from underneath blonde eyelashes. Louise was a bespectacled, dark girl, short and very young, who took copious amounts of notes on each property and, scarily, everything I said.

We arrived at the last property of the morning session and my least favourite, Villa das Avores. This particular property was not selling very well, and I was grateful for this fact. I had far fewer problems when the place was empty. All my complaints had come from this property. I could actually imagine the disappointment a client would feel pulling up outside for the first time.

The villa was a typical, Portuguese house from the front surrounded by mature trees, which gave the house a dark and gloomy feel and also its name. Inside the rooms were small and filled with dark furniture. It didn't matter how many shutters you opened or windows you threw open, it still felt oppressively dark. The owner was a Portuguese property manager, Isabel Oliveira, an older, most botoxed lady who had no intention of spending any money on the house. Recently divorced, she had managed to keep hold of the villa in her settlement but wasn't so keen on looking after it.

This was my least favourite property because it really lacked love and attention. The décor was tired and shabby and of questionable taste. Lace doilies were underneath china shepherdesses; candlewick bed throws in one of the bedrooms; fluffy mats around the toilet and sink pedestals. Put it this way, if I had paid the kind of money for my holiday that clients did and ended up there, I would be holding my rep hostage until they moved me into a villa more fitting the fee I had paid.

Sarah and Louise walked around the property, taking a lot of notes while shaking their heads and gasping.

"Have many people complained about this property?" asked Sarah.

"Um, some," I replied, "I do keep sending reports to London but they seem to fall on deaf ears, I don't know what else to do. We can't change the interior of the property."

107

"If I turned up here on holiday, I wouldn't be impressed," mumbled Louise.

"You should have seen it before I bought extra cushions for the sofa and got rid of some of the nasty knickknacks that were lying about everywhere," I replied.

I led them onto the terrace so they could look at the pool area and my heart sank. The normally beautiful pool, the villa's one saving grace, was a beautiful shade of green. The tiles were covered in algae and one of the terracotta tiles around the pool was cracked and broken.

"Right," said Sarah, "I think we might have to speak to Ellie about this place. It needs some work. It's really not up to Completes standards."

"When was the last time this villa was checked?" asked Louise stiffly.

"I don't understand this!" I said, "I did a safety check here four days ago after the last family left. It did not look like this; I can assure you."

"Well, this is completely unacceptable. That pool is bottle green! It can't have been cleaned for at least two weeks. The pumps not even on," said Louise.

I was seething inwardly while trying to keep my outward smile in place. These two were on an educational; they were not property inspectors but they weren't wrong. Ellie was going to lose it with me when she heard about this. Isabel had a lot of explaining to do about the pool. Who had turned the pump off for goodness sake?

As I drove Louise and Sarah from property to property, they only talked about work. I couldn't get any personal details or general chat from either of them. No wonder Dan was telling us all that they were, in fact, spies sent from the London office. His paranoia was laughable at times but he might be right on this one I thought.

I took them to my favourite café in Sao Bras, Café da Vila, for lunch where we had freshly squeezed fruit juice and vegetable pancakes. I couldn't resist a piece of their speciality cheesecake for dessert. Their cake cabinet called to me in the night. Well, a girl has to treat herself every now and again, especially after the morning I'd had.

Later that afternoon, I was more than happy to drop Sarah and Louise off at Casa Cecilia where Dan was waiting, groomed and oiled ready to wine and dine them for their evening.
        "Sure you won't join us Jo?" asked Dan.
        "Aw, I'd love to," I lied, "but I have a lot of paperwork to catch up on and I also need to speak to a few owners this evening," I said smiling at Louise who remained stony faced even with my smiles and thank yous. I bade my farewells and headed back east to Sao Bras and my apartment.

Back home, I spent an hour chasing Isabel across the Algarve on the various phone numbers I had for her. I left messages for her everywhere demanding that the pool at Villa das Avores be cleaned immediately. I doubted it would do any good and did not expect her to call me back at all. I sighed as I dialled Ellie's number and explained to her what had happened. Understandably, she wasn't happy at all and demanded that it be sorted the next day. If I couldn't find Isabel, I would have to call in a

109

pool guy myself and get it sorted before the next group of clients arrived. Bang went my next planned day on the beach! Would I ever get there?

I checked my messages and thankfully only had one from Emma. She sounded very excited and mysterious as she said she had something to tell me regarding the dashing Rogerio. They had been seeing each other for a few weeks now and it all seemed to be going well. I left a message on her voicemail asking her to call me at Tom's. After the day I had had, a bit of TLC from the lovely Tom was just what I needed.

Eighteen

I arrived at Tom's apartment that evening tired but relieved that my PR duties with the London staff were over. As Tom opened the apartment door, he began pulling strange faces and pointing into the living room,

"What's wrong with you?" I asked as I pushed my way past him into the hallway, "Am I glad that day is over! It's just been the worst day fending off all sorts of questions. Those London staff really do my head.....Oh, hello Gaby,"

I was stopped in my tracks by the sight of Gaby in a very short, black skirt sitting on Tom's sofa drinking red wine.

"Hello Jo. Good day with the educational?" she purred, "I hope you don't mind but I moved over to The Townhouse from Ellie's place and I got lonely. I popped in hoping Tom hadn't made any plans this evening."

"Um, err, no, that's fine! I'll just get a drink; it's been a long day!" I stammered.

I went into the kitchen where Tom shrugged his shoulders and whispered,

"I'm sorry, she just turned up. She wants to paint the town red before she flies back to the UK! What was I supposed to do?"

"Oh lord, Gaby, twice in one week! I'm not sure I can cope!" I looked at his crestfallen expression, "It's not your fault, don't worry," I said stroking his arm and smiling.

"One more night and we don't have to see her till the end of season. Promise!" he said.

After a rather embarrassing and stilted dinner at a small, local fish restaurant, we went to a small bar, in the middle of Tavira, run by an eccentric Dutch man, Ned. I don't think that was his real name, but he was happy enough to answer to it. He spoke seven languages, which is pretty impressive by itself, and prided himself on the truly international flavour of his bar. Most nights you could be rubbing shoulders with Germans, South Africans, Scandinavians, and French.

We settled ourselves at a table in a corner as Gaby went to the bar.

"God, this is the longest night ever Tom," I moaned.

"Oh she's alright, just likes talking about work a lot," smiled Tom.

"She hasn't talked about anything else all night. And she sure has it in for poor Ellie! I'm so bored though," I said pulling an imaginary rope around my neck.

"Well, looks like she's off our hands for a while," he said nodding towards the bar.

Gaby had ordered our drinks but was talking to a man at the bar. She rushed over with our two drinks and placed them on the table,

"Sorry I took so long. Here you go. I'm just having a chat with Viktor," she said.

Viktor was a tall, well built black man. His face looked like it had been chiselled with tools; the bone structure was so perfect. His toned torso was covered with a tight black t-shirt and his hair fell down his back in dreadlocks. He was one handsome man! He had also looked Gaby's legs up and down as she bent to put our drinks on the table.

112

"Gaby, be careful, won't you?" said Tom concerned, looking from Gaby to Viktor and back again.

"Tom, that's very sweet of you but I'm a big girl and I can look after myself," she purred as she strutted back across the bar to Viktor.

"I wouldn't be so sure," said Tom, "It's not Gaby I'm worried about. Poor bloke doesn't know what's about to hit him."

I laughed with a mouthful of wine and nearly spat it on the table,

"Don't worry," I said, "we'll keep an eye on her. There's no way we'll be able to leave without her knowing and vice versa. I think Viktor is also more than capable of looking after himself too."

Gaby was talking very loudly and throwing her head back with laughter as she joked with Viktor who looked only mildly amused. She placed her hand on his chest as she talked.

"Woah," I said, "she's getting a bit fresh isn't she?"

"I can't look," said Tom shielding his eyes, "she's the biggest flirt going. Look at her!"

As Gaby's hand began to move down his chest, Viktor decided enough was enough,

"What do you think you're doing?" he said, holding her hand away from his chest by her wrist. Gaby was undeterred and continued to purr at him, stroking her own hair with her free hand.

"Oh my God, Tom," I said putting my hands up to my face, "I'm so embarrassed for her. Make it stop!"

Tom jumped up and strode across the bar.

"Excuse me," he said to Viktor, "Is my friend bothering you?"

"Tom, what?" said Gaby in disbelief, "What do you think you're doing?"

I couldn't hear what Viktor was saying and I think he was talking to Tom in Portuguese. Gaby stood, arms folded across her chest, with her mouth pursed in anger.

"Tom, really I can handle this myself!" she shouted.

The whole bar was now silent; watching the spectacle unfold. Tom continued to talk to Viktor in Portuguese as Gaby left them, stropped over to me and sat down heavily. Slowly, the low level of chatter resumed as everyone realised there would be no fight tonight.

"Why doesn't he just club me over the head and drag me back to his cave?" protested Gaby.

"Who? Viktor?" I asked.

"No! Bloody Tom! If I'd known he would get jealous about me talking to a guy…"

For the second time that night, I almost spat my mouthful of vodka across the bar.

"What? You think Tom fancies you?"

"Why else would he be so bothered?" she said tucking a dark tendril of hair behind an ear and lighting a cigarette.

"Maybe," I said raising my voice, "he just doesn't like to see you sexually harassing someone in the middle of a bar! Maybe, he's just worried what could happen to you. Maybe he's just a gentleman trying to protect what little honour you have left!"

I stopped suddenly as I realised what I had said but Gaby wasn't listening to what I was saying. She was grinning at me with her red lips curled like a Cheshire cat.

"Well, well Jo! Do I sense the tiniest crush on our dear Tom?" Gaby purred at me one dark eyebrow lifted.

I blushed furiously and did my best to hide behind my hair.

"What? Don't be ridiculous! He's my friend, that's all! I don't like to see people taking advantage of him."

"Whatever Jo," she laughed, "I'll be following this story with interest," she said as she stood up and walked back over to the now laughing pair of Tom and Viktor.

I was so embarrassed and angry. Who did she think she was? I decided there was nothing else I could do. I would get drunk and tell her exactly what I thought of her.
I went to the bar where Tom joined me leaving Gaby with Viktor. It looked as if she was giving him her mobile phone number. Heavens above; she didn't give up easily did she?

"I'm getting drunk then I'm telling her exactly what I think," I told Tom.

"Well, you're already half way there," he laughed, "May I join you?"

It wasn't too long before we were both more than a little merry. We were laughing at the most stupid things and Tom had fallen off his stool twice already. My plan had fallen through, however, as Gaby had called a taxi to drive her the 500 metres to her house. She had winked at me as she left and shouted,

"Don't do anything I wouldn't do!" behind her as she wiggled out the door on her four inch heels.

After quite a few more drinks, Tom had decided it was home time. We linked arms as we weaved our way home through the quiet, cobbled streets. It was very late, and I was very drunk. An idea had started to form in my head. You know how it is when you're drunk. The most ridiculous things seem like great ideas and you carry them through without a second thought. Well, this was one time when I was going to wish I'd had the second thought.

Nineteen

As we got to the corner of Tom's apartment building, I stopped and swung him round to face me. He was laughing and singing some dodgy song.

"Mambo number 5," he sang, "duh, duh, de, de.."

"Tom," I said seriously.

"Yes, my dear!"

"What would you do if I said I was going to kiss you right now?"

As soon as I said the words, I wanted to swallow them back down. My whole body seemed to be sweating and my clothes had lifted away from my skin. My insides ran icy cold. I backed up a step and watched Tom's face in horror, which had changed from laughing drunk to seriously embarrassed.

"J..Jo, why? What?" he stuttered.

I ran around to the front door of the apartment. I had decided the best course of action was to just go with it, now I'd said it.

"You're not allowed in until you answer me!" I sang trying to make it all light-hearted and fun.

"Jo! You know I love you to death, but I do have a girlfriend. Why are you doing this? I thought we were friends!"

"You haven't answered the question, Tom!" I said quietly feeling tears prick the back of my eyes.

"Jo, move out of the way and we can go in and talk about it, eh!"

I nodded and sloped away from the door. Tom unlocked it and went up the stairs leaving me on the doorstep.

"Come on," he whispered down the hall so as not to wake the neighbours.

I couldn't move. I was so horrified and embarrassed at his response that I couldn't bear to face him or even have him look at me. I sat down and couldn't stop the tears from falling down my cheeks. I wanted a big hole to open up in the ground and swallow me whole right there and then. I had ruined everything between us and now he wouldn't trust me. How could he? He hated me and obviously, didn't find me remotely attractive. I wanted to die!

I felt a hand on my shoulder and looked round to see Tom standing over me offering his hand. I took it and stood up but couldn't look at him. I tried to hide my tear stained face behind my hair. He led me up to the apartment where I could not hold back my embarrassment any longer and more tears came. I don't know which was worse - what I had said to him or the fact that I was standing in his hall, bawling about it. He grabbed my shoulders and pulled me towards him and I buried my face in his shoulder.

"I..I'm sorry," I blubbed, "I didn't mean...."

"It's ok," he said as he stroked my hair, "it's been a difficult week and we drank too much. Don't worry. If things were different..."

"What?" I asked pulling myself back to look at him. His green eyes crinkled as he smiled down at me.

"I'll put the kettle on, yes?"

118

I nodded and blew my nose on the kitchen roll he handed me. Why did he have to be so bloody nice about it? As if I didn't feel stupid enough, here he was being so understanding and lovely. He was too good to be true. There had to be something wrong with him!

"You won't mention this to the others, will you?" I asked, "I'd have to leave the country on the first flight!"

He laughed.

"Of course I won't. What do you take me for? It's got nothing to do with them anyway. It's between you and me."

He came forward, kissed me on the forehead and handed me a cup of tea.

"Thanks, I think I ought to go to bed now. Maybe I'll wake up tomorrow and our memories will have been erased?"

He smiled and nodded, "Goodnight Jo."

I closed the door to the spare room and sighed deeply. I was such an idiot. However nice he was being about it; I was sure that I had offended him. I hoped the friendship wasn't ruined. I drank the tea and curled up on one side facing the window. I could just see the beginnings of a new day brightening the dark sky. I closed my eyes trying not to think how swollen they were going to be the next day.

I was almost asleep when I heard the door open. I was so tired; I couldn't open my eyes but knew who it was. I felt the bed depress as he sat down. I could feel my hair being stroked and was sure I heard a whispered "I'm sorry." Before I drifted into sleep, I was sure Tom had climbed in next to me.

Twenty

When I woke up the next morning, I knew that I
was alone in the bed. I was sure I had dreamed
the night before but the thrown back sheets on
the other side of the bed told me otherwise. I
rubbed my throbbing head as I rolled off the bed
and stumbled to the bathroom. The sight that
met me in the mirror was not a pretty one. I
looked like I'd gone ten rounds with Tyson with
my swollen eyes and puffy face.

I searched in vain for some painkillers and
decided I needed a very large coffee. I'd just put
the kettle on when Tom appeared waving a
small, white bottle of paracetamol at me.

"Morning, how are you feeling?" he
asked me kindly.

"Embarrassed," I answered, "please
don't look at me. I look like a monster this
morning."

"You look fine apart from your eyes.
There's some ice in the freezer. It will help to
reduce the swelling. I'm just popping out for
some milk. Oh, and Emma left a message for you
on my phone last night. Can you call her?"

He smiled and disappeared out the door. I
wrapped some ice in a tea towel and placed it on
my pop eyes. Tom was obviously embarrassed
too. He couldn't get out of the apartment quick
enough. There was no way I was going to make
it worse by asking him where he slept last night.
It was probably best not to mention anything
about anything. I would just slip out and get

back to work at Villa das Avores. There was so much to do after all.

After throwing fresh clothes on and quickly wiping a cloth round the kitchen, I was running down the stairs to my car. I just hoped I could drive away before Tom came back. I'd left him a note to say I couldn't wait and had to get to the villa before Ellie got there. Maybe a bit of space between us would help calm all the emotion down.

I pulled up outside Villa das Avores twenty minutes later. I checked the mirror and was pleased to see most of the swelling in my face had subsided. I rummaged in my bag for my make up supply and applied just enough to make me look human.
I retrieved the villa key from my rep bag and opened the front door.

The house felt dusty and unused even though the last clients had left only a week before. I went into each room and threw open all the windows. I went into the kitchen and opened the door into the garden. There was the pool, still in a state and definitely green. I'd just managed get into the pump house to turn the swimming pool pump on when Ellie came through the garden gate.
    "Hi Jo! My God! What happened to your face?" she exclaimed.
    "Oh, I think I got bitten by a mosquito," I lied rubbing my still slightly swollen eyes. I had thought I looked alright; obviously not.
    "Make sure you look after that. It might get nasty! Right then, what is going on here?" I explained again what had happened with this villa, the clients and especially the villa owner.

"Isabel is supposed to be meeting me here to discuss the maintenance; or lack of it. She's late," I said looking at my watch.

"This place needs some money spending on it," said Ellie, "if she's not willing to cough up then Complete is going to withhold her rental payments to pay for improvements. I spoke to London this morning," she said in reply to my surprised expression, "thought a bit of damage limitation was in order before the educational gets back and starts mouthing off. Look Jo, whatever you think of me, I'm on your side. When things get tough or difficult, I'm here to help bail you out. Didn't I get the car all sorted out for you?"

"Yes, yes you did," I replied, "and I know all that, but you can be a bit intimidating at times."

I immediately wished I had engaged my brain before my mouth but sighed with relief when she said, "Well, I have a reputation to uphold!"

We both stood and smiled awkwardly at each other for a moment before she said,

"The main reason this pool is green is because Jorge keeps turning the pump off! The whole thing will need draining and cleaning now. Isabel must think she's saving money but it's really not. It takes twice as long to clean all the tiles down every time it goes this green. And the rest of this place? Well, I've already bought some new things; they're in the car. If you want to make a start bringing some stuff in. We've got some work to do Jo. Ah! I think that must be Isabel," said Ellie looking at the white car that had pulled up outside the villa.

I went to Ellie's car at the back of the house and opened the boot. There were new toilet seats, towels, plants, sun bed mattresses and a whole host of other things to make this villa look as if someone loved it. I filled my arms with stuff and made my way back to the house.

Ellie and Isabel were in the middle of a heated discussion as they stood by the pool. Isabel was an immaculately groomed lady. She always looked elegant in beautiful designer suits and shoes. Her hair was professionally blow dried at least once a week. She chain smoked constantly but managed to make it look elegant like those old movie stars in the black and white movies I loved so much. Her face was the picture of disinterest as she looked at her watch, which was probably worth more than my annual salary.

"Isabel, this place is just not up to standard. Jo and I can do some cosmetic improvements but it's down to you to keep up the maintenance. You must keep the pool pump turned on all the time. Look at the state of it," said Ellie pointing to the green sludge.

"There eez no point in 'aving it on when no one eez here!" said Isabel, "I do not 'ave bundles of money." She lit another cigarette grinding out the last one with her stiletto heel.

"All you're doing is creating extra work for Jorge, who has to scrape algae off the tiles every week. I also know that he has been turning the pump off when there are clients here. It's not good enough, Isabel, and what I've heard and seen has made my decision for me. I will be informing London to withhold your rental payments so we can make improvements." Isabel flicked back her immaculate dark hair and shrugged her shoulders.

"Whatever you theenk eez right," she said flicking her ash into the pool, "I 'ave meeting now. Bye!"

She turned on her stiletto heel and, with a dismissive wave, was gone.

"Well," said Ellie, "that was worth my while. Jo, get on the phone and call Jorge. Get him over here straight away and we need someone to replace these broken tiles."

"Right," I sighed, "I'll get it sorted."

I spent the rest of the afternoon cleaning and scrubbing every surface while packing away dodgy ornaments and generally trying to make the place look like someone cared about it. We changed candlewick bedspreads to beautiful cotton ones; swapped fluffy bath mats for new duck boards. My frantic phone calls found a local company who could do the repair work on the tiles. Ellie whitewashed the back wall in an attempt to make the villa have some external appeal and brightness. We also repainted the two bathrooms and replaced the toilet seats. A lovely, smiley, rotund delivery man dropped off six new sunbeds for the garden. We scrubbed and cleaned the bbq and all the tools and jet washed the paved areas. I even cut back all of the overgrown trees at the front of the villa, opening up the front of the house and cleaned all the green algae from the window shutters. This was my second week without a day off and I was exhausted. Even all this physical work couldn't help me stop thinking about the night before.

Had I blown everything with Tom? He was being so good about it but that was just like him. He was so bloody nice to everyone that it was hard to see if he felt anymore. Did he come into my bed? I wasn't sure enough to mention anything to him. I probably dreamt it, wishful thinking on my part maybe. Ellie disturbed my thoughts by announcing the next team night out.

"I've decided that poor Emma deserves a break. She is always driving over here for us and I think it's about time that we went over to the west. We are going to have a night out in Lagos and see if we can't find some decent boys. What do you say?"

"Sounds great," I said, "sorry if I don't sound enthusiastic but I'm just so tired. I really need a day off."

"Hey, don't worry. It's always quiet in August. It's ironic that it's the height of the season but we normally manage to get more time off."

"Great! Can't wait!" I said yawning.

"Look, you get off home. I'm nearly finished for the day anyway. I'll come back to finish off tomorrow. You've worked really hard today Jo, thank you."

"Thanks Ellie. See you tomorrow."

I didn't even stop to wonder why she was being so nice or understanding. I was too tired and emotional. I couldn't even talk to anyone here about Tom. It would just get blown up out of proportion and make working relationships difficult.

When I got home, I dropped into the nearest chair, planning on making dinner and having a shower but promptly dozed off. My nap was cut short; interrupted by the ringing of the phone. It was Emma.

"Thanks for returning my calls, Jo! Where have you been?"

126

"I have been tarting up Villa das Avores with Ellie all day! And I mean jet washing and painting!"

"Oh Jo, I'm sorry but that place really needed something doing. I bet it looks fab now."

"Well, it couldn't have looked any worse, that's for sure! How are you?"

"I'm great actually," she said, and I could almost hear the smirk on her face as she spoke.

"You've slept with Rogerio haven't you?" I said knowingly.

"How did you know? You've ruined my whole story! That's not fair!"

"I believe it's what we call inevitable Emma," I said laughing. "Go on then, tell me all the gory details."

"Oh Jo, it was hysterical. Did you know he still lives with his parents in Vilamoura? Well yeah, he does, so after we'd been for our drink, we went for a drive and parked up in those woods by the golf course. Well, let's just say that the windows were getting pretty steamy when I saw a light flashing round the back of the car. It was only the bloody police!"

"Oh Em, you didn't get arrested did you?"

"God! No! Rogerio had to do some pretty nifty talking though! I swear I'm going to get arrested before the end of the season at this rate!"

"Emma, please be more careful!" I laughed, "I'd like you to be at the end of season party."

"No worries babe. I just let Rogerio take all the heat while I hid in the back seat!"

"Is it a serious thing with you two?" I asked.

"God no," she said, "he's very hot and it's nice to have something that isn't about Complete but there won't be any long term relationship here. No offence by the way!"

"None taken," I laughed. I told her about Ellie's plan for the next team outing.

"Fantastic! It's about time you lot came over here. We will get to spend a day together as well. We will shop!"

I finished the phone call promising to make the journey over to the west as soon as I had a day free, whenever that may be. Just as I'd put the kettle on, the phone rang again. It was Dan.

"Hiya! Where have you been? I was trying to call you all last night!"

"Hi Dan, I was out with Gaby and Tom. What did you want?"

"I'm bored. I've just left Silves and THE most horrendous couple and their disgusting children! I'm hungry and I want dinner now. Please say you'll come out with me Jo!"

"Ok Dan," I said ignoring my extreme fatigue, "come and pick me up!"

"Great, see you in five; I'm just round the corner!"

The last thing I wanted to do was spend the evening pandering to Dan's ego. The alternative was sitting in my kitchen listening to Antenna 3, apparently the Algarve's premier radio station, and drinking yet another bottle of wine on my own. If I couldn't have a day off, then I would burn the candle at both ends and make myself ill!

Twenty One

Dan announced his arrival fifteen minutes later
by leaning on my door buzzer. It was one of his
favourite tricks to get immediate attention. I
picked up the phone on the intercom to hear him
bellow,

"I'm in the car when you're ready!"

I replaced the phone and went down to meet him.
He was leaning on the bonnet of his car, posing
in his new Armani shades. I'd never told him I
lived above a gym and the trio of young, toned
males stood at the doorway explained his stance.

"Strike a pose, Dan!" I laughed.

"Oh darling! Hi!" He air kissed my
cheeks with great flamboyance, "you look
terrible! What happened to your eyes?"

"Mosquito bite," I mumbled. Why was
I the only girl who could still have swollen eyes
fifteen hours after the crying had stopped? I
could never cry like the women in the movies
with gentle rivulets of water dropping onto my
cheeks from my perfect inky black eyelashes. If
I was in Hollywood, no hint of red would appear
anywhere on my face except maybe just above
my top lip like Andi McDowell in Four
Weddings and a Funeral.

"You didn't tell me you lived above
The Dreamboys," said Dan peering at the boys
over his shades.

"Put your tongue away, don't you know
it's rude to stare!"

"Hi Jo!" called one of the toned boys.

129

"Hi Paulo. How you doing?" I answered and waved as I got in the car.

Dan's jaw had hit the floor. I smiled as I used my finger to close his jaw,

"You know him?" he stammered.

"He helped me carry my new gas bottle up to my flat the other day. Those things are really heavy you know!"

"I will have to remember to come to pick you up more often. Right then," he continued as the eye candy disappeared from view back into the gym, "we're going to the Chinese in Loulé. I want lots of food!"

The restaurant was exquisite; decorated to the highest standard with red and orange painted dragons breathing fire over the walls. Red and black sumptuous silks were draped beautifully around the doors and windows. All the staff dressed in stunning silk traditional dresses and black pump shoes. Black shiny hair was pulled back into tight buns and secured with chopsticks. Their service was quick, discreet and the customer barely noticed the skilful hand removing and delivering dishes to the table. Now, if there's one thing Dan could do well, it was ordering the best food on a menu. He always ordered too much and then tried to eat it all so as not to waste it. This philosophy had already contributed to him having to buy new trousers and being grateful that his uniform trousers had an elasticated waist. We ate spring rolls with sweet chilli sauce, sweet and sour chicken, prawn chow mein, beef in black bean sauce, fried rice and prawn crackers. It was enough for the whole team but Dan put in a valiant effort to finish the lot.

"I'm stuffed," I said, "why do you always order so much food?"

"Well," said Dan licking the last of the black bean sauce off his fingers, "you know what it's like with Chinese? We'll be hungry again in a few hours, so I figure the more we eat, the less likely we are to get hungry!"

"Mmm, good thinking but I'm not sure it will work in practice," I said loosening the top button of my jeans.

"So, what's going on with Tom then?" he asked looking me straight in the eye.

"What do you mean?" I said trying not to blush.

"Well, he told me that Tammy was arriving on Sunday but that mad owner Ben is supposed to be staying with him."

"Tammy's coming on Sunday?" I asked wondering why Tom hadn't mentioned it last night. It might have stopped me making such a fool of myself.

"Yes, didn't he tell you? I thought you two were joined at the hip and knew everything about each other," he said smugly revelling in the knowledge that he knew something I didn't.

"Oh, I'm sure he did mention it. I've had so much going on this week that I'm lucky I remember my own name!" I laughed, "He didn't mention anything about Ben staying with him though! What's that all about?"

"Well, I only know what Ellie told me," he said popping a prawn cracker into his mouth, "Ben's place still isn't ready for clients, partly because he's still living there, and he needs to get out so they can fix the roof and finish building the pool. Tom offered him a bed for a week or so, but it looks like the work will be delayed another week 'til Tammy goes again. Anyway, he'll still be able to come to the opening of Kadoc on Thursday night. We are all still going, aren't we? I've heard it's going to be mad!"

"Yes, as far as I know! I'm up for it! It should be a good night!"

"It's about time we had some decent fun. It's so boring around here at the moment. All we do is sit in the Klan bar or in each other's flats moaning about our terrible love lives. Well, I'm going to do something about it this week! Watch out, Dan's about!"

I smiled at his optimism. Kadoc was a huge new club, based in a massive old warehouse near the middle of nowhere and, if you believed the radio reports, the whole of Portugal was expected to be there. We might not even get in if there were that many people but that didn't stop Dan and his plans.

"Right, come on," said Dan, "I'll drop you home unless you want to come to the V Bar with me?"

"Not likely," I said, "standing around in a dark bar watching men looking at each other is not my idea of fun! You go and have fun and report back to me! I'm desperate for an early night."

The first thing I did when I got home was check the voicemail service,

"Nao tem messagems novas," said the husky voiced operator.

I had no messages from clients, and I can't tell you how happy that made me. I had no message from Tom, and I had no clue what that meant.

Twenty Two

You could almost feel the excitement building in the team as Thursday night grew closer. I actually thought Dan might pass out with excitement as the day arrived and he gushed down the phone at me.

"What are you wearing? I don't know what to wear. What time are we going? We're meeting at Beth's place; did you know that? Can you tell Tom? What's he wearing? That's call waiting – got to go. Bye!"

I smiled, shook my head and dialled Tom's number.

"Hello?" he answered in his Cornish accent.

"Hi, it's me," I said, "How are you?" We hadn't spoken since that embarrassing morning and I was hoping that it wouldn't feel strange between us.

"Jo! I'm fine, yeah! I've been helping Ben finish the roof and pool at his place! It's been really hard work and we've got loads left to do but it's been good. How about you?"

"I'm fine. Been doing a load of work on Villa das Avores and it looks a ton better. Looking forward to tonight though. You are still coming, aren't you?"

"Of course I am. I'm going to Beth's for eight. See you there?" he said.

I breathed a sigh of relief as I placed the receiver into its cradle. Everything was going to be ok. I opened my wardrobe and sighed as I began pulling dresses out trying to decide what to wear.

At seven thirty, I pulled up outside Beth's apartment. I had chosen my little black gypsy style dress that was covered in small red roses. Beth opened the door. She was flushed with excitement and looked very pretty in a simple black dress.

"Hello Jo," she beamed at me, "I'm so excited, I really am. Oh, come in! It's just us girls so far."

"Hi Jo," shouted Emma from the bathroom where she was fighting with a cow lick above her forehead.

"Jo, how is it possible that I have dead straight hair until I want to go out and then I get this big, crazy flick?"

"I'm sure it will look much worse before the night is out," I laughed helping myself to a glass of white wine.

Dan was next to arrive. He was brandishing a bulky suit carrier and was sweating slightly.

"I didn't know what to wear, so I brought everything! Oohh Jo, you look gorgeous," he said kissing me on the cheek.

"Thank you, Dan," I said really appreciating the comment. My ego needed all the boosting it could get.

Dan flapped around before deciding on some khaki cargo pants with zips at the knees and a grey t-shirt. As he applied some of Beth's mascara to his blonde eyelashes, the doorbell went and Tom burst through the door.

"Hi everyone!" he said cheerily giving all the girls a kiss on the cheek. He looked totally amazing in a plain, white t-shirt, showing off his physique, and plain, blue jeans.

"Where's mine?" said Dan pouting his lips at Tom.

"Have you got make up on?" asked Tom peering at him closely.

"You know what," said Emma slapping Tom's thigh, "you look quite fit tonight babe!"

"Oh thanks," he laughed, "what do you think Jo?" he asked with a twinkle in his eye.

"Gorgeous," I said in a Somerset accent and laughed to cover my embarrassment; I still couldn't fully look him in the eye.

As we approached the warehouse in the middle of nowhere, as I called it, the traffic thickened and slowed to a crawl.

"Has the whole of the Algarve decided to come tonight?" Dan wailed, "We'll never get in!"

We crawled towards the warehouse where men in hi-viz vests were trying, and failing, to control the traffic flow. The huge car park was already full. Poor Beth, who was driving, was starting to get quite stressed.

"Beth!" shouted Emma, "don't go in the car park, I can see a space. There! There!"

Emma was pointing to a tiny space on a grass verge at the side on the narrow road. Beth, usually so worried about breaking rules, pulled the car out of the queue and flew towards the space, where she then parallel parked in the tiny space with just inches to spare in front and behind the car.

"Wow Beth," exclaimed Dan, "that was so impressive!" He was almost drowned out by the applause from the rest of us.

"Well, thank you Daniel," smiled Beth, "I've got so good at parking living in the Algarve!"

We piled out and stood on the grass verge, trying to figure out how to negotiate the full car park to access the entrance of the club, from which a pounding bass line of music was emitting. We weaved through the hundreds of cars towards a huge crowd of people.

"What's going on?" Emma asked, "Are they taxi drivers waiting for people?"

"Oh Em, I think this is the queue," said Beth.

"No way," I said, "we'll be here for hours."

It wasn't so much of a queue as a patient crowd. People were milling around quite happily so we managed to discreetly push our way through to get closer to the front. We were achingly close; stood looking longingly at the entrance, wondering how long we would have to wait, when I heard a doorman shouting and it appeared, he was shouting at me.

"Hey you! Come in!" he was jerking his thumb back to the entrance.

I pointed at myself and mouthed, "Me?"

"Yes, you with the chest. Come on!"

"Hey guys, I think my dress just got us in. Come on."

The crowd of people parted to let us through, and we skipped through them quickly and in through the doors.

"I knew bringing you in that dress was a good idea," said Dan, "it might just bring us all some luck tonight," he winked. "Do you think if

I rub your chest, my dream boy will 1 appear and grant me three wishes?"

His hand lingered over my chest as I grabbed it and gave him a kiss on the cheek.

"Not in this lifetime darling," I laughed.

The base of the music was turned up so high that the floor was literally bouncing as we walked to the nearest bar. The main room was huge and could hold more than 500 dancers. It was bathed in an ever-changing coloured light with ultraviolet lights shining around the bar areas. Drag artists were wandering round in highly colourful and theatrical dress adding to the carnival atmosphere. Some had contact lenses in which gave them cats eyes or sunburst pupils; some were on stilts, their makeup glowing in the ultraviolet light.

"I don't think I like it," shouted Beth.

"Don't be such an old biddy," replied Dan, "this is great."

"I'm sure the posters said something about different music rooms," said Tom into my ear, "Come on, let's go for a walk and see."

We set off in convoy round the giant club, moving in time to the music to pass frenetic dancers; upstairs and down, through bars and back to the entrance. There were different rooms, some divided by velvet curtains; some actual rooms made of Perspex which had fogged in the heat and humidity; but the same pounding music was playing in all of them. It was almost tribal – there was very little melody or voice and just this pulsing, humming beat.

"I'm sorry guys, I really don't like it," said Beth, "I think I'm too old! I'm going to stay

137

in the car and wait for you lot. Have a good time!"

Before any of us could say anything, Beth had disappeared through the heavy red curtains at the exit with a wave of her hand. Dan waved a small pink ticket in my face.

"Jo, I've just put my trouser legs in the cloakroom. Please look after my ticket for me."

I looked down to see his bare calves and laughed. None of us had realised his cargo pants zipped off at the knee. I put the ticket in my purse. Once he saw I had it safely stashed, he was off bouncing through the crowd like a crazy Tigger in eyeliner.

"This music is doing my head in," said Tom, "come on, let's go on the roof."

Emma and I followed him up an external metal staircase to the roof terrace. The cooler night air brushed across my skin – a welcome relief from the hot, damp, humid atmosphere inside.

"Look at that dance room! We didn't see that on our tour," said Emma her eyes shining with excitement as she spied a separate garden room below. "Stay here, I'm going to explore."

She dashed off leaving a blur of blue chiffon and blonde hair behind her. I turned to smile at Tom.

"Looks like we've been left high and dry," I laughed as we sat down on the terrace overlooking the garden room. I spotted Emma waving her arms in the air as she danced away.

"I'm not really sure this is my thing," said Tom, "I think I'd prefer to be at the African Bar in Tavira."

"Tom," I laughed, "you only want to be there so you can bang away on the African drums, trying to make everyone believe you are very, very cool!"

"At least it's fun and decent bloody tunes! This music hasn't changed a beat in the last twenty minutes!"

"Alright Grandad! Calm down!" I laughed. "So then," I knew I had to broach the subject, "got any special plans for the weekend?"

"Erm.." he said biting his bottom lip and not meeting my eye, "Tammy is arriving on Sunday."

"Is she?" I said a little too quickly, staring into my drink.

"Yes," he replied, also staring into his glass, "for a week."

"That will be nice," I said trying not to show any emotion on my face and not daring to look at him. I feared my voice sounded sarcastic.

"Yeah, I hope it's not weird though," he said his face darkening.

"Oh?" I asked, trying and failing to sound uninterested, "why would it be weird?"

"Well, I haven't seen her in three months. I've spent more time with you than her," he trailed off as he finished his sentence.

"I'm sure it will be fine," I said with a wobbly smile squeezing his arm.

"Yeah, I'm sure it will. Of course it will. Yeah, right, thanks," he said bumbling along. We sat together in silence as the music bassline continued.

Meanwhile, when Beth returned to the car to await our return, she had fallen asleep having been awake at 6am, ready for work by 7am. The dawn was just beginning; the dark sky began to lighten and the thin sliver of bright yellow along the horizon had woken her. As she tried to snuggle back down for a bit more sleep, she noticed a group of local looking men moving along the line of cars in front of her. They looked furtively around them before trying all the doors, trying to find an unlocked vehicle. She gasped as, finding all the doors locked, they picked up a stone and smashed the side window and pulled the car stereo out. The gang were working their way up the row of cars stealing whatever they could get their hands on. Beth realised with horror that her car was next in line.

As the group of five men surrounded her car, Beth sunk low in her seat trembling. What would they do to her? One of the men noticed her hiding in the well of the car just as the others were trying the doors. He shouted something, in Portuguese, at the other men. They all bent down and peered at her as her eyes grew large with fear.

"Hello Miss!" shouted one of them through the closed window, "We're sorry if we scared you! Have a nice night!"
They all smiled and waved and moved on to the car behind smashing the window and pulling out a bag. As the fear began to ebb away from her, she spotted several policemen running up the road followed by a van with its blue lights flashing. A few moments later, the policemen were walking back past her car with three of the men in handcuffs. Beth shook her head in disbelief and relief and looked at her watch. It was 5.30am.

Back in the club, Tom and I had left the roof and were walking through the lush gardens attached to the club trying to find Emma. This really was the best part of the whole club. Tired dancers were lounging amongst the many palm trees and mini waterfalls, which tumbled down well placed rocks. It was a beautiful place and a very unexpected find inside a club. Tom had his arm linked through mine.

"I wonder where Emma and Dan are," I said yawning.

"Who knows?" laughed Tom, "how they could dance to that noise all night beats me. They must be on something!"

"Maybe they are," I said turning to face him.

We stopped just short of the doorway back into the club.

"I'm glad we've had this time together. I haven't seen you all week," said Tom.

"Yeah, well. We've both been busy re-building villas," I replied.

"Jo..." he was interrupted by Emma who came running through the door and we jumped apart.

"Have you seen Dan? He's got my purse!" She looked a fright. Her hair was completely wet from sweat, hanging in strings around her face. Her makeup had melted, and her dress was stuck to her toned body. She had been dancing all night.

We followed Emma back through the crowd, which had started to thin out a little. We found Dan just as he peeled off his soaking t-shirt, rolled it into a ball and threw it from him. It landed in an ice bucket on a nearby bar. He was now wearing only his shorts and he had rolled the legs up so far; they were more like micro shorts. He was dancing furiously in front of one of the drag artists. Tom rolled his eyes at me,

141

laughed and we turned towards the exit, deciding to leave him to it.

Dan was ignoring all Emma's attempts to get his attention.

"Argh!" she screamed, "He's so annoying when he's on the pull! I've just found Rogerio, can you believe he's here? I'll stay with him and get back home with him at some point."

She giggled as she disappeared into the dancing crowd, waving a hand behind her.

Dan had his head thrust towards the drag artist, lips pursed and eyelashes fluttering.

"I've had enough of this now," said Tom, "shall we go?"

I nodded my agreement and we made toward the exit.

The car park was still full of people trying to get into the club. It was after 5.30am and the sun was starting to peek above the horizon.

"This has been some night!" I said as we walked towards the car.

"Sure has," said Tom, "I wonder how Beth is. She's been out here for hours."

Beth was asleep when we banged on the window.

"Hi guys," said Beth as she wound the window down, "You will never guess what happened here...."

Twenty Three

That Sunday, I was standing at the company
stand waiting for the next lot of happy clients.

"I don't feel very well," moaned Dan
who was standing next to me.

"I have no sympathy for you darling," I
said handing him a mint. "If Ellie catches the
smell of alcohol on you, you'll be going home on
the next flight."

"Don't care, I'd be quite happy with
that if it meant I could go to sleep right now," he
mumbled slipping the sweet on to his tongue.

"How's it all going then? Tell all but
spare me the gory details," I asked.

Dan and the dancing drag artist, from the club
opening night, had really hit it off and had seen
each other every night since. He smiled,
blushing a little.

"He's really nice Jo. Just lush! We get
on so well, like there's no awkward silences and,
for once, I'm really interested in what someone
else has to say about stuff, you know?"

"My God! Has love struck our
Daniel?" I teased, winking at him.

"Stop it!" he said, "I've really got to do
some proper work this week or Ellie will be on
the war path and I will be on the next flight."

"Have you collected your legs yet?" I
giggled behind my clipboard. I had forgotten to
collect the bottom half of Dan's trousers from
the cloakroom when I left the club.

"No, I have to try this afternoon. I must have looked so gay wandering up the N125 in a pair of micro shorts at 10am!"

"Nooo," I replied in mock horror, "I can't believe you hitched your way home like that and someone actually picked you up!"

"Well, Jo, some of us have it, some always strive for it and some of us," he looked me directly in the eye smiling, "just don't."

"You, Daniel, are revolting when you're in love," I laughed swiping him with my flight manifest.

As the next flight landed, the queue at car hire began to build and was soon stretching across the airport concourse. I called Emma and Tom in from the car park to help placate the tempers that were starting to fray.

I spotted a couple towards the end of the queue looking particularly uncomfortable. They were Tom's clients but as he was being held up at the front of the queue, I approached the couple to see if I could help.

"Hi," I said with my best smile, "I'm so sorry about the wait. Several flights have landed close together today and I'm afraid there will be a short delay getting your hire car. If you are uncomfortable, then please take a seat or get yourself a coffee and I will keep your place then come and get you when you are at the head of the queue."

I indicated the café to the side of where we were stood.
The man, who was in his middle sixties, was leaning heavily on a walking stick and looking fit to burst, his face red and his bushy eyebrows twitching.

"I don't want to get a coffee or take a seat. I want my car now," he said calmly but with a menacing undertone.

"As I explained Sir..."

"I heard what you explained, young lady, and I'm not impressed," he seethed at me.

"What can I do for you to make the wait easier?" I asked.

"Go away?!" he said.

"As you wish," I said backing away from him.

I joined Tom at the front of the queue and pulling him away from his clients warned him.

"You've got a lively one at the back Tom," I whispered telling him what happened. "You might want to do some damage limitation."

Sighing, Tom thanked me and set off towards him to see if he could have any more luck.

The queue was finally diminishing and Tom's difficult client was nearing the head of the queue. Even with another offer of help from Tom, the man had insisted on remaining standing. Just as I thought we could begin to breathe again, the man made his own personal protest and sat down on the floor of the concourse.

"Oh my God," I said motioning to Tom. We both approached the man and Tom helped him to his feet despite his protestations.

"You, young lady," he shouted jabbing a finger at me, "are a joke! I have been standing here for an hour without so much as the offer of a chair."

"With due respect I did...." I started but he interrupted me.

"That is the problem. There is no respect these days. Now get my car. I will be in

145

the car park waiting. I will be writing a strongly
worded letter of complaint."

With that parting shot, he was off in the direction
of the exit doors – his apologetic wife, struggling
to push the luggage trolley with a wonky wheel,
behind him.

"Oh Tom, I'm sorry! You are going to
get it in the neck from him tomorrow. It's the
last thing you need with Tammy arriving today."

"Don't worry," he said squeezing my
arm, "I've dealt with worse than him before."

"I think it's going to be one of those
days!" I said forlornly.

I didn't know how right I was when I uttered
those words. Flights were delayed, including
Tammy's and Ellie had been on the warpath
about our standards of bookkeeping. Dan had
got the worst roasting and couldn't be placated
until I promised to help him with his accounts
the next week. Beth had given us the wrong
flight details for the afternoon and Emma had to
make a mercy dash back to the office to collect
the correct paperwork. However, worse was yet
to come as I checked my phone messages.

"Tem uma messagem nova," said the
Portugal Telecom lady. I groaned and pressed
the star key.

"Hello Joanne," said a chirpy male
voice, "it's John Delaney here at Casa Verde.
We arrived this morning. We have a small
problem for you. Well, I say small. A rather
large tree appears to have fallen straight onto our
hire car and we're not sure what to do about it.
Can you help? Now, there's no rush. We're not
planning on driving anywhere so could you come
round when you're ready please? Thanks!"

I replaced the receiver and, closing my eyes,
emitted a long, low groan.

Twenty Four

I could barely believe my eyes as I stood, hands
on hips, with my mouth open, staring at the
horrific scene before me. The last time I'd seen
this villa was at the lunch with The Bertram's. It
was a beautiful country villa then with two shady
car parking areas. Now, the second car port lay
in ruins; decimated by a humble carob tree.

"We don't know quite how it
happened," said Mr Delaney, scratching his
wispy head and shrugging his shoulders, "We
were sat by the pool enjoying our first holiday G
& T and the next thing we heard this really loud
creaking noise followed by an almighty crash.
We thought the roof had caved in!"
"Yes, I see, I think you are all very
lucky the tree fell the way it did. If it had fallen
the other way, it would be through the bedroom
roof! Goodness me!" I said shaking my head
and wondering what to do first.

It really was quite the scene and all the
neighbours had come down the hill to have a
closer look. The small, brand new, shiny blue
Citroen Saxo hire car was still just visible
underneath the large tree canopy. The trunk of
the tree had fallen straight down the middle of
the car roof caving it in between the seats inside.
The branches had gouged deep tears in the metal
of the doors and bonnet and there were numerous
scratches and dents. I had never seen anything
like it. Mr Delaney was the first customer to

ever drive this car and it only had 70km on the clock!

I started by calling Carlos at the car hire company and explaining what had happened.

"Oh Jo," he laughed down the phone, "you are a bad omen for our cars! How did you make this happen?"

"Yeah, yeah Carlos, it's hilarious. I need you to help me. Please! I don't know what I'm doing and I need you to stop laughing and help me!" I said growing more anxious and frustrated.

Finally, and I think his empathy reappeared, he remembered his professional demeanour and started to make the necessary arrangements to help me.

"There's a new car being sent out to you now," he said, "and also a low loader to recover the car you broke." He laughed again as I rolled my eyes in frustration but also felt so relieved the car would be taken care of and the clients wouldn't suffer in any way.

"Thanks for your help, Carlos," I said a little stressed, "even if you have laughed at me a little too much."

"I'll make it up to you, Jo, I promise," he said suggestively.

I ignored the innuendo and thanked him before hanging up. I still had plenty of work to do.

The next call was to James, the villa manager. James was a very sprightly, near eighty years old, absolute darling of a man. A close friend of the Bertram's, he overlooked the rental of the villa when they were away and, having lived in the area for thirty years, he spoke the language, knew everything about everyone and was always on hand to help anyone. He wasn't surprised to hear the news, "that old tree has needed cutting down for a while but Caroline wouldn't spend the money," he sighed, "it's probably rotten and dead inside. Leave it with me and we'll get it sorted! The cavalry is on its way!"

While waiting for James to arrive with said cavalry, I set about taking lots of photographs of the scene, including the inside of the tree, to pass to Ellie for the sake of settling the inevitable insurance claim. I had sent Mr Delaney back to the rest of his group by the pool reassuring him of my ability to deal with the whole problem. I sounded confident even though I wasn't really. I was rather pleased, however, that I was managing to deal with it all by myself and hadn't called on Tom or Dan to help me.

A small crowd of neighbours and other locals had gathered and was now standing a little way away watching the spectacle unfold. This was probably the most exciting thing to happen in years! I was very relieved when, a short time later, I spied a truck full of local men driving up the lane towards me. The elderly James jumped down from the driver's seat and walked over to the spot where I was standing.

"Shhesh," he said scratching his bald head, "how the hell did this happen?"

"I really don't know," I replied, "I think you were right, the tree looks rotten in the middle and I think it was only a matter of time before it just broke from the weight of the branches. It's just terrible timing that it decided to fall when there was a brand new car underneath it."

"Brand new, you say?" asked James.

"Seventy kilometres on the clock," I said nodding sadly.

"Gosh, that is unlucky. At least they have the other car intact," he said pointing at the second vehicle safely parked under the front car port.

"Yes, thank goodness they are great people too. They've been amazing about it and haven't kicked off at all. In fact I've only seen one of them," I whispered, "as they're all by the pool having a gin and tonic; so can we get all this mess cleared up do you think?"

"No problem," said James, "I managed to round this lot up from the Luis dos Frangos restaurant after lunch. They just want a few beers for their trouble."

"Well, I will sort that out James, thank you so much," I said thrusting a fistful of escudos at him, "please treat them all on us!"

"No problem, will do. The promise of some lubrication will speed them on," he smiled as he motioned to the men to start work and pocketed the notes.

Soon, the air was filled with the sound of chainsaws cutting away the trunk from the top of the car. I agreed the men could have the firewood for nothing in return for their hard work, which also pleased them no end. I joined the line they had formed from tree to truck and helped pass every piece of wood into the back of the truck until all that was left of the tree was a small stump and some sawdust.

The car hire team arrived and carefully loaded the car onto the back of the pickup and left a shiny new car in its place. The crushed car was still shiny but its wheels were facing outwards as if it were very tired and was having a little lie down. The roof was ugly and twisted, scratched and gouged. All the activity had caused quite a stir in the small lane. This was a very quiet hamlet where nothing ever much happened. The old widow up the hill who permanently dressed in black, had even ridden bare back on her donkey to have a closer look.

Mr Delaney came down from the pool where they had all been watching the proceedings with much amusement.

"My dear, you have worked away and beyond the call of duty today," he said handing me a cold glass of water, "you must have other clients arriving today too?"

"Don't worry, my colleagues will be looking after them for me," I smiled taking grateful gulps of the cool liquid.

"Well, you'll certainly be getting a good report from us and don't bother to visit us tomorrow. We're quite happy to explore and find things for ourselves. The notes you left in the villa are enough. You have a rest tomorrow and we'll call you if we need you, ok!"

"That's great," I smiled, "why can't all my clients be like you?" I laughed handing him the keys to his new, uncrushed car.

As the whole event drew to a close, I took the opportunity to call Emma, who was still at the airport covering for me.

"Hiya babes," she sang down the phone, "got that tree sorted yet?"

"Just about," I replied, "the whole village has been out watching! Thanks for covering for me this afternoon. Have I missed anything exciting?"

"Nah, nothing lovie. The usual miserable bunch of moaners has arrived! Oh, and how could I forget? Tammy finally arrived – three hours late!"

My heart began to beat a little faster, "Oh, of course. Well, what's she like?"

"Well, I didn't get to talk to her or anything, but she seems ok. Nothing special."

"What does she look like?"

"She's small and dark. Very pale too. Maybe she's been living under a stone."

"Emma!" I said sternly but giggling at the same time.

"Well, Tom could do better if you ask me!"

"I hope you didn't tell him that."

"Didn't get a chance! We were so busy this afternoon that he missed her coming through and she was wandering around for half an hour trying to find him."

"Oh dear! That's not the best start to the week is it?"

"Oh who cares?" sniffed Emma, "We won't see Tom for a whole week now. I don't like it when someone outside enters our group. We work so well as a little quartet, do you know what I mean?"

"Yes," I said sighing, "I know exactly what you mean."

I felt tired, grubby and was scratched from the wood. After speaking to Emma I felt heavier, sadder and alone.

Twenty Five

The alarm beeped its morning welcome far too early. I crawled out of bed and opened the window shutters. I tried really hard not to think of Tom with his girlfriend, but images kept coming to me that I had to swipe away. I was so annoyed with myself for having such jealous feelings. This place was so good for me; I was growing in confidence and dealing with some crazy situations I couldn't have even guessed at or believed I could deal with before coming here. I'd made amazing friends who made everything so much easier and I'd never worked in a more supportive team.

I gazed out across the hills, which stretched north of Sao Bras, as I sat on my balcony, drinking my morning tea. Antenna 3 was playing on the radio and the noise wasn't helping my brain. I turned the radio off telling it to shut up at the same time. In an hour, I would be telling new clients all about the 'Slide & Splash' water park, the best and quietest beaches and which restaurants they should visit. I sighed deeply as the silence enveloped me. My shoulders felt round and heavy and I felt very alone.

I pulled up outside Casa do Campo and sighed heavily as I turned off the ignition. My heart just wasn't in all this rep business today. I painted my best smile on, hoping the family wouldn't suspect its falseness. This particular family were staying for six weeks, which was great in one way as they wouldn't need much from me but could also go the other way and they could be more demanding.

I left nearly ninety minutes later on a mercy mission to the airport to try and retrieve Mr McCrae's spare walking stick, left carelessly on the baggage reclaim carousel. The family had quizzed me on every aspect of the Algarve and its many attractions, the costs, the opening times and the available parking. I wondered if London were constantly sending me mystery shopper families. Surely no other rep had this many forgetful, accident prone, demanding, angry clients?

By Wednesday afternoon, however, I really had had enough. I had been called out at 10pm one night because the McCrae's had run out of nappies for their baby. Guess who had to find the late chemist in Faro, a twenty minute drive away? They couldn't possibly go as they'd enjoyed wine with lunch and they hadn't noticed how low their supply had got.

Another couple had phoned me to ask if I could identify a pink flower in the garden of their villa. Why didn't my clients just go to the beach, get drunk and sunbathe like normal people? Instead, they had to roam around the gardens making notes on plants and flowers like Alan blooming Titchmarsh. After three whole days of smiling and running around after my clients, I was fed up and in need of normal company. I phoned Emma and told her to get her party pants on because I was on my way west.

There was a strange smell in the foyer of Emma's Lagos apartment block, which only got stronger as she opened her front door.

"What is that smell?" I asked holding my nose.

"Ooh, it might be me, I've just come from the gym," she said pulling her t-shirt away from her chest, "or it could be my cabbage soup," she said, "come in!"

"Cabbage soup? You're not doing that stupid diet are you?"

"I thought I'd give it a go; Rogerio says all the beige is making me fat," she replied holding onto a tiny piece of skin on her midriff.

"What?" Seriously? Is this guy for real? There's nothing of you!"

"Yeah, right," she said, "no beige for me this week."

She led me into the kitchen where the smell was almost unbearable. On the hob was a large, saucepan.

"Pworgh! It is a bit whiffy now you mention it!" she said wrinkling her nose as she lifted the lid, "If you eat this for a week, you're supposed to lose half a stone."

"And where exactly are you going to lose this half stone from?" I enquired as I looked at her in her gym gear.

"My arse, for a start," she moaned pinching another tiny piece of skin between her finger and thumb. "Oh lord," she laughed as she wafted the steam away from the top of the pot, "it's gone all blue!"

I peered into the pot whilst holding my nose. The mixture inside was a bright blue lumpy mess. The smell was like old, rotten eggs and was absolutely stomach churning. Emma laughed hysterically as she reached for the air freshener,

"Emma," I said, "did you use red cabbage by any chance?"

"Yes, it's all I had," she said as she held her nose and sprayed the freshener.

"Ooh, throw it away, Jo! That's nasty!"

"It would have been the red cabbage that turned it blue," I said laughing and coughing as I tipped the blue mess into a carrier bag and tied the handles together.

"Jesus! It stinks! Spray some of that stuff quick!" I laughed as I ran out of the apartment to the communal bins.

Much later, after giving the flat a good airing, downing a few drinks and lots of girly gossip and make up, we were on our way down into the centre of Lagos. As we walked down the hill, we could see the still green mountain of Monchique ahead of us. Most of Emma's properties were dotted around that area. It looked very beautiful as the sun set behind it and the whole mountain seemed to glow in the orange light.

We had dinner at the Italian restaurant where Emma dined at least once a week. She had all the waiters wrapped round her little finger. I've never had such attentive waiters serve dinner. Emma played on this, flirting with them all.

"When I phone an order through for delivery, it turns up after fifteen minutes," she winked at me, "a little flirting doesn't hurt now and again, as well you know!"

"I don't know what you mean," I said trying to look hurt and failing.

"Oh you know, Jo," she smiled, "I've never seen anyone flirt so successfully with a gay man! And Tom is well in love with you! The two of them would do anything for you and you know it!"

"What do you mean Tom's in love with me?" I screeched reddening.

"Interesting that's the bit you picked up on; the two of you spend so much time together. He was a real loner before you turned up, you know."

"Really? I thought he was a very sociable bloke."

"Of course he is," she smiled, "just more so when you're around. It's terrible what a great distance can do to a relationship isn't it?" she said mischievously, "It must be so hard when you're working so much and you're busy...It would be really hard to keep it together especially when there are so many distractions around!"

"I don't know what you're talking about, Emma," I said staring intently down at my dinner.

"Really?" she asked eyeing me from under her lashes, "It's just, well... if things don't work out for Tom, he'll really need his friends round, won't he? I mean, he'd need a lot of support. Long distance relationships, well, they can be difficult, can't they? Who knows what will happen?" Emma grinned reaching for the wine bottle.

"Now, more wine?"

Much later on, after even more wine, we were in the full swing of the evening. We were stood at the bar of 'The Loco' laughing at girls who were coming in through the door. The bar had a glass floor just inside the entrance and all the people downstairs could see straight up every poor, unaware girls skirt.

"Surely, there must be a law against that," I laughed, in spite of myself, as one girl jumped off the glass after realising what was, or rather wasn't, beneath her.

"You would think so," said Emma, "especially when some people don't wear any knickers!"

I looked at her my mouth hanging open. She nodded and giggled, wrinkling her nose.

"Oh my God Emma, and that," I said indicating the glass floor, "is disgusting."

We continued to weave our way from one bar to the next dancing our way along. As the sun started to peep above the horizon, we were sitting by the harbour in Lagos looking over the boats and yachts and finishing the bottle of champagne we had smuggled out of the last bar. Our platform shoes lay discarded on the floor. Emma had a purse full of phone numbers scribbled on bits of cigarette boxes and coasters. I scrambled to put my shoes back on for the walk home but didn't fasten them.

"Come on, time to go home," I said dragging Emma to her feet, who was beginning to nod off on my shoulder. As she pulled herself up using my hand to help, she actually knocked me off balance and I fell sideways off my shoe, bending my ankle at an awkward angle. It hurt only momentarily before I clambered back onto the high sandal and we set off home in the early morning light.

Twenty Six

There was a constant ringing coming from somewhere. It stopped for a while and, a few minutes later, started again. I felt Emma's weight shift on the other side of the bed as the ringing stopped again. Then it was there again. Ringing endlessly.
Emma sat up and putting both her hands round her head staggered out of bed and down the hall to answer the ringing phone.

I couldn't hear much but a low grumble whenever Emma managed to speak. A few moments later, she was back climbing under the duvet.
"Who was that?" I asked sleepily trying to ignore the drilling sound in my head.
"Ellie," mumbled Emma, "I have a blocked sewage tank and a backed up toilet in Monchique to deal with. She's been trying to get hold of me for ages and has called out a plumber herself. She's not impressed as I'm sure you can imagine. I have to go meet him now and get it sorted."
"Oh no, Em," I said, "If your stomach feels anything like mine does....."
"Don't," she interrupted, "I feel sick just thinking about it."
"What time is it?" I asked.
"10.30."
"We didn't go to bed until 7am," I moaned.
"I know, don't remind me! Why did I drink so much?" said Emma as she dragged

herself up again and disappeared in the direction of the shower.

One hour later, Emma was standing at the side of an open manhole cover. The smell of raw sewage was too much to bear and no matter where she stood, she couldn't avoid it. The plumber was feeding a camera down the drain to try and find where the blockage was occurring. Emma praised herself for sending the clients away from the villa for the day. It was grim.

"Could you get the pipe extension for me?" asked the plumber. There was no answer.

Emma was headfirst in the landscaped trees that bordered the garden saying goodbye to breakfast.

After Emma left, I tried to get out of bed and fell straight back down onto the mattress. The pain in my right ankle was insane. I peered down to see it swollen to twice its normal size. What on earth...? Then I remembered falling off the side of my platform shoe. I tried to stand again but couldn't bear my weight on it. I leaned and pulled on the bedstead to help me stand, balancing precariously on one leg. Hopping and shuffling round the flat, I gathered my belongings and managed to get out to the car. I had some flipflops in the boot, which I managed to get on my injured foot, as my trainers were just not going to fit. Of all the times to injure myself, it had to be today when I was due to meet Ellie for an assessment. My ankle was really throbbing now but I didn't think it was broken. My friend back home broke her ankle years before and couldn't even bear anyone near the cast; the pain was so intense.
I rummaged in my bag for some painkillers, finding one lone paracetamol. It wasn't going to

do much but I swallowed it with some water anyway and set off to Vilamoura where I was due to meet Ellie.

Driving wasn't actually that bad as my injured foot controlled the accelerator. If it had been my clutching foot, I would have been in trouble. I arrived at the marina and parked up at the agreed place. Vilamoura is definitely full of money. The marina is packed with yachts and boats of all sizes ranging from small fishing boats to huge cruisers. Surrounding the marina were many restaurants selling amazing seafood and wine, designer shops, hairdressers, nail bars and cafes. The prices here were ten times what they were back in little Sao Bras.

I sat in my car for a while wondering how I was going to explain my ankle to Ellie when there was a knock on my side window. Startled, I looked across to see Dan's face pressed up against the glass, making a fish face.

"Oh my gosh!" I said jumping a mile in the air. I lowered the window and asked, "What are you doing here? I'm due to meet Ellie."

"Hello to you too!" he replied, "Yes, I'm fine, thank you!"

"Sorry," I said, "I'm in a fair bit of pain here. Can you help?"

"What have you done now?" he asked me coming round to the driver's side and opening the door.
I waved my ankle in his direction and said, "This!"

Dan gasped as he peered at my swollen extremity. "Ouch! What happened?"

I explained the cause of the injury exclaiming, "I really need to stop drinking!"

"No," he replied, "you need to stop wearing such ridiculous shoes!"
I rolled my eyes and asked what he was doing there.

"Well, Ellie asked me to let you know your assessment is cancelled because she's in Monchique dealing with Emma and a toilet or something."

"Oh, thank the Lord, I didn't want to explain this," I said pointing to my foot.

"You're welcome," said Dan helping me out of the car, "so I'm here to tell you and was going to take you out on a cruise for the afternoon but that's probably not such a great idea, looking at you. Here, take these," he said holding out a silver foil packet.

"What are they?" I asked popping a tablet from its blister pack.

"Drugs!" he laughed, "seriously though, they're strong painkillers I take them for my back when it's bad. They might help. We need to get you sitting down and get that leg elevated."

With one arm around my waist, he helped me hop to the nearest waterfront café, deposited me on a chair and went to ask for some ice. I was left looking out at the sun bouncing off the water and watching the boats as they bobbed gently up and down. The water was making gentle sucking sounds at the marina wall. It was most peaceful and a little hypnotic.

"Here we are," he said reappearing with a spare chair, "let's get that leg up."

He gently lifted and placed my leg on a chair, draped it with a tea towel and carefully lay the plastic bag of ice on top.

"This should help, have you taken one of those painkillers yet?"

"Thanks Dan, and yes I've just taken two," I replied.

"Two?"

"Isn't that the normal dose?"

"When you're used to them or in writhing agony, yes. I was going to suggest trying one and seeing how that went. Oh well, let's see!"

Twenty minutes later, the world was such a beautiful place. I felt sleepy and excited at the same time. Everything seemed louder somehow and funny; it was all funny.

"Dan," I laughed, "what drugs have you given me? I'm off my face!"

"Hence advising only one!" he tutted, rolling his eyeballs at me.

I sniggered at him again and he pushed water across the table at me, "keep drinking too. You don't want to get dehydrated on top of those tablets or we'll never get you home."

"I don't care," I said sleepily, my eyes blinking slowly, "I like it here. Why don't we get everyone else here and have a drink"?

"With you like this?" he laughed, "much fun as that would be, I don't think it would be such a great idea inviting Tom and Tammy, do you?"

I grimaced at the sound of her name.

"Urgh, I bet they've been shagging all week. How disgusting!"

164

"Why are you so bothered Jo?" asked Dan taking full advantage of my drugged state.

"He's so fit Dan, isn't he? He's so fit!"

"Yes Jo, he is very fit," laughed Dan. "I think we're going to need some more water and some coffee." He waved to the waiter to make an order.

"Don't get me wrong," I said, "I'm sure she's deeeelightful and pretty and small." I stuck my tongue out in disgust. Blergh! My tone had become more disparaging as I went on. "I mean, I don't even know her. What would I know? I don't even know what she looks like. I'm sure she's a beautiful soul. Who am I to make judgment?" I said sweeping my arm wide and almost taking out the waiter and his tray.

"Jo," said Dan, "you really need to get over this crush you have on Tom. We all know about it. He loves you to bits, you know, but he has a girlfriend." He enunciated the last part of the sentence to really push home the message.

"Crush? Who me?" I smacked myself in the chest, "I don't have a crush. Who told you that?"

"I can see with my own eyes Jo, no one needed to tell me."

His voice was calm and soothing; almost sympathetic.

"I understand Jo, how you're feeling, I really do," he said softly and placed his hand on mine.

There was a moment of quiet before I laughed again.

"Fooled you!" I laughed, "we're just great mates! What are you going on about Dan? As if! Huh!"

Even in my drug addled state, I didn't want to open up to anyone else or confide in them. My modus operandi was to keep things to myself and brood on them; overthinking was a pastime for me. Heaven forbid anyone should know what was going on in my head. I'd made such progress during this season and had begun to trust people again and confiding things to Tom made me feel so close to him. I trusted him with everything; I knew I was safe with him.

"Well, ok," said Dan from behind his coffee cup, "whatever you say."

He removed the ice from my ankle and peered under the tea towel.

"The swelling has gone down a bit. I'm guessing you've sprained it. It may need strapping up for support until it's fully healed."

"Thank you, Dr Dan," I smiled as the world continued in its woolly state.

The subject was changed just like that and we sat in that café for a while until the sun began to sink lower in the sky and Dan was convinced enough of the drug had worn off to allow me to drive back home. I was more than grateful to him for his help, patience and genuine concern for me getting emotionally hurt. He really was very sweet under the blustering front he presented to the world.

Twenty Seven

The following Sunday, I was stood at the company sign with Dan waiting for the next group of happy clients. My ankle had recovered well but I still had it strapped up to help support it and also cover the giant black and blue bruise covering the skin.

"Thanks for the other day," I said gratefully, "you really looked after me. That was sweet."

"You were a bloody mess," he laughed, "what else was I going to do? Just leave you there in pain?"

"Some people would!" I retorted.

"Yeah, well, I'm not some people," he replied a little huffily, "we all adore you Jo. You just need to believe it."

I didn't say anything in response and actually, didn't know what to say. I felt a little foolish and embarrassed, as if I were fishing for compliments, which is the last thing I would do. I decided to change the subject completely.

"How's things going with you then?" I asked, "I didn't ask you the other day."

"With my man, you mean? Oh that's all over! He was so boring Jo. He wanted us to go see a movie. Can you believe it?"

"Gosh!" I said in mock horror, putting my hand on his arm, "how dare he want to spend time with you!"

"Don't take the piss!"

"Sorry Dan, I just really don't see what the issue is."

"I didn't come here to meet some lush Latin guy, dressed to the nines in a club, looking fabulous and then sit watching a subtitled Julia Roberts every night! I want some excitement out of life not a cosy suburban existence. Not yet anyway!"

"I see and I understand," I nodded, "It's just such a shame, you two were getting on so well!"

"I've never been one to stay with someone if it doesn't feel right just to avoid being alone. Do you know what I mean?"

I knew exactly and thought of Andrew in London, his snotty media friends and their shoe judgments.

"Never mind honey. There's always the gay bar to save you if all else fails. There's plenty more fish!"

"Don't remind me of that," he laughed, "Darling, I'm desperate but not that desperate!" he laughed throwing his head back but I thought he looked sad.

"Tammy goes home today, doesn't she?" he asked changing the subject.

"Erm, I'm not sure...yeah, I guess it must be today," I replied pasting on my best smile at the approaching family.

"Great!" he said beaming broadly too, "we get our little clique back and some gossip. Someone round here has to be having a love life 'cos it sure as hell ain't us!"

I felt my friendly smile become a grimace as Dan greeted the clients and pointed them in the direction of car hire. As I watched them weave a path towards the desk, I saw Tom chatting to Carlos and gesturing towards someone stood next to him. That must be Tammy. Emma had been right – she was petite, only reaching Tom's shoulder, she was pale, even after a week in the sun. However, unlike Emma's description, she was pretty, her dark hair falling perfectly down her back. The two of them were making their way over to us. I felt my stomach tighten and told my face to smile.

"Hi guys!" said Tom cheerily to us both.

"Hello stranger," said Dan stroppily, "I suppose you want to be our friend again after a whole week without even one phone call!"

Tom laughed, "This is Dan, Tammy; don't worry, he's always this dramatic."
She smiled up at Dan, batting her eyelashes.

"Pleased to meet you," she said.

"It's lovely to meet you too," gushed Dan, "We've heard almost nothing about you!"

There was an awkward moment of silence broken by my nervous laugh as Tom introduced me.

"This is Jo," he said, "my nearest neighbour who I've told you about."

"Hi," I said smiling as best I could. I didn't look at Tom once, terrified something in my eyes would give me away.

Tammy smiled back but the smile didn't quite reach her eyes that bore into me. It felt as if she was trying to read my mind. Could she tell my feelings?

"Ah, Jo. I've heard so much about you," she said in a sickly sweet voice. I chose to ignore her and blabbed, "have you had a nice week?"

I looked quickly from one to the other to avoid direct eye contact.

"Oh yes, thank you, we've had fun haven't we?" she giggled putting one hand on Tom's shoulder, the other stroking his cheek. "It's just a shame you still had to work and couldn't have your clients covered."

Dan shot me a glance; eyebrows raised.

"He left me in the airport for a whole day while he sorted out an 'emergency'," she gestured bunny ears with her fingers.

"It was an emergency!" protested Tom, moving her hand from his shoulder.

"I don't call fixing a boiler an emergency," she said with a smile that didn't reach her eyes. "Anyway, Carlos looked after me and treated me well, so it was fine in the end."

"I bet he did," said Dan nudging me discreetly with his elbow.

"Thanks for covering some stuff for me this week, Jo. I really appreciate it. I owe you one," said Tom grabbing Tammy's other hand and pulling it away from his face.

Tom coughed and stared at the floor as the silence deepened.

"Well," said Tammy eventually, "I best go and check in or I'll miss my flight."

"Yes, we wouldn't want that, would we?" said Dan in a more than sarcastic tone, "better to be airside nice and early!"

"Nice meeting you both," smiled Tammy, meeting my eye for rather too long again, "Tom? Shall we?" she grabbed Tom's hand and pulled him away from us.

"See you later guys," said Tom with a sheepish smile as he was pulled away.

Tom and Tammy disappeared in the crowd as I nudged Dan in the ribs with my elbow.

"Hey," he moaned, "You didn't like her either did you?"

"I don't know her so I can't say that I don't."

"Oh come on, Jo. She's awful. She barely spoke five words to us. She's obviously jealous of Tom working with such beautiful people. Did you see her stroking his cheek? VOMIT! And what was all that about Carlos?"

"They must be in love, Dan, that's why." I sighed deeply.

Dan laughed and slipped an arm round my shoulder and squeezed me toward him.

"Doubt it! I've never seen anyone look so uncomfortable in my life. Poor bloke. He's well under the thumb there. I would have thought he had more balls than that. Never mind honey. We can still have a good time together. I'll buy you a coffee once this flight's through and we can plan something fun, ok?!"

"Yeah," I smiled, "that would be nice. Thanks Dan," I said still watching Tom and Tammy as they disappeared into the crowd.

Twenty Eight

Our coffee after work turned into a drink at the gay bar in Vilamoura.

"I don't think Sunday night is the big gay night sweetheart," I said looking mournfully around at the near empty bar.

The V Bar was tucked away in a corner just a stone's throw away from the main bars and restaurants of the marina. There were a few tables and chairs outside the bar filled with a few groups of men. A red carpet led the way to the door of the bar, which was enveloped in a heavy, red, velvet curtain. The inside of the bar was mostly lit by ultraviolet light giving a blue glow to the room. A giant V in blue neon light hung on one wall and the solid wood bar stretched the entire length of the room.

We bought a drink and settled on the stools at the bar.

"Hey Luis, where is everyone tonight?" asked Dan of the barman.

"It's Sunday, what you expect? You should be here last night!" replied Luis batting his long, dark eyelashes as he polished glasses.

"He always says that to me, Jo. It's not fair I can't come down here on a Saturday night and see the local talent."

"Eh Dan, the locals don't know what they miss, eh?" said Luis winking at me.

"Is he taking the piss?" asked Dan thrusting his thumb towards a laughing Luis.

"It is pretty quiet in here tonight, but you never know," I said optimistically

"Sometimes the best nights start on a quiet note."

"Oh, bless your heart," said Dan softly as he stroked my cheek, "you're trying to cheer me up when it's clear it should be the other way round."

"What do you mean? I'm fine."

"I saw your face today. Don't worry, I didn't like her either."

"Who? Tammy? She seemed ...nice," I said rather unconvincingly.

I thought Dan was going to spit out his mouthful of drink but thankfully he managed to swallow it.

"Nice? Nice?? She was absolutely vile! She was rude to us going on about his clients being covered. You did visits for him! Cheeky cow, and the way she was stroking Tom...urgh! Totally unnecessary if you ask me."

"They haven't seen each other for a while and I guess she's a little insecure about him being out here surrounded by beauties," I gestured towards the bar where two men had slipped in, sat in the corner and looked at us under their ears.

"You can joke about it all you like, darling, but I think she's horrible and she has every right to be worried," he said as he stood up and walked off to the gents.

I didn't know if Dan had noticed anything in my behaviour or if he was just fishing for information. Both Emma and Dan had made comments about the relationship between Tom and me. I reconciled myself to the idea they were just curious. We did spend a lot of time together after all. There was nothing to tell anyway apart from a few mega embarrassing incidents. I would much rather they never found

173

out about those! I would just have to rid myself
of these ridiculous feelings. I was far too old to
have a crush on a guy; that's all it was. I came
here feeling vulnerable, alone and lonely. He
was there to pick me up and show me the ropes
and had been so kind whilst doing that. I felt
like a very different girl now but old insecurities
are hard to banish and can hit you across the
back of the head when you are least expecting it.
The swings I was having, from confident
Algarve girl back to needy, whiney London girl,
were getting less as time passed. I wanted to see
the back of that old me and keep the new one as
much as possible.

Twenty Nine

True to Dan's story, Tom had two new house guests that week, a villa owner called Ben and his dog, Lasagne. Ben was an eccentric American man with a shock of fluffy, white hair, a straggly beard and a love of naturism. He left America when he was in his twenties and set up home in Denmark, moving to Portugal when he met his wife who, sadly, died very young. He spent every winter sailing in Scandinavia acquiring an old seadog appearance with a deeply lined, tanned characterful face. His blue eyes were the azure colour of the waterfall pool. He really must have been a very handsome man when younger.

The traditional Portuguese house he owned was in a secluded valley two miles away from his nearest neighbour. He had spent the spring building a new pool for all the overheated honeymooners who loved the isolation of the valley but not the dust and heat. Tom had helped him with the renovations, disappearing for days into the hidden valley.

Now in his mid sixties, Ben was fit and tanned and looking forward to his short stay with Tom before he set off to Denmark. Tom and Ben had built a close friendship, which endured even through Ben's love of naturism. Yes, Ben loved to be naked. All of the time. Tom had told me how, even when he was mending the roof of his house, he was naked. Making dinner? Naked.

Erecting a fence? Ahem…Yep, you guessed it; he was naked.

Ben reasoned that as his house was so secluded, no-one could see his nakedness. He didn't like tan lines and yes that tan really was all over. He carried on this behaviour in Tom's flat and they both agreed that as long as the business end was covered when in Tom's presence, he could do as he pleased.

I figured I could visit under the pretext of wanting to meet this man and not feel uncomfortable breaking the silence with Tom. I stood outside the block of flats, took a deep breath and pressed the bell.

"Hello!" Tom's familiar voice echoed down the crackly intercom.

"It's me, Tom," I replied.

"Jo, what a great surprise. Come on up!"

He buzzed me into the building and I ascended the stairs feeling silly and a little nervous. I knew this was all in my own head and I just needed to get over myself.

Tom opened the door as I was halfway up the final flight of stairs, let me in and gave me a huge welcoming hug.

"Great to see you," he said, "we didn't get to speak much at the airport and once I'd finished, I couldn't find you!"

"Yeah, sorry, I went to the V bar with Dan after he'd been so good to me with my ankle and everything," I mumbled gesturing towards my right foot, which was still strapped up.

"No worries," he said, "Just, well we needed a catch up and well, here you are!"

"Hi there!" came another voice from the living room. It was a low, drawling voice and sounded like honey dripping off a spoon.

"Jo, let me introduce you to Ben. He's staying for the week until he departs north."

"So I hear," I replied following Tom to where Ben was sprawled on Tom's sofa. He had a small, white towel tied around his waist, which really didn't cover much. He beamed broadly as he shook my hand,

"Pleased to meet you Jo, come in and have a drink. Thanks Tom," he gestured an imaginary glass towards his mouth as Tom rolled his eyes and disappeared to the kitchen.

Ben sat himself back on the sofa cushion and the tiny, white towel fell open. I looked away in horror and embarrassment as he pulled the towel back round himself.

"Whoops sorry, have to get myself a bigger towel, I guess," he apologised in his slow drawl.

"Yes, you should really do that," I said blushing, looking away and taking a bottle of beer from Tom.

"Ben, I told you to be careful with that towel. You don't want Jo running out on us do you?" said Tom.

"Hey, I'm sure it's nothing she ain't seen before," Ben laughed slowly.

"No, but I wanted to see the others," I whispered under my breath.

Tom gave me a dig with his elbow and grinned at me. I breathed a sigh of relief as we easily regained our camaraderie.

"Ben, we're going out for a quick dinner. You be alright on your own or do you

177

want to come with us?" asked Tom, "It's just the Italian tonight."

"And have to wear clothes in this heat?" he asked, "No, I'm fine here with my take out. You guys go have fun! Don't do anything I would," he chuckled pulling at the towel as he crossed his legs revealing his total nakedness yet again.

"Oh, wow, there it is again," I said covering my eyes and laughing as Tom led me towards the door.

We walked into the centre of the town chatting easily until I could stand it no more and had to address the elephant in the room.

"Tammy seems really … nice," I said not very convincingly.

"Thanks, yeah I think so," Tom replied. The awkwardness had come back as soon as I mentioned her name and the atmosphere seemed to shift a notch.

"Did you have a good time last week? The weather was great…" I tailed off waiting for him to reply.

"Yes, the weather was great. It was a great week and you really helped, doing some of my visits."

"You'd do the same for me," I sang back trying to lift the mood back up.

"Look Jo," said Tom who had stopped walking and turned towards me, "the thing is - she didn't really feel comfortable around you guys, especially you."

My heart began to beat faster as I asked him, "What? Why? She doesn't even know me? She's barely spoken to me. How could she feel like that? She spent about two minutes in my company!"

He held his palms up to me in a calming gesture.

"She says I'm always going on about you lot and it makes her jealous; like she's missing out…and the one person I talk about more than anyone… is you."

The air seemed to thicken around me as he stepped toward me and looked into my eyes, shrugging.

"Oh," was all I could manage to blurt out.

He stepped even closer and I looked at the outline of his mouth as he said, "So, I think it's a good idea if I don't spend quite so much time with you from now on. I need to do this for the sake of my relationship, I hope you can understand that Jo. I think we've all got a bit too close and we need to expand our circle of friends a bit, don't you think?"

His eyebrows were raised, waiting for a response. I felt as if the wind had been punched out of me and eventually, I managed to speak.

"Has she asked you to do this?" I asked.

"Not in so many words but she did find it odd how close we all are, working together and socialising and not allowing anyone else into the group."

"That's so ridiculous!" I protested, "and unfair. She's based her opinion after being here for one week and listening to you talk about your colleagues was too much for her, was it?"

"Jo, calm down! I'm not deserting you all. Just maybe, I don't know, getting a better balance back between us and the rest of the world would be a good idea."

"Is that what she said?" I asked angrily.

"You must understand that the more time I spend with you, the worse it is for our relationship. She doesn't understand how closely we all work here together and it's just easier this way. I need this to work out, I really do."

"Easier for who, Tom?" I asked, my throat burning, "You are a huge part of our lives here and if I'm not allowed to see you..."

"It's not a question of being allowed Jo, we just need to cut back on the amount of time we're together alone. You do understand, don't you?" he'd emphasised the word "alone," so I guessed it was me she had the issue with, rather than Dan or Emma.

I didn't understand at all. I felt it was a mistake for Tom to tell me that Tammy didn't like any of us. It made me feel defensive towards my small group of friends and angry, really angry. I knew telling Tom anymore about these feelings would also be a mistake, so I nodded miserably and continued walking, linking arms with him as we headed towards the restaurant.

"Well, she must be really worried tonight," I smiled trying to ignore the thickness in my voice, "what with you having a naked man in your apartment and everything!"

"Oh God, don't," he laughed, the tension dissipating slightly, "Ben is an amazing man; he has so many stories. I've spent hours just listening to him; he's an amazing raconteur. He's also pretty easy to be around; just needs feeding every now and again and he's also partial to a spot of single malt whisky."

"Oh really?" I laughed, "there'll be no palming him off with cheap plonk from Lidl then?"

"Most definitely not!"

He squeezed my arm and laughed as we continued on our way to dinner; friends again but with the Tammy issue still hanging in the air.

Later, after some beige, a delicious dinner of clams and far too much white wine, the atmosphere had eased a little and the previous conversation almost forgotten. We chatted as we normally did and there was plenty of laughter. Not being able to do this freely and always worrying about what his girlfriend was thinking was going to be really hard. Having thought about it more, I did understand, though, in a way, I really did. If it were me, 1500 miles away, I'd be worried but, at the same time, if there's no trust in a relationship, is there anything? I did feel bad for Tammy, don't get me wrong, of course I did. It must be awful being away from the man you love and seeing him having such a good time with new friends in a hot country. But asking him to limit contact with his friends and call her every day? That's controlling behaviour and I felt uneasy for him, wondering why he was so desperate for the relationship to work.

Over dinner, we talked and talked on all subjects from politics to music and clients and the story of the tree on the client's car and it was just so easy. I never had so much in common with a man before or found it so easy to talk freely. I felt comfortable; self-confident and strong. Tom praised me for sorting out the car hire all by myself and so quickly, saying anyone else would have called in more help from fellow reps.

"You've changed so much in your time here, Jo. You used to ring me all the time about clients and what to do and now you just go off and deal with it. It's great!"

"Thanks," I said shy again; I never was any good at receiving compliments.

"I even love how you can put Dan in his place when he gets a bit out of order, and I've never seen anyone else be able to do that!"

"You just have to know how to handle him," I laughed. "I manage better with Dan than I ever did with my ex, Andrew. He didn't know much about anything except football, which bores me rigid. He never really listened to anything I said or ideas I had. I made decisions, slowly, by myself and told him when he needed to know. It really wasn't the best coupling ever. We weren't exactly Posh and Becks!"

"Would you want to be?" asked Tom giggling and swigging his wine.

"Oh, I don't know," I said, "being made to feel like a million dollars and having a wedding with my very own throne? Maybe! Couple goals!"

"Your Majesty!" he said throwing his napkin over one arm like a waiter and pouring more wine. We laughed together and drank far too much wine, as usual.

"I definitely have not eaten enough beige," I said slapping my stomach, "I'm sloshing with white wine!"

"That's because you were too busy talking to eat," giggled Tom.

"What's your excuse then? I really didn't want to drink tonight; this is all your fault you nob."

"Thanks a bunch," he replied sending the waiter a signal for the bill.

"Time for home, yes?"

We staggered back through town to Tom's apartment and collapsed through the door onto the floor laughing and screaming. We had both forgotten all about Ben being there and must have woken him up.

"Come on Queen," slurred Tom as he hauled me to my feet, "you look silly down there."

"Oh, thank you kind sir," I replied, "which one of you is going to pour me another drink?" My vision was seriously impaired and the patterned tiles on Tom's floor were making me feel a little nauseous. The sudden movement from horizontal to vertical was not the best plan and I felt my stomach lurch.

"Oh, I don't feel so good," I managed to blurt as I raced to the bathroom. I threw myself onto my knees in front of the toilet.

I felt a hand pull my hair away from my face and another rubbing me on the back.

"What are you like, you bloody lightweight?" Tom laughed as I heaved again. "Do you think Posh does this after dinner?"

"Undoubtedly!" I managed.

From another room, an American voice began to call out. It was Ben.

"Hey Jo, did you bring your friends Ralph and Huey home with you? That's all I can hear you saying!"

Just as he asked me that question, another "Ralph" was upon me and my stomach heaved again. Tom was laughing hysterically.

"Ralph and Huey, did you hear that Jo? How funny is that?"

"Hysterical," I managed to reply before "Huey" came back again.

Finally, I was done and managed to pull myself to my feet. Tom handed me a cold, damp flannel

and my toothbrush with toothpaste already on it,
a smirk on his face the entire time.
I was more than grateful and had given up
feeling embarrassed. This guy was my mate and
what an amazing friend he was being right now.
I disappeared into the bedroom and climbed into
the waiting bed.

"Tom," I called gently.

He came into the room with a large glass of
water, two painkillers and placed them on the
nightstand next to me.

"That's the last time I spend money on
buying you dinner," he quipped.

"I'm sorry Tom," I sniffed, "Thank
you."

"What for?" he asked holding my hand.

"You held my hair back," I said feebly
feeling a banging headache begin behind my
eyes.

"Can't have the queen with sick in her
hair can we now?"

I smiled as my eyes closed and the darkness of
sleep washed over me.

Thirty

The season was really moving on now and all of us were very busy in our areas. Ellie had been right though; things did seem to be settling into a regular routine and there had been few disasters. I was still battling with Isabel over the pool pump at Villa Das Avores and was making thrice weekly trips to the house to ensure it was turned on.

I hadn't seen Tom, apart from airport days, since that last night in his apartment. He was staying true to his word and promise to Tammy and, if anything, it increased my respect for him. You had to admire his loyalty even if it made me feel a little unwanted and alone. Emma was spending more and more time with Rogerio and I hadn't seen her for weeks either. Beth hardly left the office as Ellie kept her nose to the grindstone although she did ring me regularly to moan about it! I had been spending more and more time with Dan and that time revolved around eating and drinking – a lot. My clothes were getting tight and I knew I was piling on weight. I didn't like it and resolved to start making some better choices and not have quite so much beige.

I was applying my last smear of lipstick as I heard the nonstop buzz of my doorbell that told me Dan had arrived. I buzzed him into the building and opened the front door for him as I grabbed my bag and keys.

"I'm ready now so don't have a go at me for being late," I yelled rushing into the bedroom for one last mirror check, adjusting the ties on my simple wrap dress, as Dan's footsteps echoed in the hallway.

"There's no rush, babe," came the reply but it wasn't Dan's voice, it was Tom's.

I thought my heart had actually stopped beating for a second before I could move towards the door of my bedroom. Sure enough, there was Tom looking more gorgeous than ever, stood in my hallway, hands in board shorts pockets, his dark hair dishevelled and in need of a cut.

"I was expecting Dan," I managed to blurt.

"Oh right," he replied, "It's just...I was at a loose end and thought I'd just pop round to see you...you know it's been a while..." he tailed off.

"Oh..well, Dan's on his way to take me out for dinner. You're more than welcome to come, of course."

"If you're sure I won't be intruding then I'd like that," he grinned broadly at me.

"Course you're not," I smiled back as the buzzer went again, "that will be Dan, come on let's go."

Dan was more than a little surprised to see Tom descending from my apartment but happy he had decided to join us.

"So nice of you to join us darling," he said sniffily, "we thought we weren't good enough for you anymore."

"Dan!" I said warningly, "play nice!"

"I'm just saying, don't you think you can just love us and leave us though," he said defensively as Tom looked at the ground and then up at me through his dark lashes.

We had a table reserved at the Canto Azul in the small fishing village of Santa Lucia. The small restaurant overlooked the ocean and was lit purely by candles and fairy lights. Swathes of white muslin were draped along the walls giving the place a highly romantic feel. It was a popular restaurant amongst our clients, although there didn't seem to be any lurking in the dark corners this evening.

"So, Tom," began Dan, "why have you been avoiding us all?"

"I haven't been avoiding you Dan, I've just been really busy," he said as he shifted uncomfortably in his seat and avoided my gaze.

"Busy?" asked Dan, "we're all busy darling. Doesn't stop you having a life outside of the job though, does it? I thought the whole point of being here was to have fun. When was the last time you were even out?"

"Erm," replied Tom, "that would have been when I took Jo for dinner and then she puked it all back up again," he said with a wicked glint in his eye.

"Oh God, Tom, please don't remind me," I groaned, hiding my face in my hands.

"So…" said Dan thoughtfully, "are you two going to tell me exactly what is going on between you or do I have to beat it out of you?"

I choked on a large gulp of wine and began violent coughing and whooping as I tried to catch my breath. Tom slapped me on the back while Dan asked for some water. My face was puce and sweating from the exertion of trying to breathe. I certainly know how to create a diversion, that's for sure. I pointed towards the toilets and ran off in their direction, still coughing and gasping.

I stood with my forehead against the cool tiles of the bathroom wall and breathed deeply. I blew a lungful of air out and inspected the image the mirror was reflecting back to me. My hair was wild as it had come free from my clips and smudged mascara had collected underneath my eyes. I quickly wiped it away, reapplied some lipstick and smoothed my hair.

"I can do this," I muttered to myself, "stop being so ridiculous," I repeated as I pushed open the door and walked calmly back to the table.

Dan and Tom watched as I weaved my way back through the restaurant. Dan had a strange look on his face.

"So, just when were you going to tell me?" he asked sniffily while pouting.

"Tell you what," I asked looking from Dan to Tom and back again and feeling the hotness of embarrassment spread upwards from my chest.

"Just how you managed to make Tom fall in love with you, that's all," Dan said smiling, his eyes moving to Tom and then onto me.

"That's not exactly what I said Dan," said Tom also now embarrassed.

"Tell her what you did say, Tom," grinned Dan.

Tom looked down at the table and then back at me.

"I said I thought you were amazing, because you are, you know."

"And ..." prompted Dan.

"And, it's amazing how you've changed over these last few months, while still being you," he said a little awkwardly, "this is only what I told you the other week at the restaurant, isn't it, but Dan's making a big deal of it."

Tom's steady green eyes met mine as I gazed back at him, unspeaking.

"You didn't tell me you'd already told her this!" protested Dan
"Why would I?" replied Tom swiping Dan's arm with the back of his hand,
"Jo's worked really hard this season. She should be rewarded for what she's achieved."
"I'm hardly going to win Rep of the Year," I said disparagingly.
"No," said Dan, his mouth staying in the O formation before he added, "but yes, you are improving all the time. Better than the elegant but shy lady who arrived here."
"Thanks. I think," I smiled
"We all know you love each other to bits," said Dan out of the blue, "that's not wrong or disloyal," he said to Tom, "it's just how things are. But can we not have this silent distance Tom? It's not fooling anyone, least of all Tammy! Just be honest with her and tell her you are working and living your life whilst maintaining your relationship with her. If she doesn't trust you, then dump her ass and move on."

He clicked his fingers in the air with a flourish as he finished his little speech, leaving Tom, and me, rather speechless.
"Well, I'm glad we cleared that up," Dan continued, filling the silent gap, while rubbing his hands together, "now, whose turn is it to buy the wine?"

Thirty One

August was extremely hot with the temperature reaching the high thirties most days. The Algarve got very, very busy as Spain and Portugal went on summer holiday and headed for the coast. Lines of traffic stretched everywhere, and Dan struggled to park outside his apartment as families from the interior of the country came to the coast to holiday and parked anywhere near to the beach they could find.

Ellie had been right. Even though we were full to capacity in every villa, our clients seemed happy enough and all was well. I'd even managed to have some time off and spend some time on the beach, turning a golden brown under my factor 50.
The whole team seemed more relaxed and I was doing my best to just have fun. And it was with that thought in mind that we began planning our next mission.

Ellie started the thought process one Sunday morning when she announced she was returning to London for five days for meetings and reviews at head office.
        "Can I even trust you guys to behave and look after things while I'm gone," she questioned us over coffee in the airport café.

Emma was busy removing all her jewellery and plaiting her hair after her weekly scolding and was scowling. Tom was busy writing welcome notes at the last minute and not really taking any notice of Ellie.

Dan however perked up, sitting upright in his chair, "You're going to London?"

"Yes," said Ellie getting annoyed, "don't be getting any ideas while I'm away!"

"As if," sneered Dan looking at his nails, "I was just going to ask if you could bring us back some teabags. These Portuguese ones are so weak; I need at least 3 per cup. Please Ellie!"

"I'll see what I can do," she said gathering her things together and standing. "I have some packing to do so I'm going now but I'm on the mobile if you need me. I fly tomorrow and will be back Saturday lunchtime. "

"Have a great trip!" I said cheerily.

"Oh my God!" said Dan when Ellie had disappeared from view. "This is it! This is our chance!"

"Our chance for what?" asked Emma as she replaced all her jewellery and shook her long hair free from its plait.

"To go to Spain for a few days!" said Dan excitedly his eyes sparkling.

"Spain?" I asked.

"Yes, what about Seville? It's only 2 hours away!"

"Oh yes!" said Emma coming to life, "road trip! Please everyone! Let's go! When do we leave?"

"Well, we've got to make sure everyone who arrives today is happy and settled first, then I say we go on Tuesday. We only need stay away one night and be back the next day. No one will ever need to know!"

"What if one of us has a problem with a client?" I asked.

"Then we all come back and sort it out, together. One problem; four reps to deal with it. Deal?"

There was a unanimous "Yes!"

Thirty Two

Tuesday morning arrived bright, sunny and
already very hot. We all congregated outside
Tom's flat. He'd volunteered to drive us. I
couldn't believe how excited I was about this
trip. It felt so naughty and exciting. We'd been
working really hard for a couple of months,
sometimes going without a day off for weeks on
end. I'd never been to Seville and couldn't wait
to explore. Lots of my clients had made the trip
and raved about it to me. This was a fabulous
opportunity to see a part of Spain I'd never seen
before.

It was eight in the morning and it was already
boiling hot! The kind of heat when the seatbelt in
the car burns your leg, hot. Both Emma and I
were applying plenty of sun cream before we
even got in the car. I'd been caught out a few
times thinking I wouldn't catch much sun in a
vehicle only to come home from work with red
patches of burn on my arms and legs.

We piled into Tom's car, pointed the car East
and headed along the IP1 towards the Spanish/
Portuguese border, windows down, with Buena
Vista Social Club playing on the stereo. It was
just the right music for the journey to Spain with
flamenco guitars and trumpets. The warm
breeze came through the open windows and
tossed my hair around knotting it, but I didn't
care as we were off on an adventure. Everyone
was in a happy, chatty mood and the usual banter

ensued. Tom, however, was a little quieter but I put that down to his concentration on his driving.

The sea was to our right with hills rolling down from the motorway to the coast. To our left were mountains, hills and farmland. The once lush green landscape full of beautiful spring flowers was now brown and parched, scorched by months of hot sun. The sky, a seamless cornflower blue, was endless without a hint of a cloud.

"I'm so lucky!" I thought and again I thought back to that grey day in London when I completed the application form for this job, never dreaming what an amazing experience it would turn into.

We passed through the Spanish border control without incident and sped towards Seville. Dan had already checked out some accommodation, before we left, and had found the nice cheap, centrally located Hotel Goya. It was only three minutes from the Gothic Cathedral and surrounded by bars and restaurants. Exactly what we needed. It's simple stone frontage, which was right on the pavement, belied the interior, which was cool in the hot sun. There was a central courtyard, fully tiled in tones of blue, adding to the cool feeling. Circular fans spun from the ceiling and I could hear water running somewhere. Big leafy green plants lined the area and gave such a calm, tranquil feel, it was easy to forget we were in the middle of the city. The receptionist was patient and friendly and gave Tom precise instructions to find the hotel car park.

We checked in quickly and went to see our rooms. Tom wasn't too happy about sharing with Dan ("he snores like a train!") but the rooms were comfortable, cool and beautifully decorated with whitewashed walls and bright, jewel coloured bedding and cushions.

After dropping our bags in our rooms and grabbing a quick drink, it was time to explore. We headed for the Gothic Cathedral. I'd heard so much about Seville from my clients and couldn't wait to see more for myself. The afternoon sun was so intense, and the heat was extremely oppressive. The local chemist flashed the temperature next to its green cross sign – 43 degrees. Every step took so much effort and the air felt heavy. It felt like a big hand on my head pushing me down, making every movement twenty times more difficult than normal. A heat haze shimmered several feet above the ground and the tarmac was soft and melting. Office workers hurried between air-conditioned buildings and tourists hugged the side of the pavements trying to walk in the little shade provided. I'd never been in such a high heat before and welcomed the cooling interior of the cathedral.

Flocks of tourists with multi-coloured backpacks milled silently around the aisles. The only sounds were the clicking of camera lenses, the shuffle of feet upon the dusty floor and the low murmur of chatting. I gulped my warm, bottled water gratefully as I wandered around, following the slowly moving crowd.

The high, stone vaulted ceiling created a calm, cool space for contemplation and we were silent as we gazed in wonder at our surroundings. Even the usually sarcastic Emma was amazed by the detail on the carved stonework depicting

195

everything from angels to prophets to scenes from the bible. The incredible golden ceiling shimmered down on us, sparkling in the light. It was such a beautiful place; we were loath to leave and go back to the intensity of the sun outside.

Tom had disappeared during our time in the Cathedral, and we finally found him kneeling in front of the altar praying.

"Wow Tom," said Dan, "I didn't know you were the religious type!"

"There's a lot you don't know about me," replied Tom, standing up and pushing past Dan towards the exit.

"What's rattled his cage?" said Dan.

"For once in your life," I said scathingly, "try respecting other people's space and opinions."

I hurried after Tom who had been very quiet on the drive here and since we arrived.

"Tom," I shouted after him, "are you ok?"

"Yeah, why wouldn't I be?" he replied smiling, although the smile didn't reach his eyes.

"You've just been really quiet, that's all and a bit snappy."
He sighed deeply. "Sorry, I'm ok, nothing for you to worry about," he said draping his arm over my shoulders. "Come on, there's still so much to see."

Outside the cathedral, in the shade of some trees, was a row of horse carriages, waiting for tourists to climb on board. The carriages were all white and yellow wood with big wagon wheels. Each could carry four people and had a striped, canvas canopy to provide shade. It was so hot the thought of more walking was not appealing to me and I'd already drunk three litres of warm water. I hurried towards one of the carriages and climbed on board, waking the driver who I hadn't previously seen. The slightly rotund, middle aged man had been prone on the front bench seat, snoring quietly. He sat up, yawning running his hands through his messy, curly black hair and down his face.

"Oh perdon Senor," I said as the others caught up with me, laughing at the look of horror on my face.

He muttered something I didn't understand (and which didn't sound too friendly) and Tom took over having a full conversation with him as Emma and Dan climbed up and joined me in the carriage.

Dan sat down next to me and Emma and Tom faced us as we took off through the busy streets.

"Did I annoy him, waking him?" I asked Tom.

"He has a newborn son who's not sleeping well, and he was up with him all night. He takes his time at work as an opportunity to sleep," he smiled.

"Oh that's so sweet," said Emma.

"Yes," I said, "please tell him I'll pay him a tip for driving us."

Tom did as I asked and the driver seemed much happier, even slowing the carriage down a little. He even began to sing a little and his, surprising, baritone voice encouraged us all to clap along with the lively song. Once the carriage was moving, a hot breeze encircled us making the temperature slightly more bearable. The sound of the trotting horse's hooves was almost hypnotic as we made our way down the wide main streets towards Parque Maria Luisa, a huge public park. The driver pulled the horse to a stop under some trees and we were able to have some time to look around while he gave the horse some well deserved water and a rest.

In front of us was the amazing semi-circular brick building, the Plaza de Espana. There were grand tall towers at each end and in front of the building was a huge canal with fountains and decorations of beautiful tiles and ceramics. The gardens were in full bloom and the scent of the brightly coloured flowers wafted on the light breeze. The sun seemed to bounce off the brick making the building appear to glow.

"Oh, this city is so beautiful!" I said, "it makes me want to never go home!"

"Yeah, you and me both," said Tom morosely.

"Tom, what is up with you? You've been quiet all day and when you do speak, you just sound so miserable. What's happened?"

"Sorry," he said, "sorry, I just have some things on my mind at the moment and no, nothing I want to talk about, thank you."

"Ok," I said feeling put in my place. "When you do want to speak..."

"I know where you are, yes, thank you," he said kindly.

Emma and Dan were listening from a distance. Neither of them had ventured to ask Tom what was wrong. Emma shrugged her shoulders at me and Dan rolled his eyes. The conversation still carried on and Tom did take part, just not with the same gusto as he normally would. He was definitely distracted and it was obvious he was mulling something over. I didn't know what was troubling Tom but knew not to push it with him. He'd tell me, or not, in his own time.

Later that night, after a long, cool shower, we ventured out and found a very cool Tapas Bar on the banks of the Guadalquivir River. Circular tables tumbled out of the front of the open building and they were crowded with every nationality. A wooden pergola covered the seating area, and it was strung with vines and white fairy lights. It was so pretty! The sun was setting over the river, turning the water shades of red, orange and pink. The intense heat had cooled but the evening was still so warm. Laid back, blissed out tunes were playing in the bar and drifted out over the tables as the waiters passed quickly between them. We drank ice cold beer and ordered a ridiculous amount of food, all in tapas sized small portions. The waiters set down the many plates, running out of room on the table. They kindly shuffled over another table to add to ours to make enough room, as we discussed the day.

"I can't believe it's still 27 degrees," moaned Emma fanning herself with the menu, "how do people live and work in this heat? Fair play to them!"

"Oh Emma," replied Dan, "when you live here all the time, you acclimatise better. Like we have back in Portugal."

"I'm not so sure about that," I said, watching the waiter try to discreetly wipe his brow with a napkin, "I feel so sorry for the chefs in the kitchen! I hope they've got air conditioning back there."

"Just like you to worry about everyone else," said Emma kindly, "I'm sure they're ok."

I smiled and then a thought came to me, "Do you think anything has gone wrong back home?" I asked

"Oh Jo, stop worrying about the clients. They're on holiday, they'll be fine. Just chill out!" said Dan rolling his eyes.

"Hey," said Tom, speaking after being so quiet, "give her a break. It's in her nature to worry about people and want them to be having a good time and I can't blame her worrying with Villa das Avores in her portfolio!"

Everyone looked at him quietly for a moment before Dan said, "well, he does talk! And always to defend Jo. Such chivalry!"

"Oh, shut up Dan," replied Tom moodily, "I'm a bit sick of you going on about me and Jo. We're friends. Is that so difficult to understand? I'm fed up with listening to your endless innuendos about us, and your intrusion into my personal life. Maybe there are just things I don't want to share with you!"

"Wow," said Dan when he was sure Tom had finished his little rant, "chill your boots Tom. I don't know what's rattled your cage recently but don't treat the rest of us like we're the enemy!"

Tom pushed his chair back and stood up, "I've had enough today," he said, "I'm going back to the hotel. I'll see you in the morning."

"Tom?" I said looking worried but before I could continue, he held his hand up to stop me, turned and walked away towards the hotel.

Thirty Three

The next day was just as hot and sunny as the previous one. I showered as Emma talked to me through the door.

"What's Tom's problem?" she asked loudly over the noise of the water.

"I really don't know," I said sighing deeply in the warm steam.

"Must be something bad if he hasn't even told you!" she sighed, "Well, I hope he's a bit happier this morning because we have a long journey back today and we do not need a moody atmosphere from him, no matter how cute he is!"

The journey back was definitely more subdued. Tom met us in the hotel foyer and then, unspeaking, went to get the car. Dan was not for speaking and, stood with his arms folded, foot tapping, was obviously in a mood after Tom's outburst at him last night.

"Well," announced Emma loudly, "this is going to be an interesting journey home."

"Dan," I said, "please don't be in such a mood. Something is obviously really upsetting Tom and he doesn't need you adding to the drama. Just leave him alone."

"Hmmph," said Dan in response but his posture relaxed a little while we waited for Tom to pull up outside. I wondered if he would just drive home and leave us here, such was his mood. I needn't have worried though as the small blue car appeared at the door of the hotel.

We were all suffering from the effects of too much beer and not enough sleep. The day was again hot, over 40 degrees, and Emma was clinging to her bottle of water for dear life. The inside of the car was like a furnace, and even with all the windows open, it was still sweltering. The wind whipped my blonde hair across my face and, bored with constantly brushing it aside, I pulled it into a rough ponytail.

The atmosphere in the car was palpable and thick. I felt like saying something, opened my mouth and then closed it again, fearing I'd only make things worse.

It would be the last time we were altogether until airport day at the end of the week when Ellie would be expecting reports and accounts to be perfect and up to date. Once back, we would be planning those second visits to each villa and the monthly inspections were also due. A lot of paperwork and running about lay between us and the weekend so I tried not to think about it as I watched the back of Tom's head as he drove. I noticed the little curls on the nape of his neck, which was tanned and smooth.

I wondered for the millionth time what was up with him. Only the crackly radio station broke the silence today. Dan was asleep in the front passenger seat, his head lolling around on the seat back. There was an air of sadness in the car, like the back to school feeling you have every August bank holiday, knowing the fun is about to end.

I was, however, hugely relieved nothing had gone wrong during our one night away. If anyone was going to have an issue, it was definitely me!

"Dan," I said finally, breaking the silence and poking him with my finger, "can you put some tunes on please? Something chilled out?"

"Of course," agreed Dan sleepily as he pushed a CD into the player. Blissed out Balearic Beats drifted out of the car speakers as we crossed the border back into Portugal and sped towards home. Some time apart was obviously needed by us all.

However, if I'd known what I was heading towards, I would have made Tom turn the car around.

Thirty Four

Tom dropped me outside my flat. The door to
the gym was open and the cool interior expelled
grunts and the metallic clunk of weights being
dropped onto the floor. Tom drove away without
much of a goodbye and for the hundredth time
that day, I wondered what was wrong with him.
The car disappeared round the corner in a cloud
of dust, leaving me stood in the middle of the
road with my bags. I sighed and walked towards
the front door of the flat. The inside was a
welcome coolness, and I climbed the stairs
slowly up to the second floor.

As soon as I opened the door, I could see the
light on my phone blinking. "Oh yes," I thought,
"I must call mum back."
I picked up the phone and listened to the
message but it wasn't Mum.
         "Michelle, I wanted to let you know we
may have a problem here." It was Sandrine from
Moinho do Monte. "The mother and daughter
we have here? Well the mother has been having
pretty bad chest pains. We've advised her to see
a Dr and the local English one is on his way.
Please can you come as soon as you get this."

The timestamp told me the message was an hour
old. My insides turned to ice and began to churn
with worry once again. This could be serious.

Twenty minutes later, after a super quick shower
and change of clothes, I was hurtling through the
town towards the turning that would take me up

the hill to Moinho do Monte. The car tyres threw up clouds of the dry, yellow dust that made up the track as the heat of the afternoon scorched my skin through the open window. I drove quickly to what I hoped would be a false alarm; maybe pain brought on by heatstroke or overexertion, easily treated and resolved.

After twenty minutes, I pulled into the property gate and stopped outside the apartments. All was quiet as I headed up the steps towards the apartment where Doreen and her daughter, Yvonne were staying. The lazy dog, Pepe was laying in his usual place, underneath his favourite Carob tree, snoozing gently; his paws twitching gently as he chased rabbits across his dreamscape. The yellow stepping stones across the lawn led me round to their door where I found Sandrine pacing up and down on the small patio area in front of the apartment.

"Sandrine!" I cried as I quickened my approach, "any news?"
She turned towards me, one hand on her hip, the other on her forehead. Her normally tidy hair do was frizzy and raked through.

"Jo! Thank goodness you're here. The doctor is just finishing with her now. She's not good I'm afraid."

As I opened my mouth to speak, the door behind her opened and a tall, elegant man with swept back silver hair, his blue shirt sleeves rolled up above his elbows, stepped out into the sunlight. Sandrine introduced us quickly and I discovered this suave, silver fox was Dr Pereira. He shook my hand briefly; it was warm and dry.

"I'm afraid Senora Doreen is suffering quite severe chest pains and breathlessness and I'd like to get her to hospital for some tests.

She's in some distress unfortunately; I can call an ambulance…"

"No," I said, "I'll take her. It will be quicker."

"Ok," the doctor agreed, nodding his head, "you can follow me, and I'll be able to book her in rather than waiting in the emergency department."

Yvonne emerged first through the door supporting her mother, her arm around her mother's waist. The woman leaning heavily on her looked very different to the woman I'd seen a few days ago. At the beginning of the week, I met a sprightly 70 year old lady, beautifully dressed, with sleek, blonde hair. A few days ago, she looked the picture of health. The woman in front of me was leaning onto her daughter, her face grey with a soft sheen of perspiration covering her forehead and top lip. Dr Pereira had given her an oxygen mask which was attached to a small cannister with a clear tube. Doreen's breathing seemed laboured, and her movements were slow and deliberate. Her daughter, Yvonne, seemed to have aged five years in a few days, the lines on her face deepened with worry and lack of sleep.

"Hello Jo," they both said, fear buried into the lines between their eyes.

"I'm so sorry to cause you all this bother," said Doreen breathlessly, waving her hand.

"No bother at all," I said trying to sound cheerful even as my heart sank to my feet.

"It's a bit extreme all this just to meet Dr Pereira, don't you think?" I joked trying to keep both their moods buoyant.

206

"If I'd known our local doctor was this dishy, I'd have got ill sooner," Doreen joked back but she was gasping for air as she spoke.

"Oh Mum," said Yvonne tutting and rolling her eyes but smiling at the same time, "the poor man is trying to help you."

"Oh Yvonne, don't tell me you haven't noticed! He's a dish! You could do worse," said Doreen winking at me. If her sense of humour was still firing on all cylinders, then maybe all was not lost.

I went to the other side of Doreen to help support her and we slowly made our way down the lawn and steps to my car. We carefully lowered her into the back of the car, and I lifted her legs in to the footwell and I tucked a blanket around her as she felt cold to touch. Yvonne climbed into the other side of the car, reaching across to clutch her mother's hand, concern etched in the lines around her mouth. As I closed the car door, I heard running footsteps as Sandrine came flying down the steps to the car carrying bottles of water and Doreen's handbag.

"You might need these," she said kindly handing over the bag and water.

"Thank you Sandrine, I'll let you know what's happening."

"Please do!" she said looking worried but forcing a weak smile at Doreen.

Dr Pereira spoke to me in a low voice, his head turned away from the women in my car.

"We need to drive steadily," he said, "she's very ill. Do you understand? We need to keep her calm and reassured."

"W-w-will she be ok?" I stammered.

"Let's just get her to the hospital and then we'll know more." He replied with a gentle smile and a nod back to the passengers.

I followed the doctor as carefully as I could, chatting to Doreen and Yvonne about Seville as if this was a completely normal occurrence. We were almost at the turning for Faro when Yvonne shouted, "Mum? Mum? Jo, I don't think she's breathing!"

My heart pounded in my ears as I pulled over to the side of the road. Jumping out of the car, I ran around to the back door and pulled it open.
"Doreen? Doreen?" I said gently shaking her shoulder.

Her skin was grey and pallid, her eyelids almost translucent. With a trembling hand, I placed my fingers against her neck trying in vain to find a pulse.
"There's no pulse and she's not breathing!" I cried.

Thirty Five

I heard a low moan and then a cry as Yvonne
began wailing.

"Mum? Mum don't do this! Come on!"

"Yvonne, I need you to be calm, ok," I
looked ahead hoping Dr Pereira would notice we
were no longer behind him and come to the
rescue. All I could see was the dry, dust cloud
thrown up by his tyres. Everything seemed to
slow down, and a strange calm came over me.

"Yvonne, I need you to help me get
your mum out of the car and on to the grass
verge, ok?"

"Why?" she wailed, "we can't just lay
her on the ground."

"Yvonne, until the Dr turns around and
comes back for us, we're going to have to help
your mum breathe ok? Now, we need to do this
quickly."

Something in my tone must have shocked her
into action as she rubbed a hand across her nose
and nodded. She helped me shift Doreen to the
edge of the seat before running round to the door
to help me lift her out and gently onto the
ground.
From somewhere in my distant memory, I
remembered I needed to check her airway and
breathing first. I put my ear to her mouth and
nose and listened. There was nothing. Her chest
was not moving either. I felt her neck again and
could not find a pulse.

"Ok Yvonne," I said calmly, "we're going to have to help your mum breathe. I'm going to begin chest compressions and I need you to breathe for her."

"What? Oh my God! Jo, don't let her die, don't let her die. She's all I have!"

"I don't intend to, but I need you to breathe for her ok."

I placed my hands on top of each other, put them onto Doreen's chest and began to pump, willing her heart back to life. I nodded to Yvonne when she should breathe into her mother's mouth. I have no idea how long we continued like this before I heard a car brake quickly on the roadside gravel. Footsteps came towards us and a warm hand touched my shoulder.

"Jo, what happened? Let me check her!"

I could have cried with relief when I realised it was Dr Pereira, who'd realised we were no longer driving behind him. I could hear a siren in the distance.

"I called an ambulance as soon as I realised you were no longer behind me," he said, feeling Doreen's neck.

"You've done great work here, Jo, she has a faint pulse and is breathing. She's still in a bad way but you have both just saved her life."

The relief coursed through my body and I began to shake violently. Yvonne stood up and threw herself at me, crying.

"Thank you, thank you so much," she cried before kneeling back beside her mum, stroking her face.

In just a few minutes, the ambulance arrived, and Doreen was carefully loaded into the back with her daughter at her side. As the ambulance screeched off towards the hospital, Dr Pereira approached me.

"Jo, are you ok?" The Dr wrapped a blanket around my shoulders, "you did a great job. You've given her the best chance. I'm going to drive you to the hospital."

"What? But my car.." I stammered, "No, I'm fine, I can drive!"

"You're shaking Jo," he said kindly, leading me to his car. "Come. You've had a shock. Let's make sure you're ok. It's not safe for you to drive right now."

"Will Doreen be ok?" I asked turning to him with tears tipping forward and down my dusty cheeks.

"Let's get you to the hospital and make sure Yvonne has some support eh?"

The short journey passed me by in a blur of tears but very soon we were arriving in the hospital car park at Faro. I couldn't take in what had just happened. She'd died. Doreen had died in the backseat of my car. And I'd just brought her back to life.

The doctor helped me climb out of the car and guided me into the hospital entrance. I'd never been in a hospital anywhere except the UK. This was a very different experience. There was no air conditioning and the wall of windows down one side of this emergency waiting room intensified the heat. People of all ages and states of injury sat on the plastic moulded chairs waiting to be called back to a treatment room. Dr Pereira was talking to the reception clerk as I stood, not knowing what to do. I wondered where Doreen was now and if she was ok.

"Okay Jo," smiled the Dr, "come with me and we'll make sure you're ok." He guided me past the plastic chairs and into a long corridor, brightly lit with fluorescent lights. There, was a curtained cubicle where we found Yvonne, sobbing, her hands covering her face.

"Yvonne?" I asked, "are you ok? How's your mum? Where is she?"

She pulled her hands away from her face and immediately, I could see the deep fear in her eyes, the need for a friend, someone to lean on while she stayed strong for her mum. I imagined how it would be to be in her situation, her mum gravely ill and no one to be with her, to reassure her. I couldn't leave her here alone.
Dr Pereira appeared with two cups of hot, sweet coffee and handed them to us.

"Doreen has been taken to theatre. They decided to operate straight away. She's stable and in the best hands. All you can do now is wait. Someone will come and talk to you as soon as they have any news," he said kindly.

"Thank you Dr, for everything," I said with a weak smile as I guided Yvonne to a chair.

We took a seat each, Yvonne clutching her mum's handbag to her chest, her face grey with worry. Some brightly coloured plastic children's toys lay underneath our chairs and seemed out of place right when everything else was drained of all colour, seeming black and white. I placed my hand on Yvonne's and tried to reassure her.

"I'm sure she'll be ok," I said quietly, "she's in the best place now."

"I really hope you're right," she said tearfully, "it's not really the holiday I planned for us."

"Nobody ever plans these things Yvonne, you didn't know this would happen."

A tear rolled down her face and she brushed it away swiftly with a finger.

"If anything happens to her…"

"Let's just see what the Dr has to say first, ok."

"Without you, Jo, it would have been too late by the time we got here. You saved her! I can never thank you enough!"

I smiled, feeling hot tears pricking my eyes again. Unable to speak, I smiled and nodded while squeezing her hand tightly. She nodded in understanding and we sat in silence, waiting.

Thirty Six

I've never known time to pass so slowly.
Yvonne flicked through a Portuguese copy of
Hello magazine, her eyes looking at the pictures
but not really seeing them. The longer it took for
us to hear any news, the more nervous and
frightened we were both becoming. I passed the
time by pacing up and down. The physical
activity helped my brain not to overthink. The
corridor we were in was, at least, cool. I made
several trips to the coffee vending machine and
called Ellie on one of those trips.

"Ellie! I'm in hospital with a client!" I
blurted down the phone as I explained to her
what had happened. "What do I do?"

"You've done the right thing calling
me," she said, "you need to stay calm and let me
call Head Office, we may need to organise an
early flight home for them. Hopefully, it won't
be any worse than that!"

"You mean if she dies?" I sobbed
beginning to cry in panic, my voice rising.

"We need to prepare for any
eventuality," she said sounding as though she
were reading from the training manual. "The
most important thing is to stay calm and don't
feel you have to stay in the hospital with the
daughter. You've done your bit," she said
coldly.

"I can't just leave her! She's by herself
and terrified!"

"Well, that's your choice Jo but you
don't need to. You've done your bit just by
taking her there. The rest is up to the hospital,
the doctors and their travel insurance."

She sounded so cold, so mechanical. I told her I would be staying a while, promised to call her back with any news and trailed my way back towards Yvonne.

As I entered the corridor, I could see a Dr talking to her and I hurried towards them.

"What's happened?" I asked as Yvonne was crying and nodding.

Again, I had that ice-cold gut feeling of impending bad news.

The doctor was walking away as I approached. Yvonne leapt up from her chair, not knowing what to do with herself.

"Yvonne, what's happened? Is Doreen ok?"

"She's in theatre!" she wailed tears streaming down her face. I guided her back to the chair and helped her to sit down. "Can you tell me what the doctor said?" I asked again calmer this time. Even though I didn't want to hear bad news, I expected the worst, I needed to know what was going on. This poor woman was in pieces in front of me. How could I just leave her and go off home for a beer and a pizza?

"The Dr gave her some aspirin when he arrived at our apartment which must have helped but when they got her here, her chest pain got worse. Oh Jo, they think she's had a heart attack. They're going to do an angiogram and if it shows any blockages or narrowing of the arteries then they'll most likely fit a stent to try and open it up again."

"But that's good, right? That will make her better?"

"There's no guarantee. It depends if there was damage to the heart muscle. If so, she made need a bypass operation but for now

215

they're hoping this will do the job. And we can get her home."

"Right, then I'll stay with you until she's out of theatre and we know she's ok."

"Jo, you don't have to, you must have a million and one other things that require your attention."

"Nothing as important as Doreen," I smiled reaching for her hand and squeezing it.

"I'm not going until I know she's ok."

"Thank you Jo, I do appreciate all you've done to help us today. I think I owe you a coffee," she said, shuffling slowly down the corridor.

Thirty Seven

It was several hours later before a nurse came to
the corridor and motioned with her hands that we
should follow her. She held her finger up to her
lips in a shushing gesture as we followed her
onto an intensive care ward. There seemed to be
four people in this ward, none of whom looked
very well at all, hooked up to machines that
glowed with florescent lights and emitted gentle
beeping sounds and curtains pulled partially
around their beds. The nurse guided us to the
bed near the window. The green curtain was
drawn, and it was only as we rounded the bottom
of the bed that we could see poor Doreen.

Yvonne gasped as her hand flew up to her mouth
and she rushed forward to her mother.
        "Calma, calma," said the nurse and
pulled a chair over to the bedside for Yvonne to
sit down. I took a chair and sat further back as
Yvonne reached for her mother's hand.

Doreen was lying prone in the bed, wearing a
blue hospital gown, white sheets pulled up to her
chest. She had a thin tube running to her nose
with two tiny tubes feeding the oxygen directly
to her. Her eyes were closed and the skin of her
eyelids looked translucent with the tiny veins
underneath the skin clearly visible. Her chest
moved slowly up and down and she looked so
peaceful. The grey, sweaty pallor she'd had on
arrival at the hospital had gone and she was,
once again, a healthier pink colour. A catheter in
her hand fed fluid from a bag, which hung from a
metal coat stand contraption next to the bed. A

217

heart monitor sounded out each beat with a steady rhythmic bleep.

"O medico falara com voce em breve," said the nurse backing away smiling.

"What did she say?" said Yvonne never removing her eyes from her mum.

"I think she said something about the Dr coming soon," I said half guessing.

"She's a much better colour isn't she?" I asked not really expecting an answer.

"I'm just so happy she's still here!" said Yvonne beginning to cry again.

I handed her a tissue from my bag and squeezed her shoulder.

"She'll be ok now," I said quietly, "we just need to get you both home."

"Yes," said Yvonne, "but how do I do that and change the flights and …"

"Don't you worry about any of that," I said, "we'll take care of it all. You need to make sure she's looked after and ready to fly. Can I bring you anything Yvonne? You need to look after you as well!"

"I'm fine," she said, "but would love a change of clothes. But please don't put yourself out. You've done so much already and spent so much time."

"I haven't done anything different to what anyone else would do," I said.

"Oh, you have Jo! You saved her life! We wouldn't have even got this far but for you," she said smiling. "You didn't leave me alone and I thank you for that!"

I smiled back at her and we sat in silence for a while watching Doreen's chest rise and fall.

"You know, it's just been me and Mum since Dad died," she said shakily never taking her eyes away from Doreen's face. She took her mum's hand in her own tracing the fine veins, which stood up on the back of her mum's hand.

"We've always been close. People could never understand why I didn't have that teenage rebellion thing with her. She was always there through school, university, my first job." She paused as she smiled at some memory. "She's always right too. Especially about my husband. Ex husband."
She smiled and turned to look at me, her eyes red rimmed and moist.

"You ever been in love?" she asked. "You feel like you rule the world! Could take on anything! 'Slow down,' she said, 'wait for the first wave of blinding love to settle into something more stable, more long lasting. Make sure it's right. Don't rush my darling.'"
She gave a small laugh. "I didn't listen. Got married within six months, had my first baby by the end of the first year and the second a year later. What a whirlwind that was! And then the pressure of two tiny children, money worries well... it all started to fall apart but she never said I told you so. Not once. She just smiled and hugged me, said the right thing and got me through it. Those tiny babies are all grown up now and are just amazing people. Thanks to her."

I listened to this woman as she poured her heart out to me. I really heard what she was saying. Too often in life, people may listen but not really hear what you're saying. Yvonne was stood in front of me, baring her soul, maybe for the first time, vocalising what her mother had meant to her in the most difficult points of her life. For the first time, I stood there, in the semi darkness, feeling useful, feeling I was really helping someone. I think it was right there in that hospital ward so far from home when I could feel some shift in my thinking and attitude towards myself.

She turned to face me, "Jo, what will I do if I lose her?"

The tears began to fall from her eyes again and she brushed them away, embarrassed.

"Sorry," she said, "you don't want to hear all this, I'm sure. Some silly woman going on."

"Yvonne," I said touching her lightly on the arm, "what you've just said is so beautiful. How lucky you are to have such a wonderful relationship with your mum. Not everyone is so fortunate. She did all of that out of love for you. What you have will never leave you, no matter what happens."

I smiled at her and she laughed crying even more as she wiped her tears on the back of her hand, her face a mess of snot and tears.

"You, Jo, have been amazing. You need to go home and have some rest. You have more than me to look after"

"I'll go once we get some news about Doreen," I said smiling, "and that's all there is to say." I added quickly holding up my hand before she could protest further.

I'm not sure how much longer we sat there in the dim light watching Doreen's chest rise and fall. The steady beep of the machine she was attached to was hypnotic, there, in the semi darkness of a hospital ward a very long way from home.

Some time later, I'm not sure how much later, a friendly, moustachioed face appeared around the curtain. This man had dark hair cut very short into the sides and back; the top swept back. His face was smooth and tanned but his eyes crinkled as he smiled. He had blue shirt sleeves rolled up to his elbows, his chest pocket stuffed with pens and bits of paper. A stethoscope hung around his neck reflecting the room in a weird, distorted manner. The man smiled broadly and introduced himself as Dr Faria as he shook my hand in a firm, warm grip.

"Your mother is a very lucky lady," he said in heavily accented English as he shook Yvonne's hand too.

"Will she be ok?" said Yvonne, the strain, pain and tiredness of the day showing clearly on her face.

"She'll be fine, we got to her in time to prevent a more major attack. We have fitted a stent and that is allowing the blood to flow properly to the affected part of her heart. Thankfully the blockage was only partial, but she will need further care. With some rest, she'll be up and about in a few days but will need lots of recuperation time and you'll need to seek extra treatment and support when you get back home. I will let you know when she is cleared to fly."

Yvonne exhaled a breath she didn't even know she'd been holding and said a shaky thank you to the Dr. This time the tears she cried were those of relief.
The Dr gave a small bow and withdrew back around the curtain to attend other patients.
Yvonne threw her arms around me sobbing with relief.

"Oh Yvonne," I said, "I'm so happy for you both. Let me go and get you some things to help you stay here and I'll get the ball rolling to get you home."

"I cannot thank you enough, Jo, you've been amazing! Thank you, thank you!"

"It's been my pleasure Yvonne," I said, "I'll go now and get you some supplies from the hospital shop to keep you going and I'll bring you both some of your things from the apartment tomorrow. Okay?"

"I'll be writing the best review about my holiday rep," she smiled.

I laughed and thanked her as I said goodbye.

As I headed back to my car, I could only think how I would have felt in her shoes, had it been my mother in hospital in a foreign country. Though exhausted and hungry, I was proud of the decision I had made to stay with her all that time. Sometimes all we need is for someone to be there, not to do anything, but to care and that can make all the difference. Knowing you have someone by your side, looking out for you, is the best feeling in life; someone whose got your back no matter what. I'd felt something more change within me right there as I walked back to my car. This was the important stuff in life; friends and family, being a great person and doing the best you can. All the years I'd been fighting to be seen, to be appreciated, to be loved and that's what I needed to show. Reaching out to Yvonne and allowing her to give space to her emotion and to really hear her had made me realise something about myself. I needed to stop worrying about my friends' opinions on my life, choices and ambitions. The need to fit in had held me back and caused me to constantly doubt my own thoughts. I needed to believe in myself; that was the key all along. The fear I'd been

living with seemed to disappear. I felt strong
and alive for the first time.

Thirty Eight

I drove back to Sao Bras feeling significantly lighter than I had several hours earlier. The day was coming to an end and just a thin line of light peeked out from along the horizon as I headed inland and uphill. My stomach growled angrily at me in protest as I realised I hadn't eaten all day and my eyes were sore with tiredness and strain.

Seeing the road turn into where my apartment block stood was a very welcome sight as the darkness had now enveloped everything casting shadows all around.
I pulled up in front of the building, turned the engine off and with great, physical effort, hauled myself out of the little vehicle, towards the apartment front door. I checked my mailbox, which was empty apart from pizzeria flyers and began the slow climb up the flights of stairs to my door. Not for the first time, I wished there was a lift in this building, as my legs felt heavier and heavier with each step.

I nearly jumped out of my skin when I climbed the final step only to find a slumped figure sitting in the semi darkness in front of my apartment entrance. Stifling a scream, I quickly pressed the light button to illuminate the stranger and realised it was Dan, who was gently snoring, his back leaned against the front door as his head lolled onto his shoulder.

224

"What on earth?" I shouted as I kicked his foot gently with my toe.

The slumbering Daniel woke and his face spread into a smile as recognition dawned.

"What on earth are you doing here?" I asked as I helped him to his feet.

"I spoke to Ellie earlier," he yawned, "she told me what had happened and that you'd be on your way home soon. I knew you probably wouldn't have eaten so I brought dinner."

He picked up a brown paper carrier bag from where he'd been sitting on the floor.

"It might be a bit cool now but its Chinese!" he said with a smile holding the bag out towards me, "and wine!"

He pulled out the bottle from behind his back with a flourish and that daft look he gets when he knows he's done something lovely for someone else. Pulling him to his feet, I gave him the biggest cuddle I've ever given anyone. I opened the door and wafted Dan and the Chinese food in, more grateful to him than I could ever express.

Thirty Nine

I must have slept like the proverbial log because when my alarm rang, I didn't hear it at all. It was Dan, who'd crashed in my spare room, shaking me awake.

"Wow, I could sleep for a week!"

"You nearly have," laughed Dan, "its past nine!"

I jumped from the mattress and straight to the bathroom still talking to Dan as I cleaned my teeth.

"Has the phone rang? Are there any messages, Dan?"

He leaned against the doorjamb of the bathroom looking at his manicured nails.

"Ellie called. I let it go to voicemail. She's organising the flight home for those two ladies. She wanted to know if there was any update on Doreen and when she can fly. That's all."

"Great, at least she's on it! I can't believe this happened to one of my clients. Dan, it was so scary! She actually died. In my car!"

"You told me all this last night Jo; it's obviously traumatised you a bit. I can imagine it was scary but she's ok and that's all that matters!"

"Dan, it was the most frightening thing ever! I really thought she might die! Can you imagine? One minute, you're on holiday with your mum, in the pool, eating lovely food, enjoying the sun. The next, you're waking up in foreign hospital in a place where you don't speak

226

the language being told you've had an operation after your heart stopped!"

"Calm down Jo," he said rolling his eyes, "don't be such a drama queen."

"Me?" I laughed and spat toothpaste everywhere.

"I haven't even told you about my hook up the other night, have I?"

"You hooked up? And are only mentioning this now?"

"Why do you say that like it's a really unlikely thing?" I shrugged as he continued on regardless. "Remember that guy I met in the restaurant in Santa Lucia? The one who looked like George Michael?

"George Michael 'Careless Whisper' hair? The one when you fell off your chair when he said hello? That one?" I asked raising an eyebrow.

"He was very handsome!" Dan protested giving me a look and ignoring my playful naughtiness.

"Oh, I don't even know if I want to hear this and, unfortunately, I don't have time right now. I've got to go and collect some fresh clothing for Yvonne and find out when Doreen will be well enough to fly home."

Dan opened his mouth to protest but I held my hand up.

"I promise you, I want to hear all about it but not now darling. I've really got to get these ladies sorted."

"Ok, ok but I really need to talk to you! I guess I'll tell you all bout it over cocktails."

"Knowing you, I'll need a drink to hear it all."

"Right, it's a deal, after airport duties, your ears are mine over a mojito or two."

I laughed and shut the bathroom door to take a shower.

Forty

I raced up to Moinho do Monte to grab some of
Doreen's and Yvonne's things before I headed to
the airport. Thankfully, my first flight was a bit
later than usual, but I still had to get to the
airport as Ellie would be on the prowl, checking
we were there and ready in the café to meet for
the weekly budget meeting.
Sandrine had already prepared a bag of various
clothing and personal items for Yvonne and
Doreen and she handed it over as soon as I
pulled into the driveway.

"Thank you so much," I said with great
relief, "I'm super tight for time this morning."

"Not at all," she smiled, "Yvonne rang
early this morning and gave me a list to make
things easier for you. She's doing ok and
Doreen is awake and doing fine. I'm packing the
rest of their things ready for you as requested."

"That's such great news! Thank you
Sandrine. I'll see you later." I shouted as I
reversed the car back out onto the main road.

Speeding towards the coast and the airport, I
opened the window and allowed the sea scented
air to fill the car. This would never get old. The
smell of bougainvillea, sea salt, ozone and pine
trees was intoxicating. The sun was strong and
hot, burning my skin as it beat through the open
window. I pulled into the airport carpark
reserved for our car hire company and found the
last free space. I gave a cheery wave to Andrea
in the little kiosk, who was waiting for happy
people to help, and headed across the road to the
arrival hall.

229

There's always something exciting about an airport. There are so many personal, people stories being acted out each day. All of life is here. Every age, every kind of family, every reason for travelling, it's all there in the arrivals and departure lounges. Tears, smiles, laughter, sadness, grief, excitement, nervousness, fear and more. We'd worked here for such a long time and seen all these emotions and more played out on the concourse. I knew I was feeling a bit more reflective after the recent events, smiled and headed towards car hire.

"What time do you call this?" asked Carlos from behind the car hire desk, smiling his big, toothy grin.

"Time for you to give me a break!" I said smiling through gritted teeth as I picked up the pile of contracts ready to hand to clients. He tried to reach across to take my hand but I snatched it back before he could make contact.

"Honestly, Carlos! Isn't there something they could put in your tea or something? You know, to calm you down?"

He smiled his oily grin, "You wouldn't want me any other way."

"Except castrated, maybe?" I pretended to laugh, faking humour.

"What?" he said confused.

I looked up to see Emma struggling down the airport floor laden with her child sized rep bag, which was bursting at the seams.

"Hi sweetie!" she said as she dumped the bag on the ground and rubbed her shoulder. She started taking her many earrings out, putting them into a small, patterned, Indian silk purse.

230

"Better take these out before Ellie sees me," she said rolling her eyes as she pulled her hair up into a high, messy bun.

"What have you got in your bag?" I asked gently kicking some of the contents, which were overflowing onto the floor.

"Oh, just a few supplies, just in case," she said thinking out loud, "you know, all the stuff you might need on an airport day."

"Indeed," I said smiling. Emma was always like a small whirlwind wherever she went, her bag always overflowing with things you never knew you needed. Changes of clothes, snacks, plasters, deodorant, hand sanitiser just to name a few items. I also knew there was a sewing kit in that bag somewhere as we'd used it to repair a small tear in a car seat cover before now.

"Have you heard about Dan?" she said conspiratorially, leaning in and laughing.

"What do you know?" I asked, raising an eyebrow.

"What do you know?" she threw straight back at me, giggling as she did so.

"Not the fisherman?" I asked.

"Exactly the fisherman," she laughed. "He thinks no one knows."

"No one knows what? He was going to tell me the story this morning but I was running late so…" I looked at her questioningly, both eyebrows now raised.

"Oh," she said lowering her voice, "you don't know. You don't know!" She sang laughing with a mischievous tone.

"Know what?" I said raising my voice as she had picked up her bag and was off towards the arrivals area. I hurried after her with my bag, clipboard and car hire contracts flapping behind me.

"Oh my, I really want to tell you," she said dumping her bag at the foot of our stand and pulling out her clipboard, "but the reveal will be all the better when we're all together!"

"Oh, Emma, you are driving me crazy," I laughed, "when are you going to tell me?"

"Oh, I think we'll get this lot through then all will be revealed at the budget meeting later."

"Oh my, do I even want to know?" I laughed as I held my clipboard up as the arrival doors swiped open and the first holidaymakers of our first flight began to trundle through with their trolleys and suitcases.

Dan and Tom had joined us part way through the morning and it was a good thing as we had more arrivals than usual. As we continued to greet clients and direct them to the car hire desk, Dan noticed the queue was getting longer so grabbed me to go and find out why.
Carlos was still his unshakeable self at the hire desk. He was taking his time with each client as always, explaining the insurance and always trying to upsell.

"Carlos," Dan hissed, "where is Sofia? The queue is stretching over to the passenger café."

"Sick," replied Carlos never lifting his eyes from the task in hand.

"Why didn't you say?" said Dan as he put his stuff down and grabbed the next contract to help.

I decided to pre-empt any complaints and speak to the clients in the queue to explain what was happening and see if they were all happy, or not as the case may be.

Emma was helping a family of seven wheel two trolleys laden with luggage across the concourse.

"Jo, see if you can find the contract for the Williams family for me," she whispered, "they're hot and the kids are restless and cranky, and I don't want them waiting in this queue."

"I'll see what I can do," I winked as I slipped into the back of the car hire kiosk. As I was flicking through the pile of contracts, Dan jumped suddenly next to me yelling and swiping at his chest as if he were flicking something away.

"You ok, Dan," I asked wondering what had got him so excited.

"Erm, yeah, fine, it's nothing," he bumbled, "I thought I saw, well, it doesn't matter right now. We're still having that chat later, yeah?"

"Yeah, okay, are you sure you're ok?" I asked, my hand on his arm to calm him in front of all the clients.
He took a deep breath and nodded.

"Here," he said handing me a contract, "this is the paperwork for Em's family. Can you deal with that and I'll just carry on here helping Mr Dreamboat?"

Carlos turned and flashed his white teeth, winking suggestively at me as he always did.

"Carlos, why do you always do that," I asked in frustration.

"One day, you'll admit I'm irresistible and come out with me!" He spread his arms wide at me in invitation.

"Yeah, that's not going to happen," I laughed sarcastically, "I'll try to hold myself back though."

233

"You wouldn't be the first to succumb and you won't be the last," he said smiling at that next client at the head of the queue.

"Oh, dear Lord," I rolled my eyes, "I wonder what poor girl's been caught in his trap this time?"

Once we'd cleared the queue and sent everyone on their way to their villas, we headed up the escalator to the top café with other reps to have our budget meeting with Ellie.

I grabbed a coffee and some toast from the counter and weaved my way through the tables to where Ellie sat with Dan.

"Hi!" they both chorused while simultaneously stealing my toast.

"Really?" I said somewhat frustrated.

"Sorry Jo," said Dan, "I'll buy some more."

Off he trundled towards the counter as Tom appeared at the top of the escalator, flapping his clipboard and flight manifest.

He collapsed into a chair and shouted across to Dan in the queue,

"Get me an Americano please!"

"And a latte Dan!" shouted Emma as she too appeared and dropped her heavy bag at her feet before falling into the steel tubular chair.

Ellie looked around at us all, somewhat amused, somewhat annoyed.

"Nice to see you managed to take the bullets out of your ears this morning," drawled Ellie towards Emma, who ignored her rolling her eyes.

Dan appeared with a tray balancing several rounds of toast and the coffees for Tom and Emma.

"Now," said Ellie in her throaty voice. "What was going on this morning? Carlos told me there was trouble at car hire."

Dan immediately stepped in and explained how the lack of car hire staff had a knock on effect on the waiting times, with me backing him up. Ellie sighed out loud.

"Right best get an incident report done then. If it's done, got to Beth and sent to Head Office before any of the clients have a chance to send a complaint in, then at least they'll be ready for any. It's not the first time you've all had to jump in the kiosk to help out. I'll be having words with them, I think," she said writing notes in her organiser.

"Oh," she added, "Beth asked me to pass this on to you Dan."

"What's that?" I asked noticing it was a pharmacy bag with the standard green cross.

"Nothing!" Dan sang as he snatched the bag from Ellie.

"Why are you so red?" I laughed. "What's going on?"

A loud laugh burst from Emma, then Tom and even Ellie was stifling a laugh.

"Stop it," she said, "Guys, it really isn't funny!"

"What am I missing out on?" I asked looking perplexed at Dan.

"I tried to tell you this morning. I was trying to keep it quiet but obviously everyone knows." He glared at the other three. Emma was bright red from laughing; tears running down her face.

"Go on," she said, "tell her. Jo, this is classic Dan. So funny."

"I'll kill Beth," said Dan, now puce.

235

He opened the pharmacy bag and pulled out the contents. It was a box of headlice solution.

"What's that for?" I asked confused. "Does one of your clients have an infestation?"

Emma looked like she would combust she was laughing so hard. Tom was trying to save the coffees as she banged the table with her hand.

"Oh stop, its hurting!" she cried.

"Gosh Emma, calm down," purred Ellie.

"No," said Dan looking back to me, "I do!"

"You've got headlice?" I asked looking immediately at this head.

"But they're not on his head!" burst out Emma.

The penny dropped with me and I found myself lowering my gaze from Dan's face to his crotch.

"Ohhhhhh, you mean…"

"Yes!" said Dan, "I caught crabs from the Santa Catarina fisherman! Now you can all have a good laugh at my expense."

"Oh my, Dan…" I trailed off as I started to laugh. "Did you hear what you just said? You caught crabs from a fisherman!"

"Can you now see why Emma's about to have an aneurysm?" sneered Ellie.

"Alright, alright!" said Dan. "I tried to tell you this morning and you were in a rush and so I called Beth thinking, incorrectly as it turns out, that she would be discreet. I didn't know what to do and didn't want to go to a chemist and not be able to explain myself so I asked Beth to do some internet research to see how I could get rid of them myself! This is what she came up with."

"And I picked it up on the way here," said Ellie in her sarcastic way, "but it seems Beth let it slip to Emma who told Tom, and obviously, she wanted to make it a show for you to find out!"

"Alright Ellie, no need to be so bitchy!" said Emma in her hurt voice.

Ellie just shrugged and rolled her eyes.
As they were laughing, I leaned into Dan and asked, "and the swiping in the kiosk when you got a bit funny?"

"I thought I saw one crawling on me!"

I recoiled and looked down at his lap again, "oh Dan, ew!"

"Thanks Jo, thought you being the sensible one wouldn't laugh so hard at me or be so disgusted."

"Oh, I'm sorry Dan, I know this must be so embarrassing but I'll have to boil wash my sheets," I said as I thought about my spare bed he had slept in the night before.

"Thanks for the loving care there," Dan said grumpily.

"Oh Dan," I said smiling, "you know we all love you but only you could get yourself into a pickle like this."

"Again, thanks a bunch. I'm glad I made you all laugh so much. I'm going to kill Beth!"

Ellie held her hands up to calm us down. Most of the café was watching our table now.

"Oh Dan, chill out for God's sake. If it were any of us, you'd be rolling on the floor laughing and never let any of us forget it. Now that you have all had a good laugh, and before we let Dan disappear home to, ahem, treat himself, we need to talk budgets needed for the week ahead."

We all groaned and got our paperwork, ready to talk budgets and requirements for the week ahead. Ellie sure knew how to bring the atmosphere down and, for the hundredth time, I wondered what pressure she was under to submit certain returns, booking percentages and satisfaction scores. This new found me was starting to empathise with everyone!

Forty One

Later that day, once all the paperwork was completed and handed over to Ellie, I left my weary colleagues to their post airport beer and drove along the main road towards Faro hospital.

With the bag of belongings I'd collected from Sandrine that morning, I ventured into the building and navigated the corridors to find my way back to Doreen's bedside. The nurse at the desk of intensive care stopped me and here again, my lack of Portuguese embarrassed me.

"Doreen Johns, se faz favor?" I asked smiling.

"Ela foi movida para a ala 5," she responded.

"Hmm, is that ward five?" I asked guessing.

"Sim, 5," she said smiling back.

"Muito obrigada," I replied as I backed up and went back into the corridor.

If Doreen had been moved into the ward, then she must be doing better, I reasoned.
I followed the strange signage to Ward 5 and rang the buzzer at the door.

"Sim?" came the reply.

"Doreen Johns se faz favour?"

The door began to buzz so I pushed against it and the lock clicked to allow me in. A nurse at the desk pointed me in the direction of a bed, holding a finger to her lips in a shushing motion. I followed her pointing finger and found Doreen and Yvonne. They were both asleep. Yvonne was balanced on the edge of the bed on her side, one arm flung up and around Doreen's pillow. Her fair hair streamed out behind her. Doreen, herself, was lying on her back, sleeping peacefully in her hospital gown.

I placed a light hand on Yvonne's leg, and she woke immediately, looking a little disorientated at first. When she saw me, her face broke into a relieved smile.

"Jo," she whispered, "it's lovely to see you."

"I brought the things you asked Sandrine for," I said holding out the bag of belongings.

"Thank you so much," she said gratefully taking the bag from me and looking inside.

"I don't even know how long I've been wearing these clothes," she screwed up her nose and pulled her top away from her chest.

"Bless you," I said, "why don't you go and take a shower and get some clean clothes on now? I can stay with Doreen. How is she?"

"She's doing great," she smiled, "I couldn't believe they were moving her to the ward so soon, but she's responded well. Her oxygen levels are good; and they've said we should be able to leave later tonight if the doctor allows. She'll need some medicine to keep her blood pressure under check, but she should be ok."

"Oh Yvonne, that's wonderful news! I'm so pleased for you both. And flying?"

"The doctor has recommended a week's wait to be safe. We should have been flying home today! What do we do? We have nowhere to stay."

"Yvonne, please don't worry. Sandrine packed up your other things when she prepared this bag. All your belongings have already been moved. We've got you a beautiful hotel, right here in Faro, which is close to the airport and the hospital, so you don't have to make any more unnecessary journeys. It's all been taken care of."

The look of relief on her face, as tiredness and lines of stress seemed to drop away from her, was lovely to see.

"Jo, you've been just great, really. I bet if we'd been with one of the big tour operators, we wouldn't have had this kind of service."

"Well," I said, "It's what makes us great, isn't it?" I said winking and smiling.

"Now go and get that shower and take as long as you need. I'll wait until you get back. No rush."

She squeezed my arm in thanks and dashed off towards the bathrooms. I sat next to Doreen and looked at her peaceful face. The grey sheen and pallor had disappeared, and she was a healthy pink again. Her breathing was slow and steady; not like the shallow, staccato breaths she took when I drove her here. This whole experience rendered me very humble. Yvonne's gratitude for such small kindnesses on my part had changed me somehow. Much about my time in the Algarve was superficial and fun but this, sitting here with Doreen, was life. You can travel, have an amazing job, earn all the money in the world but without special people in your life, without kindness, compassion and love, what are they worth? The special relationship between this woman and her daughter made me think of my own mum. I couldn't wait to get

241

home to call her. I breathed out a long, slow, shaky breath and sent up a silent prayer in thanks.

Forty Two

My first round of visits to the new clients the
next day went without incident, or so I thought.
I returned home to see the message light blinking
on my phone. I'd got so used to these messages
now; I was almost resigned to something
catastrophic being reported. I pressed play and
waited with bated breath.

     "Tem uma messagem nova," came the
soothing tones of the Portugal Telephone lady
shortly followed by the plummy tones of Beth.
Her voice sounded thick and tearful.

     "Jo, I need you to call me as soon as
possible. Something happened at Villa das
Avores and I need your help with it. I don't
really know what to do... well, I've called a vet
and have an appointment at 3 'o clock and I'd
really appreciate you here to come with me. Call
me when you get this please. Thank you."

I played the message again in case I'd missed
something. Had she actually told me what had
happened? And what did Villa das Avores have
to do with a vet appointment? Confused, I tried
to ring her back but the call went straight to
voicemail. I decided to just drive to the office
and see for myself what was going on.

Half an hour later, I was ringing the buzzer at the
front door of Beth's building. Eventually, the
door entry buzzed, and I climbed the stairs to the
office door where Beth was waiting. Her eyes
were red from crying and she was wiping her

nose with a tissue. I thought I could hear whimpering from somewhere.

"Beth," I said, "what's happened? I tried to call but was just getting your voicemail."

"Oh Jo, I'm so glad you're here. I had a call from the family at Villa das Avores. The dad went to the main bin down the road to empty the rubbish out and heard, what he thought, was a baby crying. Can you imagine? So he climbed in the bin, really worried and found a bin bag full of ... puppies!"

She began to cry again and pulled her fleece zip down to show me three tiny little brown heads poking up from her chest.

"Someone had put these three into a bag and thrown them away in the rubbish. Can you believe it? They were going to leave them there to die! I can't believe anyone would do such a thing. So, anyway, the dad rang me after getting your voicemail, not knowing what to do with them so I drove up and collected them and well, here we are!"

I pulled one of the tiny creatures out from her fleece. It was not much bigger than the palm of my hand. Its eyes were still closed, and the umbilical cord still attached. These really were very newly born. This tiny dog was one colour, a tan brown, with a little black nose. The others had white and black markings mixed with the tan brown. I placed this tiny puppy on my chest to keep it warm, stroking it all the while.

"What makes someone do that?" I asked in disbelief.

"I don't know!" replied Beth still tearful, "and now I'm worried they haven't eaten or drank, and I don't want them to die!"

Their little bodies were panting, and they didn't look great, but I said nothing to Beth and prayed they wouldn't die on the way to help.

"Well the vet appointment is only 45 minutes away," I said reassuringly, "Let's get them in the car and get to the office there. They may be able to help us before the appointment time. It saves us sitting here worrying doesn't it?"

I smiled at Beth who looked like a mum of a new-born baby, the tiredness and worry already on her face.

"Ok," she smiled grabbing a casserole pot and lining it with her Complete Holidays fleece and placing the two puppies she was holding inside.

"Oh and those flowers over there," she indicated a huge bouquet on the side, "are for you! They're from Doreen and Yvonne."

"Oh wow!" I exclaimed going over to the huge bouquet, which was full of roses, bougainvillea, peonies, sweet-pea and other beautifully scented blooms.

"These are absolutely gorgeous," I said, "No one outside of my family has ever sent me flowers before."

I pulled the card from the little holder in the middle of the bouquet which read, 'Neither of us could have got through this without you. Thank you for your time, your care and your love, with much appreciation Doreen and Yvonne xxx'

"Really?" asked Beth, tucking the puppies into the warm fleece, "Well, you should know what a wonderful job you did with those ladies and you can see how much they appreciated what you did. Those flowers must have cost a fortune!"

"I'm extremely flattered by such a generous gift. How lovely!" I said feeling suddenly emotional and very touched by the gesture.

"You deserve it Jo," said Beth kindly, "and there's a bottle of champagne to go with the flowers. That's hidden in my desk drawer for you to take home too. Now come on, let's get going."

The vet's practice was in Vilamoura, not far from the tennis club where Ellie spent most of her time. A low, single storey white painted building, it was surrounded by palm trees, swaying gently in the breeze, and could easily be mistaken for a villa or golf club.

The receptionist welcomed us with a smile, looked over the puppies and disappeared quickly to see if the vet was ready for us. A few minutes later, we were called through to the large, white surgery. The vet was a very beautiful woman, dressed in a green scrubs. She had super thick, glossy brunette hair clipped back into a messy bun. Trendy dark framed glasses perched on her large, but perfect for her face, nose.
I carefully placed the casserole pot on the examination couch and folded back the fleece.

"I am Ms Alves," she said as she picked up one of the puppies and began to inspect it.

"Can you tell me how you come to have these animals?"

Beth told her the story, barely managing to keep from crying.

"I think your friend found them maybe a few minutes after they had been dumped there. They were very lucky indeed. They are only a few hours old and I doubt they've even had a first feed," she said concerned. She gave instructions to the assisting nurse who nodded and began pulling items from cupboards.

"First thing we need to do is remove their cords and then we can get some milk into them and give them some fluids also."

"Could one of you hold them while I remove the cord please?"

I looked at Beth who shook her head, her eyes brimming with tears again.

"Ok, I will," I said smiling and holding the first puppy. The procedure was so quick and over in seconds and the tiny pups didn't seem too bothered. The nurse had busied herself preparing special formula for them as they screeched and whimpered.

"Right then guys," said Ms Alves taking the smallest pup first, "let's see how hungry you are, eh?"

This little one needed a little extra help and the vet dropped the milk down her throat as even licking seemed too much for her.

"This is not unusual," said Ms Alves sadly, "all three are females and have probably been thrown away by some unscrupulous breeder who is breeding fighting dogs. The females do not earn anything, so they are tossed away. Unfortunately, it's something we see a lot."

Beth burst into tears again, her hands covering her mouth.

"But that's just heartless! How could someone do that to babies?"

"The world is full of people who do not value animals," replied the vet, "all we can do is love those in our care."

Beth nodded and wiped her eyes as the vet smiled kindly.

"So, I understand you want to take them home and be their mum?"

"Oh yes, I couldn't let them go anywhere else. They'll just be put down if I don't take them, won't they?"

"I'm afraid that would be most likely unless someone came forward to care for them," nodded Ms Alves sadly.

"Then there's no question," said Beth lifting her chin in determination, "I won't and can't let that happen. I'm coming forward if you can tell me what I need to do."

"It's a big undertaking," said Ms Alves, "are you quite sure?"

Beth nodded her assent.

"Well, they'll need heat, and feeding every four hours for the next six weeks until they grow bigger and stronger. They'll also need help going to the loo, which we can show you how to do. You'll have to do everything their mother would do. Can you commit to doing all of that? It's a lot to take on."

"Absolutely," said Beth determinedly.

Just under an hour later, we left the vet's surgery laden with so much puppy paraphernalia. We had feeding teats, cotton buds, sterilising fluid, formula milk, hot water bottles and puppy pads. Beth had spent a fortune on the visit and all the supplies but was determined to carry out the task that lay ahead of her.

"I know it's cost a lot Jo, but what other option was there? I couldn't let her put them down. "

"Of course you couldn't," I smiled, "It's going to be like having a new baby, you understand that don't you?"

"Well, I have no idea what that would be like so I guess I'll soon find out."

All three puppies were sound asleep on the fleece, which covered a warm hot water bottle; their little bodies expanding and contracting with their breath, which was now deep and even. Their little bellies were swollen with milk and, for now, they were content.

Forty Three

I decided to make a detour on the way back to my area and call in on Tom. I hadn't heard much from him recently and wanted to make sure all was well. Ok, I wanted to see him, I did. I was outside his apartment in twenty minutes, pressing on his buzzer. The door clicked open and I ran up the stairs, taking them two at a time. The door was open when I climbed the last few steps and I walked straight in as I always did.

"Tom?" I shouted as no one appeared immediately.

"Is that you Jo?" came a slow drawl.

"Ben? Is that you?" I asked in surprise.

The white haired man appeared in the doorway, smiling his lazy smile.

"What a nice surprise," he said spreading his hands wide. I was grateful that, for this meeting, he was wearing shorts.

"It is a surprise! I thought you had gone north for the rest of the summer?"

"Yeah, my boat was damaged on a hidden rock. She's now in dry dock getting fixed and Tom contacted me telling me there was a problem with the water at the house, so I thought I'd be best just coming back for a week until everything is sorted."

"Right," I said not knowing what else to say, "I was looking for Tom."

"I guess he's out on his visits like you should be," he smiled wandering towards the kitchen and flicking the switch on the kettle.

"Yes, well, it's been a weird kind of day," I replied scratching my head and smiling.

"Well, you're in luck," Ben said, his blue eyes twinkling, "I love weird!"

After a few minutes, we were sat at Tom's dining table, a cup of very strong coffee had been placed in my hands by Ben. I'd tried to leave when he said Tom wasn't home, but he was having none of it. I figured he lived a pretty lonely existence so a few minutes chatting to him wouldn't kill me.

"You know, you're different," he said observing me more closely than I felt comfortable with.

"A-am I?" I stuttered.

"Yeah, you're kind of, I don't know, changed. There's an air of something new. Confidence? Power? I'm not sure of the word I'm seeking? What's happened since I've been gone?"

"I guess I have changed a bit," I smiled and shrugged. "A lot has happened really and maybe, yes maybe, I've realised I can cope with all these strange things that keep happening round here! I saved a woman's life and I've just spent the last few hours helping Beth rescue some abandoned puppies."

"Indeed," he said calmly, "You have much good karma coming your way. People who love animals are worthy of much love themselves," he smiled stroking the head of his dog Lasagne, whose chin was on Ben's knee. I smiled not really knowing what to say to this man who had lost so much love in his own life. However, the sense of calm, which emanated from Ben was enviable. Maybe all the loss he'd suffered had changed him too. He was so at peace with himself and the world. Nothing seemed to faze this man and I hoped I could be more like him in the future.

"Do you know what's going on with Tom?" he asked suddenly.

"Tom?" I replied as I took a sip of the hot coffee, regretting it immediately as the liquid scorched my tongue.

"Don't tell me you haven't noticed! He's quiet, moody and downright boring that's what he is! It's like he's retreated into himself or something."
I humphed, "I really don't know. He's been a bit withdrawn for a while actually. That's why I popped round. I wanted to make sure he was ok."

"Well, he's not," Ben said shaking his head, "if you ask me, it's women problems."

"Women problems?" I asked indignantly.

"Yep, you mark my words, there's a woman behind all this."

"You might be right," I said thoughtfully relaxing my tone, "he started getting moody after his girlfriend came to visit."

"And you haven't asked him why?"

"Oh, I've asked alright, he just doesn't want to talk about it," I shrugged, "I don't know what more I can do. If he doesn't want to talk about it, what *can* I do?"

"I think the fact you're here says it all. Showing him you care. And you do care don't you Jo?"

Ben looked me directly in the eyes; his own so clear and expressive, it felt like he could read all my innermost thoughts. I blushed furiously and smiled, looking down at the floor, tucking my hair behind my ear.

"Maybe I should go," I said pushing my cup to one side, "visits to do, people to see, catastrophes to prevent, you know?"

252

"Sure," drawled Ben, "let me tell you something though before you go though. Tom hasn't had any phone calls since I've been here this time. None from back home that is, not one, why do you think that would be?"

"Is the phoneline working?" I asked innocently.

Ben looked at me a long while and smiled. "Just have a think about things Jo. I think the future may work in your favour; if you play it right."

"Why are you always so cryptic Ben? It would be amazing if you just told me what it is you're trying to say."

"And what would be the fun in that? How would you learn anything if I just told you? Life is full of lessons Jo. There's so much for you out there in the world. You just have to believe you deserve it and are worthy of it. Only then will the opportunities present themselves."

"Right," I replied, feeling touched by his care and compassion for my future. "Could you please tell Tom I was here? He knows where I am if he wants a chat."

"Yes, he does," smiled Ben winking at me with his lopsided, laidback smile.

I'd grown to really like and respect Ben and I could finally see why Tom enjoyed spending time in his company. He was quite the teacher, guiding us to see a better way, to appreciate what we have, while we have it. There was so much sadness in those amazing eyes of his but there was also peace, love and the desire to help others find the same and that was beautiful.

Forty Four

Saturday nights used to be fun. They used to mean spending hours getting dressed and made up with your best friend, having a few drinks, before hitting the town for the biggest night out of the week. Now, they meant preparing the flight manifest for the following days airport arrivals and writing welcome notes ready to hand to each excited family.

I'd already spent the afternoon in Modelo supermarket in Loule, buying the welcome hampers for each villa. The list of contents as follows: bread, milk, water, cheese, seasonal fruit, biscuits, tea, coffee, sugar, jam, orange juice, toilet roll and matches. If every villa was full and they were all changing at the same time, I could have 12 of each item in my shopping trolley, alongside colouring books and pencils if there were children in the party and any other specifically requested item. Trying to fit it all in the boot of a Renault Clio was always fun and I usually ended up with bags spilling over in the backseat. The car park at the supermarket was always rammed and I often ended up parked as far away from the door as it was possible to be. It always felt like a million degrees coming out of the air conditioned shop and the trolley always had a wonky wheel. I hated hamper shopping with a passion and it always put me in a pretty hideous, hot mess of a mood.

I did, however, sort all the hampers and delivered them either to the waiting villa or to my gorgeous maid Maria and her daughter who managed three of my villas and placed the hampers for me. Something I was eternally grateful to them for.

After such an afternoon, I'd driven straight to the municipal swimming pool back in Sao Bras for a cooling dip. I had discovered this place quite by accident one evening early on in the season during an evening walk around the town. There was a large open-air pool with diving boards used predominantly by the local boys to show off in front of a giggling group of girls and a smaller, shallow pool designed purely for younger children. There were grassy areas around the pool for lounging and sunbathing. I visited this place as often as I could especially as, being in the hills, I didn't have easy access to a beach, like my colleagues. After a restful hour with my latest novel and a few dips in the cool water, I left before the mosquitoes came out, and headed home to prepare for airport day.

I'd written all my notes, prepared all the necessary maps and packed my bag ready for the morning. I took a long shower realising how tired I was. Airport days usually meant early starts and I was often leaving before anyone else in my block was even awake. It was getting late for a Saturday night - 9.30pm – and I picked up my book to head to bed for a read before sleep when the phone rang.

"Hello?" I said, praying it wasn't a problem in a villa.

"Jo, smee Tom, pleez can you come get me!"

"Tom are you drunk?" I accused.

"Yes, maybe, I think so, I'm not sure but s'not my fault, pleez come get me.

I'm at the villa in Cacela Velha, the one on the seafront. Help me Jo. I need help. I've been chased!"

There was a click and the phone line went dead.
"What the…?" I said out loud looking at the handset in disbelief. I sighed very deeply as I wandered into my bedroom, dressed, grabbed my bag and keys and headed out the door, down the stairs to the car. I had a vague idea of where the villa was but would have to follow signs from Tavira to find the village of Cacela Velha, which was a little further down the coastline.

Tom was quite well known for dining with clients and I guessed this was what he was doing but this was weird, even for him. He'd said, "I've been chased!" What did that mean? Chased by whom? The client? Surely not? Or did I mishear?

He'd been acting a bit weird and withdrawn since Seville. Did this have some connection to whatever was on his mind? No matter how I churned it round in my mind, I just couldn't come up with a reasonable explanation of what might have happened for him to make that call to me.

The setting sun had disappeared from view turning the horizon orange and pink and purple streaks painted the sky as I drove down the mountain towards the coast wondering what on earth I would find in Cacela Velha. My mind was still whirring with all sorts of possible scenarios as I drove through the pine tree section of the route. If Tom was in a villa, then he must be with a client. If he'd decided to get drunk and call me for a lift home, I'd bloody kill him! But something in his voice told me there was more to it. I felt worried and uneasy. It was going to take about 40 minutes to get to the pretty coastal village and my mind's eye was seeing all kinds of unthinkable scenes.

Finally seeing the village sign made my stomach churn with nerves at what I was about to find. I turned off the N125 and, slowing my speed, headed down into the village. There were no streetlights here, so I drove carefully as it wasn't unheard of for foxes, and the like, to jump in front of the car. Ahead, I could see the lights of the village and I began to feel anxious twisting in my stomach. What was the main street ran alongside the beach and it was packed with people milling about as people on holiday are wont to do. I had to drive at a snail's pace, flashing my lights and beeping the horn to create a path through them. Where on earth was I going to park? I knew the villa was at the end of this main strip somewhere. I just hoped I'd be able to remember where when I got there. Up ahead, I saw a car pull out just ahead of me, leaving a small space. I punched the air in celebration as parking space was definitely at a premium here. I parallel parked perfectly first time, even with people watching me, waiting to get past. I got out of the car, feeling like a celebrity after the skill employed in the perfect parking manoeuvre, and walked a short way up the road, looking carefully at each house.

Up to now, all the houses had been whitewashed, their eaves and windowsills highlighted in blue or yellow paint, fronting straight onto the street. As I walked, the houses changed and began to get bigger, set back from the road with front gardens and gated driveways. I was looking for Tom's blue car all the while. I passed three or four of these big villas before my surroundings started to become a little more familiar. I'd visited these villas with Tom back when I'd first arrived and he'd shown me how to test the gas and complete the other safety checks but that was in daylight and several months ago. Everything looks so different in darkness. At the next house, I peered through the wrought iron gate and there, was Tom's car. Finally, I'd found the right house but where was Tom?

"Hello!" I shouted, "anyone there?"

There was no reply. The front of the building was in darkness. I looked around the gate for a way in or an intercom and found a small, black box with a button, which I pressed.

"Ello?" came a voice through the static crackle.

"Hello? Is Tom here?"

"Wait please, I'll come out," said the voice and the white noise stopped.

I stood impatiently waiting for something to happen or for someone to come and open the gate. The dark night felt enveloping and it was very quiet here, even though I could hear the noise of voices and fun from the front just a hundred or so metres away. I felt the uneasy prickles of nerves in my stomach as I waited a little impatiently for the body to appear that belonged to the intercom voice. Finally, a figure appeared from the garage area behind Tom's car, but I couldn't tell who it was emerging from the darkness.

"Tom?" I enquired.

"Ah, you must be Jo," said the figure, which was gaining features now as it moved towards me and into the dim light.

"Joao?" I asked. Tom told me often of the caretaker/gardener who looked after the villas in this area as he was always such a huge help to Tom in their management.

"Yes!" he replied, "I've heard so much about you. Come in, come in."

"Is Tom here? Is he ok?"

"Yes, yes, come on in, he's been here some time I think. I'm just locking up the pool area for the night. They're in the garden," he said in his deep accented voice.

He swung the gate open and as he was now in the light, I could see an older man who was in very good shape with defined muscles showing through his white t-shirt. His face was a lovely one, tanned, open and smiling. What a lovely looking man! I felt myself blushing as I walked through the gate that he closed quietly behind me.

"Come on through," he said, "Tom is out the back. They have big party tonight I think."

"Oh really?" I replied, my worry flipping suddenly to annoyance.

I followed the toned, muscular back of Joao through a large white kitchen, into a beautifully furnished living room, all in tones of cream, which was so well put together, it made me slow down to look around before following Joao through French doors into the garden of the house.

And what a scene I saw! The garden was large and disappeared into the darkness so I could only guess at the size of it. This section of garden was lit with lights strung along and around the trees, which gave a really beautiful feel. I wasn't really in the mood to appreciate it however, as the scene laid out before me was not the one I'd been expecting. Rather than finding Tom in extreme peril, here he was sitting at a garden table enjoying a drink with the villa client!

"Tom? What on earth?" I exclaimed, my hands on my hips, "You've brought me all the way down here just to drive you home because you decided to get drunk?"

Tom jumped up and ran, or rather stumbled, towards me.

"Jo! Thank God you're here!"

"Yes, I can see you are desperately in need of help, it must be really difficult to have dinner and drink all night in these surroundings."

"Jo, it's not what it looks like," he pleaded, wobbling slightly.

"You're steaming drunk, Tom, what else is it supposed to look like?"

"What's all this about?" Another voice had joined the conversation. I looked behind Tom to see, what must be, the client.

"We're just having a bit of dinner here, what's the problem? You come storming in here throwing yourself about..."

A red faced, sweaty looking man was stood near Tom. He was sunburnt in the way only the English can be with odd red shapes over his neck and arms.

"And you are?" I asked, folding my arms in front of me, my mouth twisting.

"Me? Me? I am, John Morton, a Complete client; the person who invited Tom for dinner, not that it's any of your business my girl," he blustered. "Do you mind telling me what's the meaning of you bursting in here like this? Who do you think you are? We were having a perfectly lovely evening before you blustered in."

He threw his arm around Tom's shoulder and pulled him into a side by side hug. Tom couldn't have looked more awkward and embarrassed, twisting his body away from the rotund man.

"What's going on here?" I asked Tom, my hands on my hips.

"As I just said…" said Mr Morton, wiping beads of sweat from his top lip

"I asked Tom," I said holding up my hand to stop him talking, "please would you give us a moment here. I need to speak with Tom. You can go back to your table and do whatever you were doing before."

To my surprise, he obeyed me and trundled his large, bulky body back over to the table and sat down heavily in the garden chair. I carried on watching for a moment, almost willing the chair to collapse.

"Tom, what the hell is going on?" I whispered angrily, turning my attention back onto him, "you're an absolute, bloody mess!"

"Jo, I'm sorry! But you've got to help me get out of here."

"Why? It looks like you're having a perfectly lovely time to me!" I hissed.

"He wouldn't let me leave Jo!" he said looking down at the ground as his face reddened.

"What? What are you talking about Tom?"

My anger abated a little as a nervous hand gripped me somewhere deep inside.

"I managed to get out to the phone box to call you, but he came out and got me, brought me back."

Tom was swaying and had obviously had a fair bit to drink.

"Are you saying this guy has held you here against your will? Tom, this is really serious! We need to call the police!"

"Just get me out of here! Please! I'll tell you everything on the way home."

"Okay, okay," I whispered, "where are your shoes?" I said looking down at his bare feet.

"They came off when I had the hosepipe and now I can't find them. I told you I needed help."

"Hosepipe? No, tell me later," I said as I took a deep breath and started to look around the garden, searching for Tom's shoes.

"What are you doing young lady?" slurred Mr Morton struggling to stand to confront me, his beige shorts stuck between his hips, "we were having a perfectly lovely time until you showed up, you've been extremely rude to me and I shall be penning a strongly worded letter of complaint to your superiors."

"Enough of the young lady," I said really angry now, walking towards him, my finger raised in warning, "if what Tom is telling me is true, you're in serious trouble. Me being rude to you will be the least of your worries. Now back off and let me find his shoes!"

"Calm down dear," he hiccupped, dismissing me with a wave of his hand, while pulling his t shirt down over his bulging belly, "I think you'll find them over there."

He continued muttering inaudible moans as he pointed to a large bush with overhanging trees. I ran over to where he'd indicated and began to search underneath the branches and foliage and found one lone brown shoe.

"Found one!" I said waving it on the air in victory, "we just need its brother now."

A further search around the garden did not find the missing shoe. Mr Morton was sat on his chair, his hips spilling over the sides, muttering into his glass of red wine. My top lip curled as I looked at him with great distaste. I turned and went back into the house and began to search around the pristine white furniture in the lounge. Crawling along on my hands and knees, I eventually found the remaining lost shoe underneath a reclining chair. I threw it across the room at a swaying Tom, "put them on and let's go!"

As Tom sat to put his remaining shoe on, I approached Mr Morton.

"I don't know exactly what's gone on here," I said pointing into his red, sweaty face with my finger dangerously close, "but if you've done anything to hurt my friend, you will pay! Be prepared for the police to be paying you a visit tomorrow."

Mr Morton's bulging red eyes almost seemed to pop out of his flabby white face, his mouth opened and shut like a fish, but no words came forth. I looked him up and down in disgust, took Tom's arm and guided him out of the house, through the gate and up the road to my car before Mr Morton had a chance to say another word.

"Get in!" I ordered Tom as I climbed in behind the wheel. I pulled away from the kerb and turned the car around to go back through the holidaymakers on the front.

"Right, start talking!" I demanded, "What the hell has gone on here tonight?" I was tired, confused, scared and worried but looking across at Tom, could see what a mess he was. He must be feeling everything I was and more.

"Oh Jo, I got myself into a right mess tonight. I'm such an idiot; I feel so woozy but I'm not drunk, I promise you."

"Keep talking," I said swerving through the crowded road beeping my horn every now and then to part the mass of people.

"Okay, he invited me to dinner. I felt a bit sorry for him, being on holiday on his own and I've had dinner with clients before so didn't think anything of it."

"Why didn't I see him at the airport?" I asked.

"He's driven here from Lisbon. He's been touring round Spain and Portugal, staying in various Complete villas along the way. He arrived on Thursday. I decided I'd go for an early dinner and then make my excuses, go home, write my welcome notes and get ready for the airport in the morning."

"So how did you get in this state?" I asked, calming down a little.

"I really don't know. I've had one glass of wine Jo, I swear. I drove there and was going to drive back. I wouldn't ever drink more than one small glass; you know that. Please say you believe me because what happened next is even worse."

264

I looked across at him; his hair was a mess, his eyes bloodshot, his face looking at me in concern. I couldn't help but soften.

"Of course I believe you," I said looking back at the road, which was now clear of people and I was able to pick up speed.

"Jo, what if he spiked my drink!" he exclaimed in surprise as if the thought had only just occurred to him.

"What?" I exclaimed in disbelief.

"How else would I be this disorientated and dizzy? I'm not drunk!"

"I arrived at the villa at about 4.30pm, what time is it now?"

"It's nearly 11pm," I said glancing at the time on the car display.

"Oh my God, I'm so sorry Jo, I didn't know who else to call. I'm such an idiot!"

Tom hung his head, a hand clenched into the hair on the top of his head. He was angry with himself, blaming himself.

"Tom," I said reaching a hand out to his shoulder, "It's not your fault! Can you tell me what happened?"

He sat back up and threw his head back against the restraint and breathed deeply several times before continuing.

"We had a perfectly pleasant dinner, he poured me a glass of wine in the kitchen and brought it to me now I think about it. The bottle wasn't on the table like it would normally be. I don't think I even drank it all but he was making weird comments like, "come and sit here, next to me so I can see you better" and "I could make your life so much better if you just let me." It's all a bit hazy after that but I do know I kept moving around the house then the garden to keep

265

my distance from him. That must have been when I lost my shoes! Oh God, this could have been so much worse, couldn't it Jo. What an idiot I am!"

I could feel the anger rising in me. I was upset but more absolutely disgusted and furious at what this man had done when a thought came to me.

"Did he touch you at all? Tom, this is important. Did he touch you?"

Tom hesitated and I could see his mind whirring as he desperately tried to remember.

"No, I think I managed to keep moving around enough to stay away from him."

"He said something about a hosepipe," I said in question, "do you remember that?"
He thought for a moment, his brow wrinkling trying to recall.

"I have a vague memory of spraying water at him. I think I was trying to keep him away from me! It's all so fuzzy," he said banging the side of his head with the heel of his hand.

"It's not your fault," I said, "he's some sort of weird predator. What kind of weirdo invites a guy round for dinner, drugs him and chases him round the house? Urgh, it's disgusting! You'll have to report this; you know that don't you! This is really serious shit."

"No Jo, nothing happened. I'm fine, right? The others will laugh at me! What will everyone say?" he buried his face into his t-shirt.

"Laugh at you? They'll be ready to launch a party to hunt him down and beat him! Tom this is assault! You must report him. What would you have done if it had been me in that villa?"

"I'd have broken in and ripped his bloody head off!" he said suddenly angry.

I smiled sadly in spite of the situation. "You see! No one will laugh at you. Report it. What if he does this to someone else and it's even worse?"

"Let me just get home and have a shower, I feel so gross even just being near him."

"You're coming home with me; I'm not leaving you alone tonight. I have uniform you can borrow for the morning and I can wash your other stuff. I'll write your welcome notes and we'll get to the airport tomorrow and sort this out with Ellie. Ok?"

I looked across at him; his eyes were full of tears.

"What would I do without you Jo?" he smiled wanly and touched my hand.

"Get in a terrible mess!" I replied smiling but inside still worrying.

Tom's clothes dried quickly overnight thanks to the wonderful climate and its high overnight temperature. I woke him with a cup of tea, giving him a gentle nudge to make sure he was awake.

"Not long until we need to get to the airport Tom. Are you ok? How are you feeling?"

"Like I've been hit by a bus," he replied groggily, "where am I?"

"You're at my apartment Tom, can you remember anything from last night?"

"Not really, it's all really blurry and weird. Jo, if you hadn't turned up when you did…"

I shook my head to quieten him, "Don't, there's no point thinking what might have happened. It

267

didn't and you're safe. Come on, get dressed. I've got all your welcome notes ready for you. We need to let Ellie know what's happened."

Tom groaned and threw himself back on the bed. "I'm not looking forward to telling her. She'll probably say it was all my fault and I shouldn't be having dinner with clients."

"Tom, listen," I said sitting down on the edge of the bed, "this was not your fault. You've been for dinner with clients before. You didn't know this one was a predator!"

Tom threw the duvet over his head, "I'm just so embarrassed Jo. I feel stupid and naïve. It's not the best feeling to get drugged by some nutter. What must you think of me?"

I pulled the duvet down off his face, "Tom, I don't think any different than I did yesterday before this happened. Why would I? You've done nothing wrong. Come on, time to face the world."

Forty Five

We arrived at the airport and went straight up to
the rep's café. Tom was dragging his feet behind
me. I sat him at a table as far away from the top
of the escalator as possible, to hopefully get
some privacy from the other reps, and went to
buy some, much needed, coffee. After a few
minutes, I sat down with Tom, who had his head
in his hands. I pushed the coffee cup in front of
him and he raised his head groaning.

"Maybe I got it all wrong," he said,
"maybe I did drink more than I thought.
Maybe..."

I stopped him by putting my hand on his forearm
and smiled as he raised his eyes to meet mine.

"It's not your fault," I had said this to
him many times but felt it needed repeating.

"You did nothing wrong Tom,"
reiterating what he needed to believe.

We both looked up as the looming figure of Ellie
was almost upon us.

"Morning," she said, "your message
sounded pretty urgent Jo. What's happened?"

A look passed between Tom and I as she sat
down waiting for one of us to speak.

"I think this needs both of us to tell you
the full story," I said in response to her raised
eyebrows.

It took the best part of half an hour to get the whole sorry tale across to Ellie who listened in silence, mouth slightly open.

"Ahem," she coughed, "Tom? Are you ok? Do you need to see a doctor?"

Her tone was not one we'd heard before. It was soft and low with compassion there.
Tom looked at her in surprise before answering, "erm, no, I'm not physically hurt and I'm guessing any drug will have worn off by now, thank you."

"If you're sure?" Ellie said with great care, genuinely taking her time with him.

Tom nodded not meeting her eye.

"What happens now?" I asked her, "this is really serious isn't it? If it had been me or Emma…"

"Yes, it doesn't bear thinking about," she shuddered, "that there's people like that. I'm sorry this happened to you Tom, I really am. None of this is your fault, you know that, don't you? We need to report this. If you come with me now, we can get that done. The police need to go and speak to this man. He's not due to leave the villa for a few days, right?"

Tom nodded but looked pained all the same.

"Jo, can I leave you in charge?" she asked me seriously.

"Me?" I asked in surprise putting my hand on my chest.

"Yes, I need someone sensible so that rules out Dan or Emma."

She rummaged in her bag and pulled out a large, bulky envelope, which she slid across the table to me.

"You need to guard this with your life," she hissed at me, "it's the weekly budget money and I'm trusting you to dole this out to the others and keep a record of who's had what. Ok? I'm going to take Tom to the police and get this reported."

I nodded and took the envelope placing it carefully inside my bag and clipping the flap closed, something I never did. Ellie stood and motioned to Tom to come with her.

"I hope we won't be too long," she said, "but can you guys look after Tom's clients as well if we're not back?"

"Of course I can, absolutely anything to help," I smiled encouragingly.

Ellie had begun to walk away but she stopped and turned back, "Jo? Thank you for looking out for Tom and getting him this far," she said, her face breaking into a thankful smile. "If you hadn't gone last night when he called, it could have been much, much worse. You saved him! I don't even want to think about what might have happened if you hadn't gone. Thank you."

Her voice had dropped to a deeper tone, she smiled at me and it was genuine and real. I smiled back in return and nodded; no words were needed this time. Tom shrugged, raised a hand to wave goodbye and followed her through the jumbled maze of tubular steel chairs and tables towards the escalator and then they were gone.

I don't know how long I sat there staring at the table before Dan and Emma came weaving their way through the tables towards me.

"Jo, what the hell? We've just had seven lots of clients through including yours and

Tom's. Where were you? And where is Tom?"
yelled Dan, his face red with anger.

"Oh Dan, chill out," sang Emma
appearing from behind him and sitting herself
down next to me.

"Look, it's fine, I'm sure there's a good
reason," she said, "but we have just had to get
Beth to fax over the maps for yours and Tom's
clients, but you wouldn't just duck out of
meeting clients for no reason. What's happened?
Where's Tom?"
I could feel my eyes moisten slightly as my
shoulders heaved in a big sigh.

Dan sat down with his mouth open, looking
worried now.

"Jo? What's happened?" he said with a
furrowed brow.

I took another deep breath and began to tell them
the story of Tom's client.
When I finished, I looked up at their faces.
Emma's face was hidden behind her hand and
Dan was staring down at the table. The silence
seemed to stretch on and on.

"Jesus," hissed out Emma eventually,
"how is Tom?"

"Well, he's not great," I replied, "he's
blaming himself for it."

"Well, he needs to stop that, it's not his
fault! That man must be a complete perv," said
Dan shifting in his chair, his tone growing
angrier as the reality of the situation sunk in,
"that's unbelievable. Who the hell is this man?
What will happen to him?"

"Well, hopefully, the police will go
round and question him," I said quietly.

"They need to throw his arse in jail!"
said Emma banging the table in frustration.

272

"Well, we'll just have to wait to see what happens, I guess. Tom should be talking to the police right now."

The mood was quiet and low as I pulled out the budget money and talked Emma and Dan through the next week's requirements. I don't think any of us were concentrating well, wondering what was happening with the police and the villa in Cacela Velha.

Little did we know, the police were already dispatched and on their way to the villa at the end of the strip in the little village on the coast. They pulled up outside the wrought iron gates, which were swiftly opened by a confused Joao who explained there was no one else in the house. The guest had left very early that morning, leaving only a note explaining he'd been called back to the UK on urgent business. The police thanked Joao for his time, bagged the note for evidence for the file and left.

It was several hours later before Tom reappeared at the airport. Dan, Emma and I were winding down for the day having safely seen all new clients through and into their hire cars. No messages had come through from any of them so we could only assume they were all ok, had reached their villas without incident and were happily enjoying the start of their holiday.

Tom looked drained and grey. Fine lines had appeared on his face that weren't there before. He also looked embarrassed as he approached us, having not seen Dan and Emma since the incident. Emma ran forward and threw her arms around his neck.

"Tom," she sang, "I'm sorry. Are you ok?"

He hugged her back, smiling sadly, "I will be, thank you."

He looked towards Dan, who stepped forward and threw an arm round him, slapping on the back as he embraced him.

"Man, I'm sorry you had to go through all that! What a creep?"

"Thanks, yeah, wasn't the best night of my life but it's over now," he said trying to be more cheerful.

"What did the police say?" I asked.

"Well, they were actually really good and took it very seriously, which I was worried about. I didn't know if they'd just laugh at me or not. They took a statement and sent some men to the villa to speak to Morton. I don't know if anything will come of it or not. I'd be happy if he just went away. It makes my skin crawl to think he's still there. And Joao has to be around him too!"

"Why would they laugh Tom?" asked Emma seriously, "they could have been investigating a serious assault if Jo hadn't got to you when she did. Don't negate what's happened here just because you're a man!"

I nodded as Dan added, "we all know what that man wanted to do and that's a crime no matter your gender."

I looked at Tom who had turned even greyer at the thought.

"I think that's what is getting to me. I keep imagining what could have happened!"

"Tom, it didn't though. You're safe and he didn't lay a finger on you," I said in my best reassuring tone.

"Only thanks to you!" he said again.

"Yes, I got there and I got you out. That's all that matters isn't it?" I said, "you can stay with me again if you want or I can stay with you, that's if you don't want to be alone, of course."

"Jo, I can't thank you enough. You totally win the award of the season for lifesaving! And you guys," he said turning to Dan and Emma, "I thought you might take the piss, have a good laugh, you know. But you haven't, and I'm so grateful."

"Yeah, I wouldn't expect that to last though," said Emma laughing, as she punched him playfully on the arm.

"Do you want to go for a drink?" asked Dan.

"Thanks mate, but I think I'm just gonna head home and rest up. It's been quite a weekend."

"No worries," said Dan, "do what you need to eh? Anyone else fancy joining me for a swift one?"

"Much as I could do with a drink after the last 24 hours Dan, I think I need my bed and some sleep more than I need alcohol," I said giving him a squeeze goodbye.

The mood of the group, the realisation of the seriousness of the situation and just how vulnerable we all were on visits had hit all of us and we would all deal with that in our own way.

Forty Six

I didn't see any of my colleagues for the rest of
that week. I think we were all dealing with what
had happened in our own ways and coming to
terms with what it might mean for each one of us
personally visiting these remote properties on
our own. Ellie was in touch with each of us,
suggesting visiting together if any of us felt a bit
worried or insecure. As a manager, she was so
supportive of us all and really understanding of
the concerns we would naturally have. Tom had
been in touch, ringing at the end of each visiting
day, to make sure I was ok and also to let me
know he was too. This event really shook his
confidence and it took a while for him to begin
to feel comfortable again.

The police shared the news of Mr Morton's early
morning flit with Tom, who claims he felt
nothing but relief that he was no longer on
Complete's property or anywhere in the local
vicinity. Police were able to tell Tom that
Morton's car crossed the Spanish border into
Ayamonte, the morning after the incident. From
there, the trail goes cold and we could only guess
at his chosen route, knowing he would end up
back in the UK eventually.

Beth contacted the head office and asked what
the company would do about this man. She was
told that the case was unproven with no
evidence; it could have been a simple
misunderstanding and there was nothing they
could so except support Tom with anything he

needed with regards to his job. It wasn't the news we wanted to hear. The thought of Mr Morton carrying on with his life, undeterred and free to carry out more potential attacks on other men was almost too much to bear.

However, time moved on and life returned to some more normality. People still arrived and departed, complained and moaned. Most enjoyed their holiday; some didn't. The season changed as the school year began back home. The only children arriving were very young, which suited them better as the searing August heat cooled into a lovely Autumnal warmth.

What had continued was Beth's care of her puppies; the news of whom had travelled across the team and every member had been to visit those tiny little orphans.
On the day I visited, it was purely to see how she was coping with the three, demanding little girls. When Beth opened her flat door, my first thought was how tired she looked. She ushered me in and shuffled into the kitchen to put the kettle on as I went to find the puppies. They were sharing a larger dog bed, which was still filled with Beth's fleece. They were currently asleep, curled around each other; their little bodies breathing in peaceful rhythm with each other.
        "Thank you Beth," I said as she handed me a cup of tea, "how are you?"
        "Oh, I'm alright," she replied smiling, "bit tired. These girls are a demanding trio through the night and then they seem to sleep all through the day. Look at them!"
        "Just like babies then?" I laughed, "how old are they now?"

"Well, we're assuming they were born on the day we found them, so now they're just over five weeks."

"Wow," I said gazing down at them, "that's gone so fast. Five weeks since the mercy dash to the vets seems crazy. Has Ms Alves still been helping?"

"Yes, she's great," replied Beth smiling, both hands wrapped around her hot mug of tea, "she also knows how to charge though! I need to have them all jabbed and certified, in order to rehome them. It'll cost me an arm and a leg. They're worth it though."

"Do you have any homes lined up for them?" I asked gently stroking one of them on the top of its soft, tiny, brown head.

"Well, yes, actually, I put an advert into one of the local English magazines and into the local paper which is like a buy and sell thing. One ex pat lady, who lives in Vilamoura is definitely taking one. I also have a couple in Italy interested so I'll wait to see what happens. I'm really pleased because they'll be with me pretty much 'til we're ready to go home now."

"Aw, that's great Beth, you've done so well looking after them night and day and running the office and everything."

"Just the same as you looking after Tom," she said raising her eyebrows, "how is he?"

"I've not seen him really," I replied, "but we are planning an outing this week actually so I guess I'll see then. We never got to the bottom of his moods before the Morton event so I think there's a lot going on there. He's definitely changed this season."

"As have you! I'm glad he has you to watch over him," she smiled, blowing gently on her tea, "I think you two have a special relationship. You've been together far more than anyone else has."

"Really? You think?" I asked in surprise, "He's been pretty moody and distant for the last couple of months now. Really, I guess it wasn't long after Tammy went back home."

"Maybe, that's something you need to ask him about then," Beth said kneeling beside me and picking up a wakeful puppy, which began to whimper. She carried it to the kitchen and came back with a small bottle of milk, exactly like you would give a baby but much smaller. She held the puppy gently but firmly and gave the whimpering animal the teat. It sucked hungrily and noisily.

"I'm so glad they can feed from the bottles now. The first few weeks was all about the dropper which just took forever to feed them all."

"You really are doing an amazing job Beth; you deserve a medal for doing this."

"Well, so do you with all your bravery, facing up to Mr Morton. What happened to that shy, scared looking girl who arrived here?"

"I know!" I said humbly. "It's been an amazing experience for me. I'm so glad I came here and met you all."

"As we are about you," she replied beaming at me. "Now go and see Tom and find out what's going on with him, then come back and tell me all about it!"

Forty Seven

Later that week, I made the trip down to Tavira to see Tom. We tried to make this a bit of a team morale boosting meeting, as we had all been working and doing our own thing since the events with Mr Morton. I drove to Tom's apartment expecting to see everyone else's car outside, but I was alone in parking under the bamboo carport.

Tom buzzed me into the building and met me at his front door.

"Am I the first here?" I asked.

"You're the only one here," he laughed, "everyone has bailed out on us. Emma is with her parents who are visiting. Beth is too tired looking after the puppies and Dan is out with some bloke he met from the V bar. Looks like it's just you and me."

"Is that allowed?" I said smirking, "I've not heard from you in ages. Have you been ok?"

"I think so," he said returning the smile, which quickly faded, "and no, I've not been great, but I needed some time away from everyone really."

I opened my mouth to ask if he was ok, but he held up a hand and interrupted me,

"I don't want to talk about it, no. Thanks for asking. Can we please just go out and have a nice time together without a load of questions?"

My head was whirling with so many thoughts and questions, but I knew Tom well enough by now not to push it so instead I closed my mouth and smiled, "'course we can."

Despite all the partying and drinking we'd done, there actually were some more cultured events happening in the Algarve. Each village had its own annual Festa, where all the inhabitants got involved decorating the main squares, providing food, music and celebrating their own Saints. Some, especially in the west of the Algarve, were pretty commercial and geared towards the tourist pound; some were more traditional and low key and had been taking place for years, mostly unchanged.
One such festival was the Olhao Seafood Festival.

Olhao, just along the coast from Faro, had been spruced up for the annual event, which was taking place adjacent to the port and canning factory. Most tourists never venture to this town and it's a shame as the seafood in this area is pretty famous and rightly so. My beloved sardine pate was made here and shipped all over Portugal and the rest of the world.

The festival was held in the lovely municipal gardens adjacent to the Rio Formosa. Strings of white and yellow lights led the way down the road to the entrance where for a five escudo entrance fee, we received a ceramic tankard full of prawns and a voucher for a free pot of seafood.

The gardens were a little soft and muddy, so I was glad I had worn flat trainers instead of sinking my heels into the grass. The crowd was made up, in the majority, by locals; families were out enjoying the atmosphere and every age was represented here. A few very English looking expats milled about, with their sun reddened skin and beige shorts, but Portuguese was the dominant language I could hear spoken. It made for a happy, lively and friendly atmosphere with a local band playing traditional music adding to the ambiance. People were smiling and singing, greeting each other with hearty handshakes and hugs.

I had grown to adore seafood during my time in Portugal and I roamed the stalls greedily, pulling Tom with me, trying oysters, langoustines, clams, crab, octopus and squid alongside all types of fish and stranger things like barnacles and razor clams. It was all delicious and so cheap! The food was cooked on the many hot barbeques that lined the gardens; the aroma sent up into the night sky was hunger inducing to say the least with lime, lemon, chillies and herbs adding to the scented air. There was even a giant, white beer tent which we did not take advantage of. Tom needed to drive home and was still a bit wary of drinking and I did not need to get drunk and blurt out more inappropriate feelings at him. We stuck to our bottled water and I bought a Cola Light to mix it up a bit.
"Eh, Tom! Jo!"

Our names were being called but we couldn't see by whom. The crowd parted momentarily and there were all the car hire guys. All the very young and cute drivers were beaming at us with their perfect white teeth. (Emma would be sorry she missed this!) I spotted those who had helped me with the tree on the car at Casa Verde and smiled and waved. The person shouting was Carlos, who was holding a beer aloft as he called our names again.

"Hey Jo! Tom! How are you? Come and join us! Why don't you have a beer?" he yelled.

"Come on, let's go and say hi!" I said, my hand on Tom's elbow.

"I'd rather not, if you don't mind," he said through clenched teeth.

"Tom, what is up with you? I wish you'd tell me! Come on, we can't pretend we haven't seen them!"

I began to weave my way through the crowd to the boy's bench. Tom trailed behind me looking morose. The long wooden bench where they sat was covered in empty prawn, clam, and oyster shells and plenty of empty beer glasses and bottles.

"Eh Jo," Carlos sang at me as he wrapped an arm around me. I felt rather uncomfortable and forced a smile. He smelled of a weird mixture of expensive cologne, fish and beer.

"Now the party can really begin!" he shouted signalling to the bar, his white teeth gleaming in the light.

"No Carlos, sorry, we're not drinking tonight," I said trying to free myself from his arm.

"Eh? What d'ya mean? Not drinking? You reps do nothing but drink! I've seen you, you know! You English girls really know how to party!" he pulled me closer to him and I could feel the anger in me begin to rise.

"Carlos!" shouted Tom over the crowd noise and music, "You heard her. No drink tonight. Let her go! It's very obvious she's not interested in you!"

"No, you English love a drink! Isn't that right Jo? Let me get you a beer!"

283

"No thank you," I said, roughly pushing his arm away from me. "Not tonight!"

He grabbed me again as I tried to push him away.

"Hey," shouted Tom wildly, "she doesn't want you touching her! Didn't you hear her? Get off her!"

Tom grabbed Carlos' free arm and pulled him away from me, knocking his beer over the table. Carlos squared right up to Tom even though he was a good four inches shorter.

"What's your problem, eh?" Carlos yelled angrily, spitting as he spoke.

"You are!" replied Tom, the veins on his neck started to pop, "you can't take no for an answer."

"Like your Senor Morton, you mean?" spat Carlos cruelly.

"What did you say?" said Tom quietly.

"I think you heard!" replied Carlos getting brave and cocky as some of the other car hire boys goaded him on, laughing with him. He'd puffed his chest out, his shoulders and arms back in an aggressive manner. "Maybe that's why your little girlfriend begged me for it, to show her some real love. Maybe she wasn't sure if you were really into her? Maybe she wanted to see what a real man could do. To see if I could make her scream," he spat into Tom's face, looking down his nose as he took a step back in triumph.

Right there in the middle of that field in Olhao, everything began to move in slow motion. My hand flew slowly to my mouth in horror as I finally began to understand Tom's mood over the last few months. Things began to slot into place.

Ben telling me there'd been no phone calls from home, Tom's sadness and moodiness. Tammy spending the day alone, starting at the car hire desk at the airport. She must have spent that day with Carlos and ... Tom must have known this all along and kept it all to himself, suffering in silence.

"You're a disgusting creep, you know that?" said Tom looking down on Carlos' grinning sneer. Tom's face reddened and a vein was pulsing in his neck. I'd never seen him so angry.

"Tom?" I reached out to lightly touch his arm, but he took no notice.

"For weeks I've been avoiding you," Tom said his voice low and dangerous, "knowing what you and she did together. I've had to let it lie; ignore it and pretend it didn't happen so I can continue to do my job. You were supposed to be a friend and colleague and you did that to me? You're a disgusting slimeball."

"Your little girlfriend didn't think so though did she? I didn't hear her complaining but she was moaning," replied Carlos smiling that creepy smile, as he moved his hips slowly back and forth.

I don't think he even saw what happened next coming. No one could have predicted it; least of all me. Tom took a step back whilst pulling his arm back, the veins pulsing and standing out from the skin. With great force, his arm flew forward, his fist slamming its way into the side of Carlos still grinning face, knocking him backwards onto the wooden bench where he fell, landing in the puddle of his own spilled beer. There he lay sprawled, the brown liquid blooming across his white shirt. There was a moment of stillness when nobody moved. The other car hire boys didn't move a muscle; they stood with their mouths open. This was between Tom and Carlos, whatever this was about. Again, I touched Tom lightly on the arm. This time he reacted and dropped his gaze from Carlos, who was rubbing his jaw; a narrow stream of blood escaped his nose and ran down his lip. His face was reddened from the punch and there were also grazes underneath his eye. I hoped it would swell into a massive black eye that he couldn't see through. I'd always thought he was a total sleazebag, but I believed he had some honour. How wrong was I?

"Tom, come on," I said gently. He nodded and stepped towards me. As soon as he moved, the noise around us seemed to start up again, as people realised the show was over.

I pulled Tom, half stumbling across the muddy ground, to a quieter area. When we had moved far enough away from the crowds, I pulled Tom to a stop and swung him round to face me. I looked questioningly at him and his face crumpled.

"Oh Jo, what have I done?" he moaned, covering his face with his hands.

"More to the point," I said, "what has Carlos done?" My voice was higher than normal, shaking after the revelations and events of the evening.

"Do you think he's alright? My hand hurts like hell!"

"No, I think he just got a well deserved punch in the face!" I said angrily, my fervour returning, "he's always so pervy round me. It's like constantly fending off a very randy octopus!"

Tom smiled despite his obvious anguish. His face still had that pained look he'd had since Seville.

"Tom, please tell me what's been going on!"

"I think you can probably guess most of it." He gave a deep sigh and rubbed a hand through his dark hair, making it even messier.

"I'm sorry, Jo. I guess it's time to tell you what's happened but not here, yeah! Can we go somewhere else, please? Get me out of here!"

"Of course," I said taking him by the arm to find he was trembling.

I led him to his car and took the keys from him, thinking it would be best if I drove as he just seemed stunned or maybe he was in shock. He wasn't the fighting, brawling type after all.

As I drove us back towards Tavira, Tom was stared silently out of the passenger window into the dark night beyond. I was worried and that old familiar, bag of snakes in the tummy, feeling was back.

I drove to a local café by the river, parked up and guided Tom to an outside table and ordered some coffee and beer. I thought alcohol might help numb whatever he was about to tell me. He thanked me and we sat for a while looking at the river flowing silently past and the children playing near the bandstand; their laughter brought to us on the gentle breeze.

"I'm so sorry Jo," he began, "I should have spoken to you weeks and weeks ago, but I didn't really know how to deal with this, and it's made me kind of...well...moody."

"No," I said in mock horror, "you? Moody? I hadn't noticed!" I smiled encouraging him to talk. He paused for a moment and I could see him wrestling with emotion, trying to keep it in check.

"So, when Tammy came to stay…"

"Go on," I encouraged. I could see this was causing him great pain.

"I was so excited about her coming, really looked forward to it in fact. We'd never been apart so long, and I'd missed her. I made plans, you know? Like we'd be on a holiday together."

I nodded without speaking, waiting for him to continue.

"Oh God," he said again, "I just punched Carlos in the face. I'll lose my job!"

"Really?" I said sarcastically, "he has been a total lech all season to everyone. It only takes me and Emma to complain and it won't be you losing your job."

"Well, we'll see," he said with a weak smile; cheered a little, "so anyway, Tammy arrived, and it all started well. It was great to be near her again, you know? To be able to touch each other after all that time just talking on the phone."

"Spare me the details, please," I said very seriously, holding my palm up towards him.

"Oh, right, yes, of course, sorry," he said trying to collect his thoughts. "Well, I guess it was when we started talking about things and what we wanted to do after I finish the season here. Our plans just didn't match up. I'd really hoped she would want to travel a bit, live a little, see some of the world and then when we talked, I realised I was being really selfish, expecting her to just fall in with my plans. She had very

288

different ideas and that would be ok if our plans kind of converged at some point, you know, but they didn't and, in the end, if you really want to be together, you will be. Don't you think? And every time I talked about us, as a team, she'd get annoyed and say I was boring going on about the future all the time. Was it so wrong of me to want to plan a future? But as the days went past, it seemed to fall apart, and I had nothing to really talk about and we ended up in silence a lot. Does any of this make sense?" he asked me, his face in anguish, pained at the memory.

I nodded taking several swigs of beer.

"I don't even know if it makes sense to me, really. We never actually said things were over between us. It was just awkward and... well...difficult. The time apart really drove a wedge between us, and we had little to talk about. She didn't want to hear our stories and she didn't want to tell me much about her either. You and Dan covered so much of my work but this one day, near to the end of the week, I got a call and had to go and sort it out; you remember, the whole thing with the screaming, divorcing couple and everything? So, I dropped Tammy at the car hire kiosk at the airport as I thought she could get a car for the day and explore, shop or whatever. I didn't see why she should suffer and lose a day of her holiday because I had to work. And I guess that's when it happened. Carlos said he'd look after her and sort her out. Well, he didn't lie, did he?"

He sank his face into his hands again, groaning slightly.

"Oh Tom, why didn't you tell me about this at the time?"

"Would you? Oh, by the way, my girlfriend has come to stay and oops, she's slept with Carlos the first chance she got. The first minute she was away from me all week after months apart."

"I think that says a lot about where she was at with your relationship and maybe she should have been more honest with you when she first arrived. Or even before she arrived. Why are you blaming yourself? This was not your fault. You didn't do anything wrong."

"You seem to be saying this a lot to me recently," he laughed ironically.

"Yeah true," I said smiling, "but that's because none of this has been your doing. You didn't make Tammy do what she did with Carlos; and you didn't make some old pervert drug you and chase you around a villa!"

Tom began to laugh, "you know when you say it like that, it sounds like a really bad movie or something. These last few months have been insane! You've always been there for me Jo, thank you."

"Ah Tom, it's what friends do; look out for each other and rescue you when needed. I'm sorry about Tammy, I really am. You don't deserve that kind of treatment and I'm amazed you managed to stay away from Carlos so long! What he said to you tonight? He was so out of order!"

"Yes, maybe but I shouldn't have hit him. That was wrong."

"And very human! He was deliberately goading you! I bet he's been dropping little bombs like that whenever he's seen you, hasn't he?" I asked.
"Pretty much, yeah and I've been able to walk away and ignore him. Up until now!"

290

"You've been holding back, knowing what he did all this time." I said kindly, "It's about time you talked about it. This must have been killing you keeping it all to yourself."

"Yeah, it has, to be honest. I've been an idiot Jo. Can you forgive me?"

"Forgive you for what? Honestly Tom, it's ok to be human you know. You don't have to be perfect all the time. No one can do that."

"Maybe," he said taking a long sip of coffee. "When did you get so confident and wise?"

"I've learnt from the best," I said smiling and placing my hand on top of his.

"Oh Jo, this has been the hardest couple of months ever. First Tammy, then Morton, do you think there's anything else waiting in the wings for me?"

"Only good things Tom," I smiled encouragingly, "only good things."

Forty Eight

As September tipped into October, the flow of
clients began to slow down. The weather was
still warm and sunny, but the nights were
becoming chilly and I'd even had heating on in
my flat. The days grew slightly shorter and the
shadows longer.
As a team, we now turned to season close. We
would be flying home in the next month and the
sadness began to envelop me. What next?
Would I carry on with the next season or do
something different? None of us had much idea
what to do next in life.

We began completing our tedious inventories,
counting towels, cots, highchairs and car seats.
We marked anything needing a repair and tidied
and re wrote villa books ready for the next
season. I worked closely with Tom, as we
helped each other with the final clients, hampers
and end of season safety checks. We delivered
thank you bouquets and cards to our villa
managers, cleaners and suppliers. With each
day, I felt a little sadder and a little heavier,
knowing this was all coming to an end. I'd be
leaving as a very different person and for that, I
would always be grateful. But what next? Tom,
however, grew more like his old self. The
moody, reclusive guy we had come to know
disappeared and the confident, handsome and
funny person I first met arrived. It was joyous to
see. Don't get me wrong. I knew Tammy hurt
him deeply but as time passed, he seemed to
revel in the freedom she had unwittingly given
him when she said yes to Carlos.

October also marked the end of my flat rental agreement, so I began the arduous task of clearing out six months of accumulated paperwork and other rubbish, before I could pack my suitcases and move out. Emma volunteered to come round to help if wine and food was involved as payment. I didn't disappoint her, putting on a vat of chilli to cook, which used up loads of food from my freezer, and buying several bottles of wine. We worked the whole day, filling black, rubbish bags to the brim and carrying them down to the large, communal bins. Next came the big clean. Luckily, most of the flat just needed a quick wash down to lift the dust as I had looked after the place through the summer. Emma kept me going with a string of dirty jokes and outrageous stories. Finally, as the evening sun shone through the kitchen patio doors, we sat down for food, wine and a catch up.

"Thanks for this Jo," mumbled Emma as she shovelled chilli and rice hungrily into her mouth.

"No, thank you so much for helping me clear up," I replied smiling, "I hate doing all this kind of stuff by myself. I have no motivation when it comes to cleaning."

"Yeah, t'is a bit boring," she mumbled through a mouthful of rice, "though we did alright at that apartment with the babies and the spaghetti, didn't we?"

"That's true, we did! We make a good team, Em," I smiled clinking her glass with mine.

"We really do, Jo, it's been such an amazing Summer! I'm sad it's over."

"Oh God, me too, I'm devastated to leave. I have no idea what comes next."

"Me neither!" she laughed, "so, let's not dwell on what we don't know and talk about what we do know! Tell me about Tom."

"I've told you everything there is to tell, really," I shrugged pushing my fork through my chilli.

"I can't believe Tammy did that, to be honest. Why didn't she just say, straight away, things had changed between them and talk about it at the beginning of the week, when she arrived? To do that to Tom! With Carlos of all people! Urgh! He's such a sleaze and he's not exactly choosy, is he?" scoffed Emma.

"No, indeed he is not! Maybe she didn't want to say anything and end her holiday. Maybe she hoped things would get better as the week went on. Maybe she planned to end things but couldn't do it when she got here. Who knows what was going through her head? But I agree about Carlos; there's no excuse for what she did with him. That was just nasty!"

"Poor Tom," wailed Emma, "he's not had the best season has he? We'll have to cheer him up before we all leave. I think you're probably the best person to do that and it's my birthday this week," she smiled excitedly.

"Oh yes, so it is! Why am I the best person?" I answered innocently, lowering my eyes in case they gave something away.

"Oh, come on Jo, it's so obvious how you feel about him and I think he knows it too. It's the end of the season. What have you got to lose? I don't know what's stopping you. Go for it!"

"Mmm…I'm not so sure. I think I'll just see what happens."

"Argh, you do like him! I knew it! Honestly, you're both as bad as each other, keeping secrets and feelings tucked inside. Just bloody well get it on, will you!"

I laughed at Emma and her exasperated face as I drank more wine and tried to change the subject.

"What will you do about Rogerio?" I asked.

"Oh, nicely swerved," she giggled, "good subject change! Rogerio? Well, it's been going really well still. I just don't know what will happen. I'm trying to go with the flow and tell myself I'm not emotionally involved with him but, well, we've been seeing each other nearly six months now!"

"That's quite a long time for a fling," I laughed.

"I still think that's all it is," she said more seriously, "I don't think he feels the same way I do."

"Oh Emma, I'm sorry, I didn't know you had feelings for him," I said smiling wanly,

"Of course I have! I was bound to wasn't I! Get all emotionally attached to someone who is completely unavailable and unwilling to even discuss our relationship!"

"Have you told him how you feel?" I asked.

"God, no!" she exclaimed, "I think he wants this all over the minute I leave Portugal. It's just been a distraction for him. It is what it is!" she said shrugging.
She paused for a moment and drifted away, lost in thought before zooming back and bursting out, "We'll be leaving soon! And speaking of leaving Jo, there's something I wanted to put to you."

"Ooh, sounds intriguing," I said putting my fork down.

"Well," she said leaning forward slightly and smiling, "how do you fancy delaying the flight home and having an adventure with me?"

"What? Can we even do that? What kind of adventure?" I asked surprised and intrigued.

"I've been thinking about it loads," she said excitedly, her blue eyes shining, "we could keep one of the cars, if the car hire let us after the whole Carlos thing of course, and have a trip round Portugal. We've not seen Lisbon or Porto! There's so much to see! Then we could go across to Seville, down to the coast and across to Morocco! What do you think?"

"Well, wow!" I said trying to take it all in, "you certainly have thought about it!"

"Oh, come on, live a little! We've been working so much; I don't think we've spent much of our salary. Why don't we do something exciting with it?"

"Do you think we could? Would London allow us to delay the flight?"

"Well, we'll just have to ask them. They can only say no! But what if they say yes? Are you up for it?"

I thought for a moment about all the times I'd allowed opportunity to pass me by; how bored I'd been in London on a low wage; how I'd promised myself to live life as much as I could and not pass up amazing opportunities.

"Yes!" I shouted, "it all sounds amazing! Let's do it!"

"Argh!" screamed Emma in excitement, "I can't wait! Let's call London as soon as we can!"

Forty Nine

The next day dawned bright as I woke up in the unfamiliar apartment. Sunlight was streaming through the window, scorching my corneas. I sat up slowly and took a breath. Today was the day Beth was delivering two of the puppies to their new parents and I knew it was going to be an emotional one for her. I decided I'd go with her to offer some support. She was so attached to those tiny dogs and had invested so much time into caring for them. Beth was the gentlest soul I'd ever met. She was a great listener, made the best tea and her heart was open to everyone which meant she often got hurt easily. Giving these puppies to their new family was going to upset her. I couldn't let her do that alone.

When I turned up at her apartment, Beth burst into tears.

"I've been so anxious about today," she sobbed, "and here you are to help me!"

"There's no way I could let you do this alone Beth," I said giving her a hug. "Now come on, what do we need to take with us."

Beth chewed her nails as she shouted out items needed for each pup and I packed them into the boxes she bought specially. We put the pups into their travel cage and set off towards Vilamoura where they would live out their new best lives.

"How are you feeling Beth?" I asked seeing her biting her thumbnail anxiously.

"Oh Jo, I'm so happy they have a home but so sad to see them go. I'm worried about going home, finding a job and somewhere to live!"

She paused to take a breath and a little sob escaped from her as she exhaled.

"Oh Beth, you're not alone there! I think we're all worried about what the future holds. Maybe you should have come with me and Emma."

"No, I have to get the last pup to Italy and I'm really looking forward to that trip. It will delay the inevitable for a while, I guess. I also really need a holiday and it will be amazing to stay with my friend for a couple of weeks and still be around the last pup for that time."

"You've done so well Beth. Raising these pups from new-born to finding them new homes and still holding down your job and looking after all of us and our nightmare paperwork. That's been no mean feat. It's lovely your friend has taken the smallest pup too."

"Thank you Jo, that's really nice of you to say. And yes, I'm so happy she's decided to take the last little girl. It puts my mind at rest! And it's been a pleasure to support you. You've certainly changed over the last six months. Watching you grow in confidence has been amazing and now I see two of my favourite people getting closer too." She smiled across at me. There was no innuendo or malice in her at all.

"Tom?" I asked as she nodded and raised an eyebrow. "Yeah, it's been a strange Summer. I've never known so much to happen in such a short time, but it's been amazing too. Tom is a fabulous guy and I'm so glad to be in his life."

"Hmm," replied Beth, "you might end up being in his life a bit more. I'd love to see you guys together. You just...fit."

"You really think so?" I asked as I turned into the pup's new driveway.

"Absolutely!" she smiled as she took a deep breath. "Let's get this done, shall we?"

The new owners of pup number one were an ex-pat family who'd lived in Vilamoura for five years. There were two children who were very excited about their new pets and happily took the two off to play as Beth handed over all the paperwork, toys and food to the new parents. Once complete, Beth tucked her dark hair behind her ear as she shouted her goodbyes after them into the house. The family lived in a beautiful, white house in a small urbanisation, a two minute walk from the wide, expansive beach backed by golden cliffs. The little dogs would have a very happy life here.

It had been a difficult day for Beth, giving up two of the little animals she'd worked so hard to keep alive and she looked tired but content.

"Good job Beth," I said as I dropped her off at her apartment. "See you at Emma's birthday?"

"Wouldn't miss it for the world," she smiled, hugging me. "Thank you for helping me today Jo. It's one of the nicest things anyone has ever done for me."

I drove away from Beth wondering how anyone could be as lovely as her.

Fifty

The day of Emma's birthday was a beautiful,
sunny Autumnal day. The temperature still as
warm as the UK in August and I was spending
the day on the beach with a book and some
peace. The sky was a clear blue without a cloud
to be seen. I'd not managed to have many days
like this and now the clients were dwindling, my
villas were quiet and empty. I had one family
only and they were very low maintenance,
having been to the area many times. I pushed
my toes into the warm, golden sand and exhaled
deeply, watching the turquoise sea roll in and
out, leaving white foam in wriggly lines along
the shoreline. I was going to miss this so much.
I had no plans for my future return home at all. I
guessed I'd have to move back home with my
parents for a while until I got back on my feet
and found a new job. I pushed all that to the
back of my mind and thought about the
adventure stretching ahead. With Beth's help
and guidance on who to call, Emma contacted
the London office and they agreed to push our
flights back a few weeks, if we flew home before
the end of December, we wouldn't have to pay
any additional supplements. That gave us nearly
a month from the end of our contract to have an
amazing adventure.

We spent the days following, making plans of
where we would visit and for how long, how
much cash we would need, train times etc. We
were so excited to explore a lot more of Portugal,
southern Spain and Morocco and Emma has even

bought a couple of Lonely Planet guides to help us get the most out of our few weeks. I packed up my entire flat into my two suitcases and stowed them in the storage facility in Faro airport. All I had now was a backpack with the essentials in. Ellie had been moved into a swish new apartment in Vilamoura and was settling in ready for the winter season. Our scores had improved so much over the summer and I guessed the new apartment was the reward for her endeavours in managing us.

It felt so strange being back in the apartment where this journey began and I remembered the girl who stayed here the first night, all those months ago, feeling terrified. The memory made me smile. If I'd known what was to come, would I have stayed? Or would I have fled back to England?

Tonight was Emma's big birthday celebration and our last night out together as a team. I went shopping to buy Emma her present; a collection of items she'd love like travel journals, a silk purse and some big knickers as a nod to her love of teeny, non-existent ones! A table was booked at the Mexican restaurant in Vilamoura for our final meal and a cake delivered to the staff to bring out as a surprise.

The excitement of the evening ahead was tinged with the sadness of the end of the season. Dan decided to return for another season with Complete but in Spain, as part of a new team; Beth was flying to Italy, for a short break and to deliver the remaining puppy to her friends who were providing a new life on the Amalfi coast; Tom was heading home, unsure of what lay ahead. Me and Emma would have an adventure

301

for a few weeks then be back home too. I tried
not to worry about the future as I lay down on
my towel and allowed the sun's rays to warm my
skin and bleach away the worries in my mind.

Fifty One

Waiting for my taxi, I felt nervous and excited
all at the same time. I'd spent extra time on my
make up and hair, curling it carefully into starlet
waves. I had a dress and heels on. I'd gone full
on glamour for this last meal together. Emma's
presents were in their gift bag ready for her and I
felt excited and nervous at the same time.
A car horn sounded from the car park and, taking
one last look in the mirror, I closed the flat door
behind me and descended the stairs.

The restaurant was loud and busy as the Maitre'd
showed me to our table, which was at the back of
the room. Heavy drapes were used to give
certain tables more privacy; specifically those
tables for larger parties. Some of the walls were
mirrored making the room seem much larger
than it was, as there were only twenty or so
tables here.
Sitting alone at the table, as I approached, was
Tom who was nursing a beer and fiddling with
his napkin. For once, his normally messy hair
had been brushed and resembled a style. He was
wearing a simple black shirt and jeans and
looked so gorgeous, I had to catch my breath
before speaking.
        "Tom!" I exclaimed as I rounded the
table towards him.
        "Ah Jo, thank God, I thought no one
else was turning up," he said as he stood and
pulled me into a big hug. He smelled gorgeous
as he let go momentarily to stand back and look

at me, his arms still around my waist, "You look...incredible, by the way."

"Thank you," I said smiling back at him, our eyes locked for longer than was necessary.

"Please sit down," he said breaking our eye contact briefly to pull my chair out for me.

"Wow, I've never had this kind of treatment before," I said appreciatively.

"Well, it's about time you did," he replied confidently, "you are such an amazing person Jo and you deserve the best of everything."

I blushed as he continued, "I mean, look at you! The girl who arrived six months ago would never have seen off Morton the way you did."

"Yeah, well, he had it coming. Great big pervert! No one messes with my Tom."

Yet again, that extended eye contact and the air sizzled with...something that made my insides flip over.

"Listen Jo, there's something I've been wanting to tell you..."

The atmosphere was broken by the arrival of Dan and Ellie. We heard Dan before we could see him as he blustered through the tables, talking loudly to Ellie about something.

"And then it turned bright red," he said as he approached the table, "can you believe it? Oh hi Tom! Jo!"

He air kissed us both as he waved a bottle bag in my direction. "Are you collecting the gifts? I picked up a bottle of fizz for Emma as well."

"Aw that's really sweet of you Dan," I said stowing the bag with the rest under the table.

"You two were looking very cosy as we came in," said Ellie to Tom and me.

"Really?" said Tom, "shall we order some drinks?"

"Best thing you've ever said," replied Dan rolling his eyes, "I've had the worst day. My last set of clients have been an absolute nightmare. They've had me running from Silves to Vilamoura and back again, booking golf lessons and spa treatments. Why they just didn't stay in Vilamoura beats me."

"Careful Dan," drawled Ellie, "you're in danger of doing some work finally."

We all laughed at Dan's expense as Emma arrived looking absolutely stunning, wearing a cerise pink bodycon dress and huge Perspex shoes making her at least three inches taller.

"Happy Birthday!" we all cheered.

"Thanks Guys," she said gratefully, "Beth isn't coming; she's knackered looking after those puppies and won't leave the last one alone."

"Oh no!" I cried, "but it's our last meal together."

"I know but after dropping the two bigger ones to their new owner today, she's a bit distraught saying goodbye. She's a right mess. Lord help her when she delivers the last one."

"Aw she's been amazing with those dogs," said Tom kindly, "she's got the biggest heart."

"I thought she was coping with it too well," I said, "I went with her today to give her some emotional support," I said in answer to their questioning faces.

"That was really good of you Jo," said Ellie.

"Thanks!" I said surprised by her praise.

305

"She's a sap," said Dan grumpily, "bloody dogs have stopped her coming out with us for ages and now she's missing the last meal."

"Well, maybe some things are just more important to her," said Emma, "I'm ok with it and it's my birthday! So you should be too! I'll catch up with her before we leave. Come on, let's get some drinks on the go and some food. I'm starving!"

It wasn't long before the table was groaning with food. Nachos loaded with cheese, salsa and guacamole, fajitas and sizzling chicken, beef strips marinated in chilli and quesadillas were all served alongside bottomless margaritas.

"Here's to another amazing beige meal!" cheered Emma holding her margarita aloft as we all chinked her glass in cheers.

Dan challenged himself to finish his pot of fajitas and had already eaten ten filled with chicken, beef, peppers and onions.

"Come on Dan," goaded Emma, "there's still five left! You can do it!"

Dan pulled another fajita onto his plate and filled it with chicken, "yes, I can. Watch me!"

We watched fascinated, slightly nauseated, as Dan forced the eleventh fajita down.

"That's it!" he exclaimed, "I'm done."

"But Dan," I said, "what about cake?"

On my cue, the waiter brought out the large birthday cake I'd sent to the restaurant earlier in the day. It was a spectacular twelve inch wide cake, covered in white buttercream. On the top, a little sugar paste Emma was sitting on a deckchair holding aloft a glass of champagne.

How life imitates art! The staff added some indoor sparklers and were advancing upon us with the sparks and flames illuminating the waiter's face. The music changed to the Mexican 'Happy Birthday' and the whole restaurant sang along, much to Emma's enjoyment and she sang along with glee.

As the song reached its peak ending, Emma looked down the room and her face fell into an expression of dismay. She looked aghast as she spotted a very familiar figure helping a strange girl on with her jacket. She was a petite Latina, as far removed from Emma as it was possible to be. The man's arm slipped round the girl's slim waist as he kissed her gently on the lips before leading her towards the exit.

I followed Emma's horrified gaze to see the back of the couple disappear through the door. When I looked back at Emma, she was again smiling her best grin as everyone applauded her birthday at the end of the song. She blew out the candles and a cheer rose up from the floor. The rest of the room went back to their meals and Emma began to cut generous portions of cake for everyone.

"Emma?" I began, not sure of what I'd seen but pretty sure.

"Cake?" she replied in an overly cheery voice, handing me a plate laden with sponge, ignoring my sympathetic tone.

"Are you ok?" I asked my hand on her arm. "Was that who I think it was?"

"I knew this would happen Jo, didn't I tell you? It's nothing I didn't expect and I'm not letting it ruin my birthday."

The tears in her eyes told a different story. She passed cake round to us all but there was still at least two thirds of the large vanilla and chocolate cake left. Emma picked up a spoon and dug in.

"Are you going to eat all that cake?" asked Dan, oblivious to Emma's emotional state.

"What if I do?" replied Emma smiling, her chin defiantly in the air, "it's my birthday and I'll do what I like!"

She continued to eat and eat until half the cake had gone, leaving a small amount sitting forlornly on the silver plate. Dan was already sitting with his bloated belly in the air and now Emma joined him. They sat together comparing bellies and arguing over who was the fullest, while still chugging margaritas. Ellie was engrossed in her phone messaging someone repeatedly. The atmosphere was weird as Emma was being loud and brash, not her usual bubbly self.

Underneath the table, I felt Tom take my hand in his, wrapping his fingers around mine. My heart leapt and when I turned to look at him, his eyes sparkled in the candlelight as they crinkled into a smile. I returned the smile and hoped the moment would never end.

"Jo! Jo?" It was Emma, who was now attempting to stand, "can you come with me, please?"

Reluctantly, I let go of Tom's hand and stood trying to guide Emma towards the ladies' room. He didn't drop my gaze until I had to look away towards Emma, attempting to walk on her ridiculous shoes. I got her into the Ladies room where she took her shoes off before disappearing into a stall and closing the door.

"You saw Rogerio with that girl, didn't you Jo? What the hell? Can you believe he's two timing me with that fat lump out there?"

She was spitting the words out and her anger and upset was very evident.

"Oh Emma, I know and I'm so sorry. It's such bad luck they were in the same restaurant as us."

"No! It's great luck! Now I know! If they hadn't been here tonight, he would have carried on lying to me. I just feel so stupid!"

"Don't do that!" I said sternly, "don't feel bad about yourself because he's been an asshole!"

"Oh, whatever," she said, "I'm done and it's my birthday and I've eaten a lot of cake. I'm going to drink more margaritas and celebrate being 25! This is my night and I won't let him ruin it! And by the way, don't think I haven't noticed the hand holding going on. For God's sake, just get on with it, will you!"

She washed her hands and tripped back out into the restaurant. I smiled in admiration at her strength and picked up her shoes. I knew she'd be in tears later on. I followed her back to the table and the rest of the celebrations.

Much later, the table was full of empty glasses. Dan's head was on the table with his face on a piece of cake. He was groaning slightly. Emma was hiccupping and laughing almost maniacally. She'd opened her presents, loving each one she pulled from the bag and insisted on wearing the giant knickers over her dress! Tom and I watched in amusement as Emma and Dan bounced jokes and insults off each other. Ellie had already departed, deciding to go before it got too messy. She'd spent a lot of time on her phone through the meal.

"Booty call," decided Dan as she left.

"Right, Emma, time for home," I said standing and wobbling slightly on my heels.

"Noooo! I want to go dancing!"

Dan's head shot straight up from the table.

"Did someone say we're going dancing?"

"Yes Dan, come on! Tom? Jo? You coming?" asked Emma, her hair messy and eyeliner smudged but still managing to look absolutely beautiful.

"Definitely," said Dan, "I'll call a taxi." He wobbled off towards the reception desk.

"Guys? You coming?"

Tom looked at me with a raised eyebrow and I responded with a smile.

"No, I don't think so Emma," I smiled, "we are due to set off on our trip tomorrow, remember?"

"We don't have to go until the afternoon," she said dismissing me with a wave of her hand and pulling her dress down with the other, the big pants falling down her legs.

"Well, it's up to you but I'm going to call it a night," I said smiling at her as I helped her back into her shoes.

"Ohhh, right, I see," she smiled, punching me lightly on the shoulder. "It's about time! You guys have a good night!" She winked theatrically as I hauled her to her feet.

"Taxi's here!" yelled Dan from the front of the restaurant and headed straight out the door.

"Come on, we'll walk you out," said Tom, helping Emma with her coat, while pulling the big pants off her shoe and leading her through the tables.

Dan was already sitting in the front of the car as we left the building. Tom and I were on either side of Emma, guiding her in her perspex shoes.
"Are you sure this is a good idea?" I asked Emma as I opened the rear door of the car.
"If I don't dance some of this cake and cocktails off, I'll be sick all night," said Emma belching, "I need to keep my mind off other things Jo. You understand, don't you?"

I smiled kindly and nodded. "Take care you two, and ring in the morning, ok? Or I'll come and find you!"
"Yes, Mum," sang Dan, "wonder what you two will get up to now?"
"Goodnight Dan," said Tom smiling as he closed the car door.

We were left standing together as the car pulled away. Once the red lights at the rear of the car had disappeared round the corner, Tom turned to me and pulled me round to face him. He took one hand in his, all the while looking me deep in the eyes.
"I've been a total idiot Jo," he said softly, "all this time worrying about a relationship which was already dead in the water. I couldn't see what was right in front of me! I've been stupid and afraid. Well, I'm not doing that anymore."

He stroked my cheek before he entangled his fingers into my hair and bent his head down to mine. I closed my eyes as he drew closer, I was sure my heart stopped, and when his lips touched mine, I swear there was an electric shock between us. Our bodies pressed closer together and I wrapped my arms around his broad shoulders as his encircled my waist. As the kiss grew deeper and longer, our surroundings disappeared and all there was, was us, right there in that moment.

Fifty Two

I woke the next morning and immediately, a smile spread across my face. For once I knew exactly where I was and with whom. The room was bright and a cool breeze was wafting across my skin. I tried to sit up and found I was pinned down by a heavy arm and then I remembered last night and that kiss, which had been the beginning of everything.

"Morning," a deep voice behind me said sleepily.

I twisted round to face him and smiled, "Morning!"

He kissed me deeply again and even with my worries over morning breath and smudged makeup, I found I actually didn't care as I folded myself into him again.

A few hours later, we were breakfasting on leftover birthday cake on the balcony overlooking the main road when the phone rang.

"Jo? Are you ok? I've not long got in. Me and Dan went to Blackjack's and danced 'til dawn!"

"Who is it, Jo?" shouted Tom.

"Oooohhhhhh!" said Emma, hearing Tom's voice, "don't tell me you two finally got it on? It's about bloody time but on the last night? Bad timing Jo!"

"Yeah, I know," I said sadly, "so if you want to go a little later, that's ok by me!" I said, watching Tom's bronzed torso as he made coffee in the little kitchen.

"Look, I've not slept yet. You probably haven't slept much either! Tom's flight is

313

tomorrow, right? So, let's just all go to the airport tomorrow and leave together, eh? What do you say? I also want to track down Rogerio and have a quiet word!"

"Absolutely fine by me!" I said, "take it easy on him! We don't want you getting arrested!"

"Don't worry," she said, "I just need to exit this with my head held high without him thinking he's fooled me all this time. Have a great day and I'll see you tomorrow. Say hi to Tom for me!"

I put down the phone and turned to see Tom, his hair messy and his eyes sparkling green in the sunlight. He was so beautiful. I smiled and said, "how do you fancy spending the day with me?"

"Really?" he replied his smile growing broader. "You're not leaving today?"

"Nope," I smiled in return, "looks like we'll all be leaving at the same time tomorrow, more or less."

He was across the floor in one stride, taking me in his arms and kissing me.

"Then let's make it a day to remember," he said.

The next day, I pulled into the airport car hire car park for the last time. Tom was following and pulled up alongside grinning at me all the time. We made our way to check in and handed over Tom's luggage before going to the rep's café for the last time. Dan and Emma were already there, drinking coffee and rose to greet us as we approached hand in hand.

"Oh, you guys are the cutest," whined Dan, "why did you wait so long?"

"Just how things worked out Dan," said Tom squeezing my hand as I sat down.

"It's been a weird few months and certain things had to happen for us to get here!"

He smiled and went to buy coffee.

"You two look so gorgeous together," said Emma, "look at you, you're glowing!"

"Thanks Em," I replied beaming with happiness, "what happened with Rogerio?"

"Oh, he tried to deny everything, saying that girl was his sister. I've never seen anyone kiss their sister like that! Can you believe him? Well, I'm gutted but what future was there for us? He's here, I'll be ...not here. It was a lovely Summer fling and that's that I guess. I'll get over it! Aw Jo, I'm so happy for you two but what now?"

Tom arrived back with our coffee, overhearing the question and said, "well, I'm going back home, at least until the new year. Jo will be with you for the next month on your exciting adventure and then we'll meet up when she's back in the UK and take it from there."

He smiled and took my hand, "I'm not letting her go that easy now."

"Oh man, pack it in," said Dan, "or I really will be sick. Seriously, we all need to meet up in the New Year. We'll have to have a reunion of some sort, maybe in the West Country seeing as two of you live there already!"

"Great plan," said Tom nodding and smiling, squeezing my hand.

"Right then," said Dan, "I need to go through for my flight. I'm always the last one onto a plane but today I'll be the first."

315

We all stood and hugged Dan. Tears sprang from my eyes as the reality of saying goodbye hit me hard and the pit of my stomach ached.

"I'll miss you so much!" I said holding Dan close. "Be careful and stay away from strange fishermen!"

"Hilarious!" he responded in a dull voice, hugging me close.

"Don't worry," he said, "I'll be in touch, you don't get rid of me that easily."

He picked up his small holdall, threw it over his shoulder and disappeared through the tables to the escalator and was gone.

We finished our coffee and descended ourselves, finding Beth in the departure area with a small crate with the remaining puppy inside.

"Oh, you guys, this is too sad. I was hoping to get through without seeing you actually as I'm just no good at goodbyes."

"No way," said Tom, "you don't get away that easily."

"Group hug!" yelled Emma, dragging us all in and crowding poor Beth into our embrace.

"Okay, okay," she said, a tear escaping down her cheek, "I'm going now. No prolonged goodbyes. I'll see you all soon!"

And with that she, and the puppy, was gone.

I wiped away my tears and laughed. I didn't know what else to do. The hardest goodbye was yet to come. Emma gave Tom a massive hug, kissing him on the cheek and instructed him to be good to me before retreating discreetly to the small coffee shop opposite the car hire desk.

"Oh, Jo," said Tom looking up to the heavens, "this is going to be harder than I thought. I know it's not for long but I'm going to miss you so very much. I wasted a lot of time this summer. I didn't realise what I had right underneath my nose. What will I do without you?"

"You'll be ok," I replied my voice thick with tears, "just don't forget about me!"

"Not possible!" he smiled and pulled me in for another kiss, wiping my tears from my cheek as he did so.

The airport tannoy came on and the booming voice announced, "Would Passenger Dan Davies please make his way immediately to gate number 3 where your flight is waiting to leave."

We listened in disbelief and laughed at Dan's ineffectual attempt at timekeeping.
I looked at every part of Tom's beautiful face, memorising every part of it before he left me. I placed my hands on his chest as he kissed my forehead and stroked my hair.

"I'll see you in a month then?" he said questioningly.

"Try and stop me," I said smiling through a veil of tears.

He began to step backwards, still holding my hand before the distance between us made physical contact impossible. He smiled, turned and walked towards the departure gates.

Emma came back from the coffee shop and wrapped her arm around my waist.
Before Tom disappeared from view, he turned, grinned and raised a hand in a wave. And then he was gone.

317

My heart had stopped, I was sure of it. I was happy and sad all at once. Emma squeezed her arm round me even tighter.

"You two definitely have horrendous timing, but thank the Lord you sorted it in time!"

"Yes," I smiled back my heart aching, "It's been an amazing summer! I wouldn't have missed this for the world!"

"Right then," she said squeezing my hand, "enough of the sadness and tears. Are you ready for another adventure?"

"Oh yeah," I smiled wiping my tears, "you bet I am!"

Printed in Great Britain
by Amazon